Ritual River

Ritual River

A NOVEL BY

Nancy Sales Cash

Nancy Sales Cash

CHAPEL HILL
PRESS, INC.

Cover shows the Charlotte, NC skyline as seen from the Mile-High Swinging Bridge on Grandfather Mountain, a scenic travel attraction and internationally acclaimed nature preserve. Photographer is Hugh Morton of Grandfather Mountain. www.grandfather.com

ISBN 1-59715-020-7
Library of Congress Catalog Number 2006923650

First Printing

This book is dedicated to my husband,
Charles Reid, for his unfailing love,
support, and endurance of the writerly life.
Our love, too, will last forever.

Thanks to the following people for their help with research: Dr. Barbara Duncan, Freeman Owle, Jerry Wolf, O.L. and Linda Yates, Joan Shuford, Deborah Smith, Dale and Betty Price, Harry Martin, Wanda Stalcup, Bill and Barbara Hughes, Annette Saunooke Clapsaddle, Zeb Conley, and others.

"As long as your story is alive, you're alive."

Native American saying

CHAPTER ONE

ASHEVILLE NC, APRIL 1999

Anxious to find out how her brother was, Carol Mattox pushed open the door of the hospital room. The sight of him gave her a terrible shock, as though someone—or something—had reached in, grabbed her heart, and twisted it.

Dimly she registered her whole family's presence. She tried to put on a smile, although she could feel it wobbling. "Phil, it's me, your pest of a sister. I got here as soon as I could." He'd been asking for her, and she had traveled a long way to see him. Feeling a rare helplessness, she took his hand, and he opened his eyes.

But he began to moan, and struggled to raise himself. It was a mournful noise that reminded Carol of things she'd heard in rituals related to her work. Automatically, the trained part of her mind tried to characterize the sound, note it for future reference.

Then, to her consternation, Phil fought to pull the oxygen line from his nose. When she tried to keep it in place, he blurted out, "I saw him! You'll know what to do about him."

Puzzled, she bent closer. "Saw who?"

Looking past her now, Phil shouted, "That Indian!"

Startled, Carol drew back.

"No, don't!" Screaming now, Phil lunged at her, his eyes wide and staring. "You'll kill me!" With surprising strength, he fastened trembling hands around Carol's neck, still without registering her presence.

With an effort, she pried loose his fingers. Frightened, she looked at the others.

Her mother, scarlet lips shaking, said, "He keeps talking about it. Says he saw an Indian open the flood gate at the dam."

Carol's blood ran cold. "Could that have happened?"

"Of course not. Especially not when he saw an Indian wearing buckskins, with a gold nugget on a red hat." Marcie's lips now twisted with scorn. But the look she gave Carol's father was uneasy.

"He's just raving; it's the drugs they're giving him," Stanley Mattox pronounced. "Go along with it, like we do."

Phil collapsed back onto his bed and lay unmoving, seeming barely conscious. What had he meant by, *"You'll know what to do?"* Carol wondered.

As she gazed in bewilderment at her parents, her grandmother whispered, "Don't pretend he doesn't know what he's saying. I'm telling you, the Mattox curse has killed him, too!"

Carol jumped. "What are you talking about, Grandma?"

Her father, looking at his mother, replied, "Hush, now. We won't discuss something so silly as that, especially at a time like this." He made it sound like a reprimand. Her father, still every inch the senator, Carol thought, was still giving orders, still telling people how to live their lives.

Senator Mattox began to pace, managing only a subdued nod at her. Her mother put a hand on her shoulder, then took it away. Well, Carol thought, as they hadn't said much of a goodbye when she left two years ago, why would they say hello now? Grandma Harriet, thinner but dressed as elegantly as ever, sat in the recliner and snuffled into a handkerchief. Phil's fiancée, Ellen, wore a sad smile and seemed the only one glad to see her.

Anxiously, Carol noticed that Phil's normally ruddy face was a sickly yellow. Always a big man, he looked shrunken. Tubes sprouted from him like roots. *Why does he look so yellow*? she wondered. The phone call to her office at the research station had been brief. In another call she'd made from the Phoenix airport, her mother had sobbed so hard that talking was impossible. So Carol knew practically nothing about what had happened to Phil. Aloud, she whispered, "How is he?" to anybody listening.

Ellen glanced at the Mattoxes and, when they failed to answer, motioned Carol outside. Carol gave Phil's hand a squeeze before following Ellen into the hallway, where Carol choked out, "What happened to him?"

Ellen's slim hand rose, then fell again. "Nobody's sure. He was fishing on the lake. You know how much he loves to fish."

Carol made a fist and pressed it over her mouth, forcing herself to listen.

It was a moment before Ellen, too, could continue. "He knew the schedule, so the dam seems to have opened *un*scheduled. Of course, nobody will admit that, especially after your daddy's threats to sue them. Anyway, Phil's boat was—was—swamped." She faltered. "He was half-drowned when they pulled him out." Finally her control crumbled.

"Ssh, ssh, now." Carol stood on tip-toe, took Ellen in her arms and held her close. They rocked back and forth a little, not speaking.

After a while Ellen pulled away. "Did you fly all the way from Phoenix today?"

"Well, I started last night; it took five hours to drive from the research station," Carol told her, suddenly feeling that her head was too heavy for her neck.

Ellen's arm slid around her. "You must be exhausted. Have you had anything to eat?"

Carol shook her head. "Don't want anything."

"You might feel better if you did. There's a canteen down on the fifth floor. It isn't much, but it's quick. I need to get back to Phil. We'll try to talk later."

"You go ahead. I'll be right there."

When Ellen had gone, Carol leaned against the wall, thinking about going back into the room where Phil lay and her parents waited. A cup of strong coffee might help her face them. Everything had happened so suddenly—the midnight rousing, the desperate dash across the country—that she hadn't had time to prepare herself for any of it; not for her disapproving parents, nor for leaving the safety of the anthropological past for the uncertainty of the living present. She was still shaking from seeing her parents again, from the violent tussle with Phil, and from the strange vision he'd described. Nothing like that ever happened to her in the remote, supposedly uncivilized, areas where she lived and worked.

Terrified through the endless night, all the way to North Carolina, she'd held on to the hope that Phil would be better by the time she got here. But he wasn't. Finally, the tears rushed out in a flood like the one that had overcome him. She turned to the thick wall and cried against it, so that no one could see her red, wet eyes, the gaping hole of pain that was her mouth.

Suddenly a disturbingly familiar voice said, very close, "Carol?"

She whirled around and saw the man she'd loved since she was sixteen.

CHAPTER TWO

"Winston?" Carol whispered.

At the sight of him, overwhelming memories tumbled through her mind, like the rushing river from which he'd once pulled her, saving her life. It had been over ten years ago, but the memory was still sharp. She could still taste their youthful passion. Winston Wolfe had given her incredible, heart-stopping joy. He had also given her desperate unhappiness. He had been her first love. And he had been her last. Since her father had forced them apart, no other man had interested her.

"Yeah . . . hey, Carol." He looked at her intently, with very dark eyes that had always seen inside her. "I'm glad it *is* you, or I'd be feeling pretty silly by now."

Dashing away her tears, she looked up at him. A decade hadn't changed him, although he looked even better than she remembered, especially in a suit. Hers was a jeans-and-T-shirt world. She shook her head to clear it. "Where . . ." she began, then stopped, trying to keep her raw, grieving nerves from blurting out, *I've missed you so much.* Because, after all, he'd never tried to see her again.

"Got a minute?"

She hesitated before saying, "Sure. But then I have to get back in there."

He glanced at the name plate beside Phil's door, and his eyebrows rose. "Sorry if I'm prying, but what's wrong with your brother?"

"He had a bad accident."

"Oh, my God! I'm sorry to hear it." He put out a hand, and for just a moment she thought he might touch her. But then he ran it through his hair, making it stand up in spikes. Just the way she remembered.

"Thanks." Suddenly she asked, warily, "What are *you* doing here?

"My grandfather had a heart attack. He's in that room right down the hall. I'm afraid he doesn't have much longer."

"I'm so sorry." Carol spoke slowly. "Wasn't he the Chief for a long time?" Then her eyes widened. Had Winston—or his grandfather—been the Native American Phil had seen?

"He's been Chief for over twenty years," Winston said with a proud expression. Quickly she banished her thought.

"I remember him." She remembered everything.

"At least he's lived a long and productive life. Not like your brother, who can't be more than what... early thirties?"

"Thirty-two, to be exact."

After a moment he asked, "Have you lived in Asheville since... since the last time I saw you?"

She thought he'd tried to make the question sound casual, but maybe that was just wishful thinking. "No. Yes. Well, I went to school, then I got my doctorate. For the last two years, I've been working with a tribe called the Nanjinas, in the southwestern desert." Seeing his puzzled look she added, "I'm an anthropologist."

His eyes lit up. "That's great. I think you said something about that when ..." He stopped, then murmured, "It's great that we've both fulfilled our dreams."

Both, she wondered? Maybe he had. Hers had been to love him. "I guess, from that, and the suit, you're a lawyer?" He nodded, and suddenly she felt a pang of yearning. They had sworn to help each other be the best they could be. She wondered what that would have been like. She drew a deep breath. "I'm glad for you. And now I need to get back in there." She moved toward Phil's door.

"Of course. It was nice seeing you."

Carol bit back polite words that would have told him how nice it was to see him, too. But she was worse off now, and not just because she hadn't had that bracing cup of coffee. How could she cope with Phil's accident and seeing Winston again, both on the same day?

Winston watched her slip back into her brother's room.

He was rocked by running into Carol Mattox. When he'd recognized her, he'd hesitated to speak. There had been trouble between their families, nearly two hundred years of it, although no one knew exactly why it had started. Though Winston had a pretty good idea.

There was one thing he knew for sure: her family didn't like him. He shuddered at the memory of Senator Mattox telling him, that summer's day at their pool, never to contact Carol again. Not that he'd obeyed, but it hadn't got him anywhere, either.

Now, he was glad he'd talked to her. Thinking about Carol without the bitterness that had become a habit surprised him. It was a relief, after so many years. It was like he'd repaid some ancient debt, and he felt good about it.

CHAPTER THREE

That night, Phil began to make a different sound. Carol ran to the waiting room and urged the rest of the family, "You'd better come."

By the time they got back and resumed their sad, silent vigil, the sound had become a rattle as Phil gasped for breath. His chest rose, stayed up, then fell, and stayed down so long Carol worried it wouldn't rise again.

She sat close to him and held his hand, to reassure herself as much as him. He quieted, and Carol clung to him, as she clung to hope.

Gradually, though, she noticed that Phil's color darkened. His hand grew purple-black, the same as his face. Then it became cool and firm. Finally, it took on a waxy look. But she kept his hand in hers, even after a nurse confirmed the worst. Phil was dead..

As Ellen sobbed, and her parents held each other, Carol leaned her forehead on Phil's arm. Her big brother was the only person who had never left her. Until now.

She remembered all the times he'd interceded for her with their father. They hadn't always won, but Phil's courage had made her stronger. She'd looked up to him even before he'd urged her to reach for the future she wanted, instead of the one their parents had planned for her. She owed him a lot.

She owed him respect for his final moments, even if they had seemed like raving to her father. If Phil thought he'd seen a Native American at the dam, then he had, she thought loyally. And he had been convinced she could do something about it.

But what? And who could it have been? Once more, she thought about Winston. No, Phil's Native American seemed to be from another time, another place. He seemed nothing like Winston.

She was so relieved by this that she told one of her old eerie feelings, the kind she'd had since childhood, to go away.

Still, just thinking about the coincidence made her uneasy.

CHAPTER FOUR

The Mattox home had been built over two hundred years ago in the Queen Anne style. Carol had always thought the house flew so many gables, roofs, and cupolas that it looked ready to sail away on a strong wind. According to family history, one of the early Mattox matriarchs had seen it illustrated in a London magazine that had come from Charleston.

The house was so large that several generations usually lived there together. The wing behind the kitchen was Grandma's. Phil and Ellen had been making themselves an apartment upstairs next to his old room.

Remembering this, and the run-in she'd just had with her mother, Carol's heart weighed heavy again. She knew her offer had been premature; Phil's funeral had taken place only yesterday, but as she had to return to Arizona soon, she had offered to help her mother sort through his things. She'd wanted to help, but her mother had acted offended.

So Carol had fled to the den and curled up on the leather sofa, hoping the cozy, book-lined room might soothe her. The pitfalls of family relationships were the reason she'd gone to Arizona in the first place. Well, now she was back, and she wanted to figure out a way to start mending fences with her parents.

Just then, Grandma came in and lowered herself stiffly into a yellow corduroy armchair. Carol sat up. "Grandma, I was just thinking..." Her grandmother might be able to suggest a way to make peace with her parents.

But Harriet commented, "I hope you're thinking about what I said."

Perplexed, Carol repeated, "What you said—when?"

Her grandmother let out a sigh of impatience. "About the Mattox curse."

Carol remembered Grandma's outburst at the hospital. Older people took things harder. So she turned her smile of skepticism into one of sympathy.

"Don't look at me like I'm retarded," Harriet said, so fiercely that Carol flinched. "Like everybody else does."

"I'm not," Carol protested. "I'm just feeling sorry for you. I'm sorry for all of us. As a matter of fact—" She got ready to broach the subject of her parents.

But this time her grandmother interrupted in a hoarse whisper. "You don't need to feel sorry for me. You should feel sorry for yourself."

"Why?"

"Because, now you're the next in line to die from the Mattox curse," Harriet pronounced in doom-like tones.

Carol could hardly believe her ears. "Grandma, I know you're upset, but you're being—"

"Silly?" Harriet finished for her and then nearly spat her next words, through a mouth contorted with grief. "I said that once, too. You should listen to me, like I should have listened to my mother." She nodded slowly at Carol. "She refused to let me marry your grandfather because she knew about the Mattox curse. Back then, they took those things seriously."

"But you did marry grandfather," Carol reminded her gently. "And you must have loved him very much if you married him in spite of that."

"Oh, yes," her grandmother sighed. "I argued my mother around to it. I thought such talk was nonsense, about curses and things. Just like you." She gave Carol an unhappy look. "But she turned out to be right. Look what's happened to me. If I'd married one of the McKeever boys, like Mother wanted me to, I wouldn't have had so many tragedies. The McKeevers never had anything terrible happen to them. Preston the Third, who proposed to me, lived a happy life, even if he was in business instead of the law profession. But look at me now. God should never have allowed me to outlive both a son and a grandson." Harriet began to sob. "And all because I married a Mattox." Her thin chest heaved; tears dropped on crisp navy linen. "There's a lot you've never been told, and you need to hear it." Eager to make her point, Harriet leaned toward Carol. "You need to listen."

Carol remembered hearing Grandma say something about a family curse years ago, after Uncle Richard died, and Carol was in the kitchen with her and Mama. Through the bony hand grasping her arm, Carol felt her grandmother's entire body shaking. Whatever the Mattox curse was, it was obviously highly upsetting to Grandma. Whatever crazy thing her grandmother was trying to say, she must let her say it and try to calm her down. So she asked, more kindly, "About the Mattox curse? But what is it?"

Straining even closer, Harriet nearly toppled out of her chair. "I'll tell you. But you've got to promise me you'll listen," she repeated. "Don't be like the others. They don't believe me."

"I promise to listen," Carol assured her. Getting up, she put an arm around her grandmother's frail shoulders and brought her back to the couch. "Come sit beside me. That way it'll be easier for you to tell me about it." When Grandma had settled down, Carol took the old woman's hand and asked, "Will you explain it to me?"

Harriet dabbed at her eyes with a thin handkerchief, and replaced a hair comb that had loosened. "It started with that woman—Isabelle—the one who went out to Cherokee country and married an Indian and disgraced the family."

Carol sat back. "The one who started the Museum of Mountain and Indian Handicrafts, who some say was the inspiration for the Folk School?" She was incredulous, but her interest had been piqued. "I always thought Isabelle was the heroine of the family. At least a celebrated and honored lady."

"Hunh." Harriet drew herself up. "All that came later. But she started the trouble, for sure. The family disowned her, so that Indian put a spell on us."

'That Indian.' These were the same words Phil had used just before he died, and thoughts of Winston shivered through Carol once again. But she tried to shrug them off by correcting her grandmother, gently, "Grandma, they're called Native Americans now."

"Call them what you like. They know things other people don't. Believe me, he put a spell on this family, and it has worked."

"What makes you think that?" At least Grandma's tears had subsided to gulps.

"Because I heard it from your grandfather's grandmother, who was still living in this house when I came here as a bride. She had known Isabelle, after Isabelle was brought back to Asheville." With an arthritic finger she prodded Carol's knee. "And she had it from Isabelle herself that that man put a curse on the family! What do you think of that?"

Carol chose her words carefully. "Life was full of dangers way back then. It isn't very safe even now. Look at poor Phil; his death could never have been predicted. People do die, you know."

"Not every first-born in every generation," the older woman stated flatly.

"What on earth do you mean?" Carol felt astonished.

Looking at Carol as though not even seeing her, Harriet explained, "In every generation of our line of Mattoxes, the first-born has died young. It doesn't matter whether they're male or female. All from accidents, but 'accidents' like Phil's. Don't think Phil's death was any accident. That dam wasn't due to open."

Something fluttered down Carol's spine as she remembered how Phil had thought he'd seen a Native American—and not just an ordinary one—open the flood gate.

Still, it was far-fetched, to say the least, and she leaned forward. "Do you seriously believe there's a curse on this family?"

Her grandmother's voice was shaky, but her conviction was solid. "I've never been more serious about anything."

Carol was taken aback. "But this is nearly the 21st century, not the Middle Ages." *And we're in an American city, not a primitive jungle or a desert like Nanjina,* she could have added.

"See, you're being just like the others. And you promised," Harriet accused, slumping back on the sofa.

"I'm sorry, Grandma. You surprised me, that's all. I promised to listen, and I have, but I just can't believe it. And in my work I hear about lots of strange things."

Harriet stared at her. "All right. You may not believe me. But will you believe the Bible?"

CHAPTER FIVE

Carol was startled by her grandmother's challenge. The Bible couldn't be refused. For hundreds of years, before official records were kept, the family Bible had been the sole and unquestioned source of births, marriages, and deaths.

Harriet took her silence for agreement and got up. "Come over here." Her bony finger beckoned, and Carol followed her to an antique bookcase. Carefully Harriet opened its wavy glass doors and selected a huge, ancient-looking Bible. With effort, she passed it to Carol, who laid it on the coffee table.

Its stiff leather cover had been tooled with the family name and crest, the gold worn but still gleaming. Harriet explained, "This one is from your great-great-great-grandmother's day—the one who knew Isabelle."

Well, it might give some insight into Grandma's tales of mysterious, premature deaths, Carol thought; something she could use to disprove them and bury the idea of a curse once and for all. She'd listen, for Grandma's sake, if for no one else's.

When they had settled again, Harriet pressed open the Bible to a flyleaf loosened and yellowed with age. "Isabelle's own brother died young, but he was in the Army, so nobody connected it. You know that he was in charge of moving the Indians out of these parts?" At Carol's nod Harriet indicated, on the crowded page, the bold line through the name Isabelle. "That happened when the family disowned her."

Carol shivered again. Then her grandmother tapped another part of the page and said, "Now, these are Charles' children. He was the one who finally brought his sister Isabelle back from Murphy, although she wouldn't come 'til he promised to bring all her Indian things. She called them 'treasures'. Here's your great-great-grandfather Jeremiah, his sisters Anne and Eloise, and his three brothers."

Carol peered at the page of faded, elaborate handwriting. Birthdates were listed, and in different writing so were the dates of death, reasons sometimes recorded beside each name. *'Killed by a horse,'* said one. "I don't see—" she began.

"Well, just look here—Jeremiah's oldest brother Daniel died when he was only nineteen, in a fire," Harriet finished emphatically.

"There were lots of fires, Grandma," Carol said.

"Look further. Look at the next generation," Harriet insisted. "Jeremiah had five children. His oldest, Jocelyn, was born in 1872. She had two sisters and two brothers, one of whom was your great-grandfather Andrew. See, all the other four lived to reasonable ages. But Jocelyn, the eldest, died in 1875. She was only three years old. And there's no reason given."

Carol tried to be kind. "It might have been an accident, or a disease. There's no way of knowing. People weren't as healthy back then."

Grandma's look was one of disgust. "You sound just like the others."

Carol pressed her hand. "I'm sorry, I didn't mean to. It's just that, in my work, I'm trained to ask questions about things like this. I do want to hear more." The trickle moved another notch along her spine, and she confessed, "In fact, I have to admit, Grandma, it is a little strange." Correction, she thought; it was downright weird.

She thought of the Australian Aborigines' custom of 'pointing the bone'—making somebody die by nothing more than wishing it. If that could happen, then anything could. What Grandma was saying was really no more extraordinary than any of the world's belief systems Carol had mastered as an anthropologist. Throughout history, people had always believed things that were outside the bounds of empirical science, or even religion. Many things still couldn't be explained scientifically, including the biggest mystery of all: human life. And death?

Strongest of all, Carol knew, was the simple power of belief. Maybe the simpler the better.

Mollified, Harriet closed the huge Bible, struggled back with it, and selected another, as large but without the elaborate cover. She opened it. "The next generation is your grandfather's, and his oldest sister died at fifteen. They said she was killed by lightning…" Grandma shuddered "… that must have been a horrible death. Then, my son Richard died. He wasn't even forty. Choked on a fish bone, they said. Phil has just drowned at thirty-two, and you know what I think about that." She slumped again, losing another hair comb.

The mention of Phil, his loss still so raw, plucked at Carol, bringing to a head the doomsday feeling that had grown as she listened to her grandmother's litany of family deaths.

Harriet was looking steadily at her. As if firing her last salvo, she announced, "Now you're the oldest child!"

Carol flinched. "Grandma, you said that before." She tried to laugh, but it fell flat. "Daddy didn't die after Uncle Richard…"

"No." Harriet pursed her lips. "But Phil was already born. Whereas, Phil has—had—no children." Her stare was unrelenting. "I just wouldn't like to be in your shoes. Or to be your eldest child."

"Grandma, now you're really scaring me." Carol hugged herself.

Her grandmother's mouth twisted in a sad little smile. But her gaze was still determined. "You need to do one more thing—go look at all that stuff Isabelle collected that we gave to the Asheville Art Museum."

Carol brightened. "Why, yes, I think I will."

Harriet didn't notice. "Thank goodness we got rid of them. They used to give me nightmares, just being in the same house with them. Why, there were things I wouldn't even look at, for fear they'd put a spell on me, and I think one of them has. You know about all that witchcraft. Go see if you can find anything that could be responsible for the curse."

Carol smiled to herself. Unlike Grandma, she would enjoy looking at the Mattox Collection again. Long ago, when she was a little girl, Aunt Isabelle's treasures had been housed in a spare bedroom. "I don't know about that. Every time I saw them I became more fascinated," she told Harriet. She'd spent hours imagining the people who had used or worn them, and for what reason. It was better than playing dress-up.

"Hunh," her grandmother scoffed. "I never went into that room."

"Well, I looked at them a lot. I wanted to know what everything was, and what it had meant to Aunt Isabelle and her life, which always seemed so interesting, so different. I always pretended I was her."

"Her life was different, all right," Harriet said acidly. "And as for pretending you were her, you might have done that too well."

"You're partly right," Carol conceded. "The collection—and Aunt Isabelle—inspired my interest in anthropology, for sure." Some of Isabelle's treasures were astonishingly similar to things from all over the world that she had later studied, or had seen in museums, or on field trips. Even now, her work would benefit from seeing them again. She would definitely make time for a trip to the museum before she had to leave. Her boss, Brian, wouldn't mind if she stayed through the weekend. She needed a little more time, anyway, to try to reconcile with her parents.

Yes, familiarizing herself with Isabelle's world again would be a good idea. For there was one thing she'd noticed in the family Bibles that even Grandma hadn't mentioned.

All the deaths seemed natural. But they had also been caused by one of the four elements of nature: Water. Fire. Earth. Air. Except for the fishbone. Well, she supposed, after all, a fish lived in water.

Suddenly, she saw an Indian man standing at the top of a huge concrete dam. On his head he wore a red cap, and it glistened with gold.

It was the same vision Phil had experienced as he was dying.

It was gone almost as quickly as it had come, but it had been sharp and clear, and it left her shaken.

It also left her more determined to see Isabelle's collection.

CHAPTER SIX

"What's on your agenda today, honey?" Marcie Mattox asked Carol at breakfast.

"What?" Carol's attention was focused on a front-page headline in the newspaper her father had opened: *Wolfe Keeps It In the Family.*

When her mother repeated the question, Carol replied absently, "I'm going to the art museum to see Aunt Isabelle's collection."

Her grandmother looked up with satisfaction, but her mother said, apprehensively, "That's nice." She continued, "Well, I'm glad to see you've at least dressed pretty for it." Then she observed sardonically, "I was beginning to think you hadn't brought any clothes besides jeans and T-shirts." Sweetly she added, "And if you've forgotten your nail polish, I can loan you some."

Frustrated by her mother's thinly disguised criticisms, and by not being able to read the article, which she suspected was about Winston, Carol groaned inwardly. She didn't like long nails, or polished ones; they got in her way, for her hands were always active. As for her blue-printed blouse and skirt, she said, "There wasn't much time to pack at Nanjina. But there are still some old clothes, like these, in the back of my closet, so I'll try not to disgrace you."

Marcie seemed mollified. "It's for your own good, honey."

How many times had Carol heard that? It was the first inkling she'd had that her mother would start the old criticisms again. They were just excuses for bossing her around. And her father would be next. It hadn't happened yet, due to their grieving, she supposed. But she knew it would come.

When Stanley left the table, Carol picked up his *Asheville Citizen-Times,* and read how Winston was closer to fulfilling another of his ambitions. He was running for chief of the Eastern Band of Cherokees, to replace his grandfather. And he seemed to be the sentimental favorite.

Thoughts galloped through Carol's mind. She thought about calling him up to wish him well in the election. After all, it would be merely the polite thing to do, the sort of thing she'd do for any friend. Suddenly, her heart began to beat so fast it scared her. She knew Winston wasn't just any friend.

He was close, in the town of Cherokee, just fifty miles away. Should she look him up? She'd like to. Was he married? She tried to remember if there had been a wedding ring. But she'd been too worried about Phil to notice that in the hospital.

How was she going to keep from seeing him again?

As soon as the thought hit her, she felt a sharp pain at the way he'd left her, all those years ago. If she looked him up, she'd probably just get hurt again. Better to let sleeping dogs lie. Good thing she didn't have time to look him up, anyway.

Harriet said, pointedly, "I hope you'll find what you're looking for at the museum."

Marcie was instantly suspicious. "And what would that be?"

"Oh, just something Grandma and I talked about." Carol shot Harriet a warning look. There was enough trouble going on without stirring up more. Then she quickly gathered her things for the trip downtown. The sooner she got out of the house the better.

When she had left, Marcie picked up the newspaper and read the article that had captured Carol's attention. Then she went straight to her husband's study.

"I saw her reading the article about that Wolfe boy. I told you I saw him at the hospital," she insisted, "and Carol could have seen him, too." A thought struck her and she whispered, "D'you think he could have been the Indian Phil saw?"

With a stern glance, Stanley looked up from the papers on his desk. "Of course not."

Marcie didn't feel convinced. "Well, now she's gone to see Isabelle's old stuff at the art museum." Despite trying to stay calm, her voice rose. "It's happening all over again, just like before. And your mother's telling those stories again, about the Mattox curse."

"Just stop listening to her."

"I don't listen to her, but I think Carol does."

Impatiently, he said, "I've explained to you about the family vein trouble. That's all the Mattox curse is, believe me. And it was all a very long time ago."

Marcie said quietly, "Phil didn't have vein trouble."

Her husband replied tersely, "Something went wrong at that dam, and I intend to get to the bottom of it." He slammed shut a ledger he'd been working on. "As for Carol, I don't want her upsetting Mother. You let me know if she does. I just don't want any of my family having anything to do with an Indian, even if it has been nearly two hundred years."

Marcie said quickly, "Promise me you'll help, by talking to her if I bring it up?"

The senator let out a long, reluctant sigh. "She's never taken my advice about anything yet, but I'll try."

CHAPTER SEVEN

Carol wandered through the Asheville Art Museum, entranced by a photographic exhibition of people of the Southern Appalachians in the last century. While color photographs might be more pleasing to the eye, she thought, there was nothing like the contrast of black and white to show character and speak to the soul. Some of those faces could have come out of the very earth they stood on.

Still marveling at them, she headed for her appointment with the director. The museum's new premises, conveniently fronting Pack Square right in the center of town, had been finished since she'd gone to Arizona, so this was her first exploration. It was a wonderful place, she decided, looking at the airy, well-lit rooms, a great improvement on the old, cramped section of a run-down building.

A compliment was her greeting to Pamela Stewart, who replied, "Thanks. The renovation took a long time, and was terribly inconvenient, but it's been worth it. We're so grateful to the civic fathers for seeing it got done." The young, blonde-haired director, whose previous job, Carol knew, had been with the Museum of Modern Art in New York, motioned to a chair near her desk. "Nice to see you again. Are you here for good now?"

Remembering her latest phone call to her boss, Carol said, "No, I'll be here a few more days, but then I'm going back to Arizona. I still have to find out how the Nanjinas know, without keeping any written records, who they can marry to avoid the problems of incest."

Pamela smiled. "I wish we could tempt you to stay, but our work probably wouldn't be in your field, anyway. As far as The Mattox Collection is concerned, you've come at the right time. We've had several requests from the Museum of the Cherokee Indian, over at Cherokee, to loan them your Aunt Isabelle's artifacts on a more or less permanent basis. And we've more or less agreed."

Carol was unsettled by the possibility of a strong connection to Cherokee. It was too much like a connection to Winston. "Why?"

"Well, Dr. Ralph Raxter, the museum director over there, thinks that because there's so much Cherokee culture in the collection, it should be displayed there."

"But there are lots of things from the pioneer culture, too," Carol argued. "And here, it's the only collection of handicrafts. Over in Cherokee, it'll be just one of many."

"Yes, but there it will have more pertinence." Pamela smiled and tried again. "It's sort of the same theory as returning the Elgin Marbles to Greece. Everybody but the British Museum, who has them, seems to agree on that."

"Makes sense, I guess," Carol finally said.

"Especially as we've had to keep moving the collection around due to space constrictions. Most everything in it's about two hundred years old, and gets a little more damaged with each move. It needs a stable home. Besides, our museum is more fine art than artifacts, and we need to use our resources, including space, accordingly." She wound up her argument. "You can be sure Ralph Raxter will give it the prominence it deserves, and a permanent home with the right conditions to preserve it for another two hundred years."

Carol had to admit it sounded sensible. "I'll talk to my family about it," she agreed reluctantly.

"I'd appreciate it. Let me know when you'd like me to set up an appointment with Ralph for you." Then she added briskly, "And now, I know you want to see your collection. I've arranged for Mrs. Sally Rhoades, one of our best docents, who's helped out here for many years, to take you down to it."

CHAPTER EIGHT

Carol followed a tall, gracious lady to the museum's basement. The docent unlocked several doors en route to an airless underground storeroom. "It's kind of creepy down here," Mrs. Rhoades apologized.

It was not upstairs' airy new spaces, Carol agreed, as she looked at dim, dingy walls, and a neon light that was bright but not illuminating. She was beginning to think the sooner Aunt Isabelle's artifacts were taken out of here, the better.

Eagerly she approached the five glass museum cases that held them. It was like discovering old friends, or distant relatives. "Oh, look," she heard herself exclaiming repeatedly to Mrs. Rhoades, as she went from case to case. "I'm sorry, I don't seem to know what else to say," she smiled.

"They're beautiful pieces," the lady agreed. "It must be interesting to study things all the time. I'd like that."

"It is; that's why I became an anthropologist," Carol answered. "I always thought the past was fascinating. It has a lot of importance for the present, and the future, too. One way or another, it's caused everything that's happening in the world today. Wouldn't you love to know exactly how everything happened?"

Mrs. Rhoades replied with a chuckle. "That would be fascinating, but I don't think it's going to happen."

While she talked, Carol had been looking for one item in particular: the medicine bag. It had always intrigued her. Where was it? And where was anything that might have made Grandma think there was a curse on the family?

She could see nothing but exquisitely made handicrafts. Each item had been neatly labeled with a white card on which had been typed its date, origin, and use. The museum had worked hard to make the collection accessible.

There were finely woven Indian baskets, their patterns a perfect geometry of red, brown, and black against natural river cane, the colors as clear today as they had been two hundred years ago. Clay pots had been stamped with similar designs. There were hand-woven mats and rugs, most of them geometrical, too, but one an unusually artistic design of a tree-lined river bank.

Everything was beautiful, the best workmanship of its type. Nothing was threatening.

There was a particularly lovely Cherokee dream catcher; some gourds of both beauty and practicality; spinning tops carved from wood; cornhusk dolls; brooms with handles made from deer antlers. And then there were the clothes: fringed and beaded bags, bear-claw necklaces and bracelets, deerskin shirts and skirts.

Most eye-catching of all was a man's turban-like hat, its red cloth faded but still vibrant. But what grabbed Carol's attention was the large gold nugget bound to it with a strip of leather.

It was exactly like the cap that Phil had seen the Indian wearing when the dam gate opened. And like the vision she'd had when Grandma had spooked her about the Mattox curse.

Carol's legs buckled.

CHAPTER NINE

Carol had to sit down on the closest chair. Rubbing her wrists to re-start her circulation, she remembered the fear on Grandma's face as she spoke about the Mattox curse. It wasn't possible, Carol told herself repeatedly. Like her, Phil had seen this cap in his youth, among Aunt Isabelle's 'treasures', and was hallucinating, as Daddy had said.

Mrs. Rhoades looked at her closely. "Are you all right?"

"Yes." With an effort Carol forced herself to get up and look at another glass case. But its vicious-looking arrowheads and bone knives made her shiver.

Then Mrs. Rhoades remarked, "I don't think I'd be much good at finding things, but I'd love trying to figure out what they were used for."

Carol grabbed the chance to get her thoughts off the red hat. "Aunt Isabelle was good at finding them. The story goes that she visited every mountain valley and cove between Asheville and Knoxville, buying the best things she could afford. Of course, people gave her a lot of things, too, just because she appreciated them. Mountain people are generous that way." She knew she was babbling, but couldn't stop herself.

As the docent nodded, Carol moved to another case. Ah. Here, at last, was the medicine bag. Strangely, it had no label. Looking at it gave her not the rush of pleasure she had expected, but a sudden, involuntary, shudder. Instead of the welcome an old friend might offer, it gave off a strong feeling, almost of danger.

To try and shake this, she told Mrs. Rhoades, "That medicine bag, now, was something almost every primitive culture had, our own included. It held things people believed provided cures or protection, or brought good luck. Like a snail carrying his house on his back."

"I don't know about luck—that looks evil to me." Now it was the docent's turn to shudder, Carol noticed.

Warily, Carol approached the case. A faded scrap of paper with the same old-fashioned penmanship she had seen in the family Bibles said:

Medicine Bag
of my husband
Tallaquoyah Wolf 1838

She was struck by the name. Funny how she hadn't realized ... must have known ... or had she? ... that Isabelle's husband was named Wolf. It was called The Mattox Collection, then, just because the Mattox family had donated it.

Remembering this morning's newspaper headline, thoughts of Winston Wolfe flashed through her mind. She hadn't been able to dismiss completely the idea that he'd been the Native American Phil had seen. Had her aunt's husband been related to Winston? The name was spelled a little differently, but that didn't much matter. If so, she and Isabelle were more alike than she'd ever dreamed.

Her emotions rising, she wanted to sit down again, but forced herself to concentrate on the medicine bag until she could trust herself to speak again.

Finally, bent over the case, she observed, "My grandmother would agree with you about it being evil. May I look at it more closely?"

"Of course. I'll get it out for you." Mrs. Rhoades selected a small key.

But a look wasn't enough. "May I handle it?"

The docent hesitated. "I don't know. Normally, it wouldn't be allowed."

Carol assured her, "I'll be careful. I'm used to handling things of great age and value."

"I know, and you are a guest of the director. It seems to me these things are yours, in a way." She shrugged. "Go ahead."

"Thanks." Carol scrutinized the medicine bag. Amazingly, the material, probably a deer's stomach, was still soft and pliable. Thus its lumpy contents caught her attention, and carefully she spread them out. There was a large, perfectly preserved white tooth from an animal slightly bigger than a dog. Carol guessed it was a tooth from the Wolf clan's power animal.

But when she saw the pebbles, she stiffened. Black pebbles were connected with death. These were yellow, but they were still pebbles.

After a while she looked at the other things that had been in the pouch. Less shocking but more curious were some dried roots, one of them a distinctive shape, like the tentacled root of a molar, and what looked like dried worms, also well preserved.

As she studied the bag's contents a while longer, she felt she was looking at something that was, if not evil, then certainly powerful, that she couldn't completely understand, and this increased her fear.

This medicine bag was the only item in Isabelle's collection that had clearly belonged to her husband. Tallaquoyah Wolf had collected each of the things inside it, and for a reason. Carol wished she knew what those reasons had been. What had he used them for? Why? If Grandma was right, these things could have been used to put a spell of death on someone, just like the Aborigines' bone. What if Wolf's objects had been used to put on a death spell? And what if that spell had been put on the Mattoxes?

Carol's nerves began to tingle, and a chill of foreboding settled over her. Omigosh, she thought. Had her aunt been married to the man who'd put a curse on their family? Worst of all, had Carol herself been in love with a man whose family had put a curse of death on the Mattoxes?

When she spoke, her voice shook. "Mrs. Rhoades, can I ask you a big favor?"

"Of course. What is it? And do call me Sally."

"I want to borrow this medicine bag. Can you cover for me?"

Now the docent was less certain. "What do I have to do?"

"Just don't tell anybody that I'm taking it. It's only for a little while. Nobody will be looking for it, and I'll bring it back, I promise. I want to try and find out what these things in it are, what they mean. It could be terribly important."

She didn't want to add, *and it might tell me if I'm going to be the next Mattox killed by an ancient Indian spell.*

How could she find out if Grandma's—and now her own—suspicions were true?

Feeling worse by the minute, Carol wished desperately that there was some way of finding out what had happened, two hundred years ago, to Isabelle and Tallaquoyah.

CHAPTER TEN

THE NANTAHALA GORGE, WESTERN NORTH CAROLINA, AUGUST 1837

"Heelllppp!"

The cry was a woman's, high-pitched, long and frantic. It so startled the rider thundering along the narrow, stony river trail that he slowed his horse.

It came again, even more urgently. "Heelllppp!" Alert now, Tallaquoyah Wolf raised his head. As if it impeded his hearing, he snatched off the dark red cloth fastened with a gold nugget that bound his head—a mark of his tribe and his high station within it—releasing long locks of dark hair that had been pinioned underneath.

That the voice was female was more surprising than its hysterical plea. This track was nearly impassable, and few women ventured into the isolated mountains of the Nantahala Gorge. Fewer still spoke English.

"Heelllp!" was now followed by a cascade of frenzied calls. "Help … oh, help me, somebody, please!" Wolf had no doubt she was in mortal danger. He brought his mount to a full stop and listened, hard, rising even taller. There was no saddle; he had no need of one.

He turned his head first in one direction, then another, trying to pinpoint the cries. At the same time, he sniffed the air. The dense forest held mostly the sweet sourness of leaf mold. The scent of people was faint. But then, water lessened the power of smells. Thus, the shouts for help, he reasoned, were coming from the rushing, twisting river itself. Doubtless the trouble lay around that sharp bend. He touched his horse's flanks with soft boots that wore no spurs; they were for men who did not treat animals as equals.

Then he noticed ruts in the softer dirt near the edge of the embankment. They had been made by a wagon, for they were wider and deeper than a buggy's. There was also the sign of many horses' hooves. Such trampling had been done by frightened horses.

As he rounded the bend, he met a sight that stopped his headlong gallop. Sprawled down the river bank was the wreckage of a wagon and team. His old friend Flapjack Foster was pinned underneath it, not moving. He might be unconscious. Or he might be dead. Wolf decided to save the living. She couldn't be too far away.

Just then, the screaming started again, diluted to a splutter from the water she was swallowing. "Ahggh! I'm drowning! Help! Help me!" Wolf's stomach muscles contracted. It had been many moons since he'd had a woman, and he was ready.

Then he saw her. Instead of one of his own tribe, or even another tribe, he was surprised to see a white woman, small and with the palest skin he'd ever seen, and hair that curled and glinted gold even when plastered to her head by the river. Immediately, his lust to possess her turned to an equally strong desire to save her. Or maybe they were the same. "Ahhgghh!" she gurgled as she went under. Finally, she came up again, thrashing at the water. She was in the deepest part of the boulder-strewn river and was being carried swiftly downstream. She would either drown or be dashed against the rocks. Even if she could swim, which was doubtful, she was weighed down by all her clothes. Another reason to wear few of them, he thought, peeling off his suit and shirt, and the fine calfskin boots bought on his last trip to Washington City. Then he dived into the river.

Watching him, Isabelle Matttox choked out a mouthful of water. "God, please help me!" She had regarded the man on the bank with horror, unsure which would be worse: drowning in the icy torrent or looking at a naked man. He might not be so much her savior as her enemy. They had crossed into Cherokee country, so he might even be an Indian. At this thought she screamed again. "Oh, God! Help me!" It caused her to swallow more of the river, and she began to sink.

She feared his help had come too late, anyway. In its rage, the river had torn her bonnet from her head. Her shoes were heavy, her long dress and three petticoats dragged her down. Chin barely above water, she shut her eyes, unable to cope longer with the horror that had befallen her. She gulped more water and, resigned to her fate, began to sink.

But immediately his body was against hers. She felt its length, its solidity, the cords of muscles running from his shoulders down long legs. Knowing he was naked made her shiver, but no longer from fear. With his great strength, he lifted up her head and kept it out of the water, cradling her in a strong arm as he swam to the river bank. Once again torn between the upsetting option of being saved or being aroused, she was both sorry and grateful to stumble against the rocks that edged the water.

Then he threw her down on the bank, heavily, on her face, smashing her nose, and slapped her roughly all over, particularly on her back. This forced the water out, a most unpleasant experience. She cried out, only to bite into the dirt. She tried to spit it out, wipe off her face, but it hurt to breathe, and moving was painful. Best, she decided, to lie still for a time.

After a while, Isabelle felt somewhat recovered, although her body hurt, as much from his thumping the water from her lungs as from fighting for her life.

Nevertheless, she sat up to thank him and nearly choked again at the sight of him. His skin was slick and glistening, and he was so close she could reach out and touch him. Mercifully, though, he crouched beside her in a way that masked his manhood.

His face was smooth and bronzed, the cheekbones so bold they seemed crafted out of the river rock. Around this curled long, wavy black hair running in rivulets down his neck and shoulders. Now that the shock had passed, he was, she thought, possibly the most imposing figure of a man she had ever seen.

He held out her bonnet, its fine straw limp but intact. "You'll need this."

She took it with trembling hands. "Thank you. And thank you for saving my life," she stammered.

"It was my pleasure," he replied.

Feeling a little uncomfortable at the way he put it, she ventured, "What's your name?"

"Wolf."

He was an Indian. A chill went through her battered body, whether from this knowledge or her wet clothes, she couldn't judge. Quaking, but curious, she managed to get out, "I thought... Indians... fear rivers."

"Indians fear nothing," Wolf told her firmly, "although we think rivers lead to the other world, and it's best to stay away from them. You should have taken that advice."

"I – " In consternation, she looked around for Flapjack. Then she saw the wagon, and the grizzled old man who had driven her over the mountain from Dillsboro. He lay halfway in the water, whip still in his hand. "Is he dead?" she cried. "Oh, I pray God he's just been knocked out!"

Wolf rose, very tall, and she averted her gaze. "I've saved your life; now I need to see to Flapjack and the horses."

"You know him?"

"Of course." But instead of elaborating, he leaped across the crumbled bank that had caused their trouble. This time, she tried but failed to keep her eyes away from him.

The wagon, Wolf saw, had slid off the path, crashed into a boulder, and turned on its side. The two horses were just managing, through hard struggling, to stay on their feet, but were inflicting injury on the driver.

The old man roused when Wolf slapped his face. "Chief!" Flapjack yelped, grasping his hand. "It's the woman you gotta help. She went in the water, and I cain't get out from under here to get to her. Oh, Lord, my leg hurts somethin' awful."

CHAPTER ELEVEN

"I've already seen to the woman," Wolf assured Flapjack, reaching for the wagon's seat cloth and tying it around his waist. "Now I'll get those horses off you." He caught both mares by their bridles and calmed them, untangled their traces, and tethered them to a maple tree already blazing red in the late summer. This done, he put his shoulder to the wagon until the old man was able to crawl out, moaning and wincing every time he moved his right leg. Then Wolf heaved the heavy wagon upright.

But when he tried to coax the horses back, one refused to budge. Wolf used a soothing tone, but it made no difference. He ran his hands over her front left fetlock. "There's some swelling, but I think it's just a bruise. It will heal if you rub it with liniment and let her rest it," he told Flapjack. "As will your own leg."

The wagon master sat on the bank holding his injured leg. "I know you're better'n any man alive 'bout horses, and most everythin' else, too," he gritted, "but I gotta get going."

Wolf shook his head. "You can't move that horse until she's rested, and that's that. You can't go anywhere, anyway. Look there." He motioned to a deep dent in the right rear wheel. "Even if it'll turn, we can't get the wagon up the bank 'til both horses can pull it. As soon as your leg improves, you'll have to ride your good horse into Valley Town and bring back somebody to help you fix the wheel."

Flapjack was aghast. "No tellin' when I can do that!"

"You'll have plenty of food. The woods are full of game."

"It ain't that. I can't keep *her* here," he yelped, looking at Isabelle, then put his head in his hands. "Her daddy'll kill me. He's an important man, a state senator, and I promised him I'd take care of her. And I took his money, a lot of it, fer making such a damn fool trip. I'm supposed to get that there lady to Fort Butler by nightfall."

Wolf stiffened. "Why?"

"'Cause she's goin' there to stay with her brother." Flapjack looked at him, unhappier still.

Wolf was silent for a long while. He was not thinking about the boisterous river, even as he watched how it ran swiftly, tumbled over rocks and boulders, foamed white from its effort, then gathered into deep pools to rest a spell before tumbling off again. He was thinking of other things.

Flapjack began testing his leg, pulling himself up by a sapling. On the fourth try, it held.

Finally Wolf spoke. "I'll take the lady to Fort Butler."

Flapjack gasped. "Are you crazy? You can't do that, it's too dangerous. Her brother's in command of the fort." His warning got louder. "Her name's Miss Isabelle *Mattox*."

Isabelle had crept close and now looked from one to the other. "Does that make a difference?"

"Only if ye want the man who just saved yer life arrested by yer brother," the old man mumbled sourly.

When she recoiled from this, Wolf told Flapjack, "You're exaggerating the danger. There've been no arrests up here. And I'm on my way to Washington City again with John Ross, our principal chief."

"Humph," snorted Flapjack. "He just enjoys all them parties they give him up there. You won't change this president's mind, any more than ye did Andrew Jackson's. At best ye'll just get it put off."

"We'll see," Wolf replied firmly.

"What are you talking about?" Isabelle wondered.

"I'll explain later." In deference to her, Wolf turned his back to put on his clothes. He added the string tie to his white shirt but looped his black suit jacket around his waist. "And now I think Miss Mattox and I will get on our way. Fort Butler is about a twenty-five mile ride from here," he told her, putting the red cap into his pocket.

He was amused to see that she had once again turned away her eyes. "Well, I thank you, sir, especially as it seems there's some problem. You'll have no trouble from my brother, for he's a gentleman, and a fair one. He'll be thankful I am rescued, and doubtless give you some reward for it, especially as you're a chief, as I heard Mr. Foster say." Her smile was large in her small face.

Flapjack snorted. "His reward'll be handcuffs and chains, most likely, maybe worse."

Once again she looked from one to the other. "I don't understand."

Once again, neither man gave an explanation.

Exasperated, as though giving up trying to understand their mute conversation, she asked, "What will happen to my trunk and boxes?"

"Flapjack will bring them when he and his horse are well and his wagon is fixed." Wolf smiled at his friend. "Won't you?"

"Ye can count on it." Although addressing Isabelle, he threw Wolf another woeful glance. "At least *I'm* scared of yer brother."

Wolf led up his black and white horse and untied his bedroll. From it he took a broad-brimmed felt hat which he set low. Next came a pair of deerskin pants and a shirt. He thrust them at Isabelle. "Get behind that big hickory tree over there and put these on," he commanded. Looking at her small waist, he handed her a long strip of hide. "You'll need to tie them on."

It was a fancy outfit, the shirt embroidered with colored beads. She shook her head. "I can't; they're too good."

Flapjack jeered, "Don't worry about that. He just wears his Injun clothes for showing off to the president and them congressmen."

"Don't you need to carry out your important mission instead of going to Fort Butler?"

But Wolf smiled at her, a sudden flash of very white, strong teeth. "Nothing is more important than getting you out of harm's way, Miss Mattox. I am fully at your service, to see you reach your destination. I can catch up with my party in a few days. We've traveled this route many times, so I know where they'll be camping each night. As for clothes, there are more where those came from." He watched her carefully and added, again with amusement, "Besides, you cannot travel in those sopping wet clothes. My pinto is strong, but he could not bear the extra weight. These are light." Again he held out the buckskins.

She was beaten. "All right, I'll do as you say, but what's to be done with these?" Ruefully, she looked down at her wet clothes.

His glance lingered too long for her liking, but he said, "Roll them up, and let Flapjack bring them with the rest."

She accepted his clothes and went behind the tree. As they waited, Flapjack moved around, stretching out his bad leg.

Realizing his maneuvers were also calculated to sneak a look behind the hickory tree, Wolf cautioned him quietly. "Mind your manners. She's a lady." But when a dainty foot appeared for a moment, he did not avert his own eyes.

"What was it ye said?" Flapjack mocked.

When she reappeared, despite the strange garb far too large for her small frame, her golden curls askew but drying, she seemed the most elegant lady Wolf had ever seen. But he said, laughing, "You make a mighty fine man, ma'am, if you'll excuse me saying so."

She was too embarrassed to enjoy his compliment. "I appreciate your generosity," she said primly, tying on her soggy bonnet, "but how will I get your clothes back to you?"

"I'll come and get them." He pulled his hat brim lower against the afternoon sun.

Flapjack slammed her bundle of wet clothing into the wagon bed, shook his head, and then scratched it.

Wolf mounted his dappled horse and kept him still while, with a strong arm and Flapjack's help, he hoisted Isabelle up behind. She clutched at his shoulders, then snatched her hands away as if she'd put them in a fire, before reluctantly putting them around his waist. He turned. "If it bothers you that I'm Cherokee, you can call me Gordon Reid. It's my Scottish name, from my father."

After a moment she told him, “I prefer to call you Wolf.”

“As you wish, Miss Mattox.” He grinned, and pressed his heels into his horse’s flanks.

“And my name is Isabelle.”

In acknowledgement he touched his hat brim. Soon they were trotting at a reasonable clip over the rocky trail toward Fort Butler.

It was a fort, Wolf knew, which had been built to imprison Cherokees.

CHAPTER TWELVE

Isabelle asked, addressing his broad back, "Now will you explain what you and Flapjack were talking about?"

"What do you want to know?"

"Well, first, are you really going to Washington?"

"Yes, I'm going to see President van Buren," he replied.

"But . . . will he see you?"

"Of course. He's expecting us." Then, amused at her tone, added, "He invited us. I'm part of a delegation going with our principal chief, John Ross."

Her silence was reverential. Even her father, a member of the North Carolina state legislature, didn't meet presidents. "What will you be talking to him about?" Questions might not be polite, but her curiosity was overweening.

"We're petitioning the president once more against Indian removal, while we still have support from important senators like Daniel Webster."

She was perplexed. "But there's no doubt of the removal, is there? That's why my brother's in command of Fort Butler. I suppose, in a way, it's why I'm going to stay with him."

Wolf was silent for so long she thought he might be reconsidering his decision to deliver her. And when his answer finally came, it was terse. "There are those of us who still believe we won't have to leave. Ross says there's a chance, by seeing the president again, and we're going to take it. In particular, I'm trying to get citizenship for our people, to enable us to stay."

Isabelle digested this. If that were true, would she have to return to Asheville? The quarrel with her father was still fresh in her mind. It made her speak boldly once more. "I didn't know there were Indians such as you—people who deal with presidents, and Congress."

"There are many of us; we're not all savages." His amusement returned. "My father came here from Scotland; he was an important man and was made a chief. He ensured that I became part of the white man's world and was educated, so that I could help our people understand and become part of this new country. That's why I'm pressing for citizenship."

"You were educated?" She couldn't help showing her surprise.

"I went first to the missionaries in Brainerd, in Tennessee. Then to the Foreign Mission School in Cornwall … Connecticut."

She commented, "You've had it better than most, even white folks." Quickly she added, "That's not to be critical."

His was the easy laugh, she thought, of a strong man. "All we want is to have our ownership recognized, be treated like everyone else, and live peaceably among our white brethren."

Not such an unacceptable idea, she thought.

"And that's why I'm going to Washington."

"Is your father going, too?"

"My father is dead." The terseness was back in his voice, and she could feel him stiffen.

"I'm sorry." Hastily, she asked, "How will you travel to Washington? Surely not all the way on horseback."

He patted the pinto's neck. "I would not travel any other way. And Weenook would not allow me to."

She smiled again. "How far have you ridden today?"

"Only from Huntington, where Fort Butler is. My home's in the northern part of Georgia, near New Echota, where we've built the capital of our Cherokee Nation. It's as fine as Washington City," he told her proudly. "But yesterday I came through Huntington, to visit my mother's clan. That's why I took this path. And another reason I'm taking you back to Fort Butler, so I can visit with them again. I don't get to see them often, and family is very important to the Cherokee."

Wolf's horse climbed a small rise, which caused her to clutch him closer. Conversation seemed the only way to take her mind off things she'd rarely thought about. "Don't you want to move west, then?"

This time, when he turned to look at her, he was astonished instead of amused. Then he swept his arm in a broad circle. "Look at this land! It's beautiful, and it's our home. It's where our ancestors are buried. How would you feel if you were forced to leave your home?"

That's exactly what happened, Isabelle thought, her hands clenching at the memory. Although she had been sent only a hundred miles, and temporarily, she understood his feelings.

As if reading her mind, he commented, "You must be a far piece from home, too."

"My home's in Asheville. East of here."

"I know where it is. Why are you going to Fort Butler?"

"I'm to housekeep for my brother, James." As that was still a sore subject, she asked a question of her own. "Why are you doing this for me?"

In trying to answer, he thought about her bright, fair hair, and the way it curled around eyes so wide and blue they looked like the cornflowers that grew around his porch in Georgia. Her eyes crinkled nearly closed when she smiled. Then he thought about her wet cotton dress; the full bosom, slim waist, and slender legs he had grasped in the icy water. And there was the glimpse he'd caught of a pale, finely-turned ankle behind the hickory tree.

It also had to do with the way she had looked at him when he rescued her, although this was something he felt rather than understood. He knew that a closeness between an Indian man and a white woman wasn't well tolerated, even though two of his friends were married to white women they had met up north.

It was all right the other way around; his father had once ridden through this same gorge, met his beautiful Indian mother, Naomi, at the trading post and taken her back with him to Georgia. Because he was a gentleman, he had made her Mrs. Reid, although it had been neither usual nor expected.

But Wolf had to admit that even those things didn't fully explain the dangerous mission he had undertaken, and voluntarily at that. And so he answered, just as honest as she'd been, "I don't really know."

As they rode on, her cheek now resting more comfortably on his back, Isabelle was silent. She had never met anyone like Tallaquoyah Wolf. Or Gordon Reid, whichever he was. She had much to contemplate as they rode through mountains towering so steep they blocked out the sky.

They sped through Valley Town and began to follow the Valley River instead of the Nantahala. At a shallow ford Wolf stopped to let his horse drink, dismounting in a single, smooth gesture, and handed a gourd full of fresh, cold water up to her before taking one himself.

When at last they left the confines of the gorge for more open country, he urged his horse into a full gallop. "It's another ten miles or so," he told her. "We'll be there by sundown."

The evening drew in as they rode, she clinging to him by now.

Then, suddenly, he stopped his horse. Over Wolf's shoulder Isabelle could see, atop a long hill, the gate of a fort, where a soldier stood sentry. She began to get down. But, curtly, Wolf ordered, "Stay where you are." He drew on his suit jacket, and put away his hat. He pulled out his red cap, and bound it around his head with the loop of deer hide fastened with a gold nugget. Then he set it at a rakish angle before galloping straight up to the fort.

Startled, the soldier pointed his long musket at them and demanded, "Stand! Who are ye?"

CHAPTER THIRTEEN

FORT BUTLER NC, AUGUST 1837

Isabelle stiffened with fear, but Wolf merely glanced at the musket. "I bring a visitor for the captain," he announced.

Looking at the unsaddled horse, the soldier sneered. "Whatta ya take me fer, an idiot? Who could you have fer the captain, ya Injun bastard? I oughta kill ye right now. It'll save doin' it later. And I'd sure like to have that gold nugget in yer cap."

As Isabelle grasped him closer, Wolf said importantly, and rather formally, "This is Captain Mattox's sister, come to stay with him."

The soldier guffawed. "Oh, yeah, his sister—and my Aunt Fanny," he leered, his musket unwavering. "Now get on yer way, afore I make up my mind to shoot ye."

Isabelle felt it might help if she intervened. "Please bring your superior officer or, better yet, my brother, Captain James Mattox, here at once."

The soldier kept his eyes steady but the musket wavered as a corporal advanced warily. "What's goin' on here, Homer?"

"Durned if I kin figger it out," replied the sentry. "We got a Injun that looks like a white man, and a woman says she's white but looks like a Injun man."

"I wish to speak to my brother, Captain James Mattox," Isabelle repeated.

"Well, if you don't sound just like the captain." The corporal scratched his neck. "Maybe you are his sister. Leave her off, then." He barely glanced at Wolf.

"Yes." Once again Isabelle moved to dismount.

"No," Wolf countermanded, stopping her with his arm. To the corporal he announced, "I am Chief Gordon Reid, and I wish to deliver her directly into the captain's safe keeping."

The sentry spewed, "You don't think we kin look after her as good as you can? Why, I oughta…" He took aim again.

"You shouldn't have done that," Isabelle hissed in Wolf's ear.

"I do not leave ladies stranded in the woods," Wolf reminded her with a smile, as if they were conversing pleasantly.

The corporal's expression hardened, but he scratched his neck again. "Well, I'll tell the captain you're here. But I don't guarantee nothing. My friend here may kill ye yet. It's fer sure the captain will." He laughed to think those two expected to get away with anything, looking such a sight as they were. He walked, cocky, toward a small log cabin set against the perimeter fence. Captain Mattox would soon put the bastard straight, he thought, glad they had their first prisoner. Or corpse. "Let 'em on in, Zeke."

As he opened the wide door, Zeke gave Wolf an unpleasantly hospitable grin. "Come in, why don't ye? 'Specially if you're ready to be put in chains. Although I confess, I'd still druther kill ye." Once again, he eyed the gold nugget.

As Wolf gave his horse a silent, barely perceptible command, Isabelle hung onto him, feeling once more that her life depended on it. Wolf, returning the soldier's stare, rode past him proudly, straight into the fort, before halting Weenook on the hard-packed parade ground.

CHAPTER FOURTEEN

Captain James Mattox strode out of his cabin, musket at the ready, trailed by the corporal whose grin, he knew, anticipated bloodshed.

Wolf said, "I bear no arms, sir, and I would think it a kindness if you put yours down, and ask your men to do the same."

James growled, "Indians always have more weapons than the eye can see," and ignored the request, fingering the barrel of his musket, issuing no orders. Almost as badly as the corporal, he was itching to arrest the Indian. But the Army's official policy was hands-off, until the removal order was enforced. He wished he could just shoot the man. Of course he could—never mind official policy. Anything could happen in a remote fort in the wilds of Indian country. Had they been alone, he might well have killed the Indian for simply touching his sister. However, there were a lot of soldiers around. Not that that mattered much.

Barely relaxing his grimace as he finally turned to his sister, James' mouth fell open at her appearance. He was unsure which problem was the worst, or which he should deal with first. Finally, he burst out with the only question he could muster. "Isabelle, what's the meaning of this? You were supposed to be brought by Flapjack Foster."

Peering around Wolf, she asked, "Aren't you glad to see me, James?"

"You know what I mean," he replied, impatient. "Of course you're welcome, but why are you with an Indian, dressed in that outrageous way? Where's Flapjack, and your things?"

Wolf sat taller, pulling his cap down to shade the fire of the setting sun. The muskets followed him. "Mr. Foster is indisposed," he replied calmly, "so Chief Tallaquoyah Wolf is delivering your sister, sir, due to the troubles she has encountered."

James measured the chief with eyes intended to be as hard as the lead in his musket. He had heard much of this man. It was said that he had more courage than most others. Not to mention lands and wealth, and the respect of both white and red men, all of which galled James. What other Indian would ride straight up to an army fort and demand an audience with the commander? "I suppose you didn't have anything to do with those 'troubles,' nor with her wearing an Indian get-up?"

As if eager to enlighten him, Isabelle rushed in, "Wolf saved my life, and Flapjack's!"

"Whatever can you mean by that?"

"It's true. The wagon wrecked into the river, and we would have drowned—myself especially—if the chief hadn't rescued us."

James saw that more soldiers, all with muskets, no doubt alerted by the commotion, had arrived, led by a sergeant. They surrounded the pinto which, as if not caring for the sight of so many strangers, snorted, and stepped around, frisky, tossing his long, pale mane. The firearms followed the horse's every move. Fingers tightened now on a dozen triggers. James felt hopeful, but noticed that Isabelle had closed her eyes and looked like she was praying. Wolf simply spoke quietly to his horse, calming him.

Finally James said, "I suppose I'll hear about these calamities in time." Grudgingly, he continued, "Well, then, Chief, it seems you've done my sister a service, after all." He lowered his weapon but still gave no orders to his men. Their beads remained on Wolf. "Get her down, Sergeant."

And when his sister had been brought down, James finally moved to welcome her. But, getting a closer look at colorful beadwork incongruously topped by a limp straw bonnet and bottomed by high-buttoned shoes, he was overcome with disdain, and stopped short of the embrace he'd intended.

She looked back up at Wolf. "How will I return your clothes?"

James' mouth fell open. "They're your clothes? Isabelle, really!"

Ignoring him, Wolf told her, "I will come for them."

James sputtered, "I think not, sir. We'll see they find you." He walked a few paces, then whirled back to Wolf. "In gratitude for my sister's rescue, I should recommend that you accept the government's offer and go west voluntarily, as many of you have done."

"Thank you for your advice," Wolf replied shortly, "but I'd rather live on my lands and work in my businesses."

"You'll get good compensation for them, and if you wait until the removal is enforced, you may get nothing."

Wolf's mouth curled with contempt, "I don't need a blanket and rifle, which is pitifully little, and all the government is offering to most of our people."

James set his mouth in a thin line. "There's the huge sum of five million dollars for them to share, and you know it."

Wolf's mouth curled again. "Our lands are worth far more. We have over twenty million acres left, and much of it contains gold."

James glanced at the adornment on Wolf's cap. "Most of your people would be glad of a rifle and blanket," he retorted. "There aren't many with the riches of Chief Gordon Reid." Once again he wished he could just shoot the man, but now he was concerned about what Isabelle would think. There was the inescapable fact that the villain had rescued her from some mess she'd gotten herself into.

"I've worked hard for my money," Wolf asserted as he gathered Weenook's reins and turned him around. "I intend to keep it a while longer." He looked at Isabelle. "Goodbye, Miss Mattox, and good luck." Then, giving the horse his head, the tall, striking figure, dark hair flowing like a banner behind him, moved smartly out of the fort.

When the muskets lifted again, Isabelle cried out, "James!"

James made a downward gesture, and could feel the soldiers' disappointment. Then he explained to his sister, "You may think me hard, but he got a warmer reception than he deserved. His actions will not benefit him in the end."

Isabelle said, softly, "It seems to me that he's damned if he does and damned if he doesn't."

"You'd better not use that sort of language around here. The soldiers will think you're one of them, especially as you're wearing trousers." James smiled in an attempt to be more cheerful. He wanted to embrace her, but as soon as he touched buckskin, his body stiffened. Still, he forced himself to say, "Welcome, sister, to your new home." Then he swept his arm out and crooked it for her to take, in order to lead her inside.

CHAPTER FIFTEEN

With a last look at Wolf's departing back, Isabelle hitched up her trousers and, forcing gaiety, accepted James' change of mood and his arm. They had walked only a few paces, however, when she had to relinquish it to pass through the narrow doorway of his quarters. What a shock she experienced!

Of course, she had known his accommodation would be different from their large, gracious, veranda-encircled home in Asheville. Even so, her face fell as she looked around, although the whole could be seen at a glance.

There was just one room, which was the kitchen but also served as what parlor there was. The room's only furniture was a rough wooden table and chair that stood opposite the wide fireplace where a small fire burned. The floor was not wood but hard-packed clay, the same red color that chinked the logs that formed the walls. Nails driven into them at random provided hanging for a few clothes and even fewer utensils. The logs were covered with a layer of pale red dust.

A rough wooden cupboard sat, lopsided, against a half-wall of wooden slats at the far end. Needing to take only two steps to reach it, she saw behind it another room, just big enough for a trundle bed covered with a lumpy mattress. She supposed it to be James'. "Where will I sleep?" Her voice trembled in anticipation of his reply. A pile of hay on the dirt floor would not have surprised her.

But his chivalrous answer did. "You may have the bedroom."

Her relief was great. "Where will you sleep?"

"I'll bunk in with the men. My real worry is what on earth you'll do with yourself here."

"You make it sound like I'm here for a holiday. I'm not; I've come to keep house and cook for you."

He waved his arm. "As you can see, there's not much house to keep, and I eat with my men in the camp's kitchen."

She was troubled by that. "But Father has ordered me to. I'll have to cook anyway, as I could not eat with the men. And surely my cooking will be an improvement over the camp's kitchen?"

He looked doubtful. "Can't say as I've ever tasted yours." When she was silent he offered, "I'll bank your fire; it'll last you all night."

Two blackened tin pots hung on the wall, but there were no iron ones, although the fireplace did have chains and pulleys for holding them. "How will I cook without pots?"

"Darned if I know." His answer was muffled by his efforts. "I've never thought about it."

She seized on the cupboard, as if it held all the answers. Inside it, though, she found only a greasy tin plate and cup, a hunting knife quite inappropriate for dining, and an oversized two-tined fork. "There's not only nothing to cook with, there's nary a scrap of food!" she wailed.

"I've never needed to cook. I'm sure you can get whatever you need from the camp's cook."

She felt doubtful, mostly because she barely knew what to ask for.

He seemed to notice. "Isabelle, are you sure you even know how to cook?"

She drew herself up, wishing she were properly dressed, for it would give her more authority. "I have full instructions from our housekeeper. Emily has been teaching me every day since Papa decided to send me. And what she didn't have time to teach me, I shall learn by myself. But . . ." her resolve suddenly weakened, and she looked helplessly around the sparse room. "Emily has so many devices for keeping house, spoons and ladles, pots and cranes and bowls, ovens for the fireplace. I see nothing here that she has even instructed me about."

James began to laugh. "This is a fine how d'ye-do. Whatever was Father thinking when he sent you out here?" He took a deep breath. "I'm sorry he did, sorry you had that arduous trip, the accident, that Indian, everything. You must have been scared to death by it all. This is no place for a lady, and Papa should know that."

She turned away so he couldn't see her chin tremble or the resentment that lingered as she remembered her father. He had become so angry at her that he swept a potted plant onto the Persian carpet, making a dark stain. "There were not many choices of places to send me. And you know that once Papa decides on something, he never changes his mind."

"What on earth did you do to deserve this kind of punishment?" James drawled, draping a uniformed leg over the table's edge.

Her smile was rueful. "I refused to marry Preston McKeever, Jr."

"His best friend's son? And the son of the second richest man in Asheville?" James gawped.

"The very same," she sighed.

He whistled in amazement. "Still, it doesn't sound bad enough to warrant exile."

"Oh, well, there's more. Preston's wasn't the first proposal I've turned down." He nodded. "And I made the mistake of telling father my reasons, each time. He didn't agree."

"What were they?" James made himself more comfortable.

"Well, Preston disgraced himself by getting drunk at the Fourth of July picnic," she said, not adding the rest. "I could not contemplate a lifetime of that," she finished firmly. "The others were cruel to their horses, or merely boring."

"Isabelle…" James shifted, choosing his words. "Those are just the things that make men… *men*."

"I don't agree. And they were not interested in my handicrafts. And besides being oafs…" her body stiffened, her face saddened, "…they made it plain they're more interested in father's money than in me. I don't call that manly."

"But surely Preston wouldn't need father's money."

She could hide the secret no longer. "He would, indeed, to keep his harlots." She brushed back a tear at remembering how she had found him glassy-eyed in the embrace of the town trollop. She turned to James for comfort. Awkwardly, he put his arm around her. Into his shoulder she continued, "And as this was the third time I've turned down one of Father's choice young men, he exploded in a fury I've never afore experienced." She plopped down in the chair. "You see, as I'm nearly twenty, I'm a complete disgrace to him."

"Now, now, I'm sure that isn't true."

She sighed loudly. "If only mother were still alive, she could reason with him. Why doesn't he harass you about being unmarried?"

"It's different for a man."

"I don't know why."

James waved away her opinion. She knew he thought her ideas unconventional. "Don't take this the wrong way. I'm happy to provide you with a haven away from your troubles with Father. But you can see it won't be easy. How long do you think you'll be staying?"

She shrugged. "Until you take the Indians away, I've always supposed. I can hardly stay on here after you leave." She frowned. And neither could she exist here like an animal, which seemed to be her new lot in life.

"Well, try to put up with things. I know it's rough, but you won't be here long. We've got orders about the Indians. I can tell you the situation is very close to being resolved, by which time Father should have relented his fury."

He lit a tallow candle, stuck it into a knot of pine wood, and handed it to her. "This will see you to bed. I know you're tired and the worse for wear after your accident. In the morning, I'll see you're sent some breakfast and some clothes." He went into his bedroom and threw out one of his shirts. "That'll do for you to sleep in, and for wearing tomorrow." Mouth twitching in amusement, he drawled, "We don't happen to have any dresses around. Even the ladies in the town have to make their own. When do you think your clothes will arrive?"

"I've no idea. But thank you." She embraced him more warmly. James was her oldest brother, and her favorite among the three, even over baby Charles. It was the reason her father's exile had seemed tolerable.

"Well, you can at least put on some proper trousers tomorrow. You sure can't go around in Indian buckskins. Somebody would shoot you."

She winced. "And when Wolf returns for his clothes?"

James' amusement faded. "See that you set them outside the gates of the fort as early as possible tomorrow," he said harshly, "so that he won't come in. That's for your protection as well as his."

She laughed a silent, tired laugh to think of needing protection from the man who had just saved her life, risking his twice in the doing. But she was too weary, and too eager to save Wolf another dangerous encounter, to argue.

"I'll bid you a good night."

When he had gone, she took off the buckskins that had so offended him, folding them neatly. Wearing James' shirt, she lay down on the uncomfortable mattress, which she discovered was filled with dried corn shucks. Its cover was rough, too, and had a musty odor. It was doubtful she would sleep much on it.

But, exhausted by the ordeals of the day, she felt herself losing consciousness almost immediately.

CHAPTER SIXTEEN

ASHEVILLE NC, APRIL 1999

Carol paced the veranda that curled around the Mattox home. It was so wide there was plenty of room, even though her mother's porch furniture seemed to have expanded in the last two years.

Carefully she held Tallaquoyah Wolf's medicine bag, which she'd taken from the museum, and was peering again at its contents when the floorboard underneath her right foot gave way. "Ohhh!" she screamed, as she fell onto hard-packed earth, landing with a one-legged jolt, doing a painful split.

She managed to slip the deerskin pouch into the pocket of her jeans and free her hands. Should she try to pull her right leg up, or her other leg down? Would she fall further if she leaned on her elbows? Would the surrounding boards give way too? "Help!"

The Mattoxes' housekeeper came in answer to her cries. In no time Geraldine had helped Carol climb out, and without further damage. "You could have broken your leg," she fussed.

"Tell me about it." Carol was glum. "Don't they check for rotten pieces?"

"Yes, it's checked regular—and nobody's noticed any problems lately." Helping Carol into a chair, Geraldine fussed some more, then went to fetch a glass of iced tea.

Carol brooded, nursing her bruised foot and scraped leg. Was it an accident? Correction: an 'accident' like Phil's? Was it the Wolf curse on the Mattoxes?

Grandma's theory was becoming more plausible by the minute. There were a lot of accidents in the Mattox family.

She took out the medicine bag and, still slightly dazed, addressed it, like Snow White: "Pouch, Pouch, in my hand, Who will be the next to die? Will Grandma be right about that, too?" A heavy shudder passed through her, the kind that make people say, "somebody's walking over my grave." What if there really were a curse on the Mattox family? One put on by the Wolfs? "I have to find out more about this," she whispered to herself. And she owed it to Phil. *'You'll know what to do,'* he'd said.

Geraldine returned with the tea and a slice of coconut cake, her remedy for every ailment, Carol knew. "Hunh. Don't talk, just get this down you. And then tell your daddy to fix up this place. It may be a mansion, but it's downright dangerous."

Carol, however, knew that repairs weren't the answer. As surely, she knew the answer was in the town of Cherokee. She needed an expert. Dr. Ralph Raxter, the man who wanted the Mattox Collection for the Indian museum, was the person most likely to know what the pouch contained. And what it meant. She would have to see him.

Even though Winston, too, was in Cherokee.

CHAPTER SEVENTEEN

CHEROKEE NC, MAY 1999

Gambling machines clacked through Cherokee's vast Harrah's Casino as though it were a huge factory. Today Wanda Running Bear and two fellow nurses had felt like getting out of the hospital for a while and exchanged their canteen for the casino's Deli. It was a favorite lunch spot for gamblers and non-gamblers alike, and they had settled at a back table.

As Joan Teesateskee bit into her tuna sandwich, Wanda asked, "When did you say that council election is?"

Inez Campbell replied, "Next Tuesday. Don't worry, everybody says Winston's a shoo-in for Chief."

"I hope so." Wanda decided to share a rare confidence. "I'd like to be the wife of the chief."

Joan stared. "Does that mean you're going to be Winston's wife?"

"Of course." Wanda tossed her long black hair. "Anyway, I should be the chief's wife."

Joan swallowed another bite. "How do you figure that?"

Although distrusting the feeling, Wanda decided to be completely honest with them. "Because I'm the most beautiful girl on the reservation, and Winston Wolfe is the handsomest man. And I'm one-eighth Cherokee, and that's better for a chief's wife." She stroked her hair. "The more pure-blooded, the better. I'm more Indian."

The neon 'lightning rods' in the ceiling started a blinding display that meant someone had won a jackpot over a hundred dollars. Tossing her hair again, Wanda failed to see Joan and Inez exchange a look before they chorused, "Right."

When the light show above them had finished, Inez commented, "Well, he seems devoted to you. He's never dated anybody else."

"We *are* engaged," Wanda reminded her acidly.

"You are?"

This time Wanda saw the look of surprise Inez exchanged with Joan. "Of course," she replied impatiently, inspecting her long, oval-shaped nails, admiring her favorite pale lavender frosted polish. Then, her mind jumping to other things, she began to drum the table with them. *Ccclliick. Ccclliick.* She had decided. She would wait until after the election, but then she would make Winston decide, too.

She would make him set their wedding date.

CHAPTER EIGHTEEN

ASHEVILLE NC, MAY 1999

Carol looked at the clutter of books and keepsakes in her childhood room. When she was about fourteen, she'd proudly chosen the chintz bedspread and matching curtains. What a long time ago that seemed. And it was a long way, both literally and figuratively, from the Nanjina research station. Preparing to call her boss again, she thought of her home there. It did not have chintz. It was a rough wooden hut which she shared with lizards and anything else that felt like crawling through its large cracks. In its single room she ate, slept, and did her paperwork. She thought of the office her call would reach. It would have a bare wooden table, and it would be mostly empty. Anthropologists spent most of their time in the field. And the field, in this case, would be a desert that was ninety degrees and climbing. If there was any breeze, it would be making whirly winds that blew dust into everything and made you feel hot even when you weren't.

She looked at her watch. Right about now her boss, Brian Keating, would be starting to check the reports from yesterday. At the end of every day, three anthropologists, herself included, sifted through the data they had collected, and wrote a precis of it for Brian. Every morning Brian read over these summaries, and if necessary made suggestions, pointing them in new directions, for the next day's work. For a moment Carol yearned for the familiar routine of the research station, instead of the emotional roller coaster she'd been on since she got to Asheville.

The researchers' current project was a study of the Nanjinas, a nearly intact tribe, culturally speaking, of southwestern Native Americans. For anthropologists, studying meant recording everything about the people, their customs and beliefs. Everything from their diet to their sex life, Carol thought, smiling inwardly. It wasn't easy to wrest such intimate information out of people, even when they'd agreed to give it.

Carol reflected on the many months she'd spent trying to unravel the Nanjinas' marriage customs. It was hard when the men refused to discuss them, the young girls were forbidden to, and even the older women were reluctant. Just before she'd left, she'd spent nearly a week talking to Frankie Moose, a Nanjina woman, and had actually been making some headway. She'd grabbed the tapes at the last minute and brought them with her, intending to do some work while she was in North Carolina. But thanks to all the upsetting things happening here, she'd forgotten about them. It was time she refreshed her memory, or she'd have to spend a lot of time catching up when she went back. Right now, she thought wryly, as she turned on her tape recorder, she was closer to working out the Cherokees' belief systems than the Nanjinas'.

"How do you know if you're marrying somebody related to you?" her recorded voice floated through the room.

"Well," came Frankie's soft reply, "first we make sure the man comes from a different place than the girl."

Sweet Frankie. As the tape wore on, her shy explanations revealed, to Carol's trained mind, that rather than having the random, and seemingly miraculous, system first suspected, the Nanjinas had highly selective marriage customs, and observed a string of taboos. It explained why such an isolated group showed none of the usual problems of intermarriage and, once again excited by her progress, Carol bent closer to her tape recorder. "One woman, in each place, is in charge of that," Frankie confided. And then the tape ran out.

Sighing with frustration, Carol put in the next cassette. "You can't say that dreams aren't real," exploded a man's voice, and Carol sat up in surprise.

Hunh? This wasn't the next tape of Frankie. This was a tape of her conversation with the Nanjina elder they called Prophet, who was unofficially the head of the clan. In her haste, she had grabbed the wrong tape.

"Of course we have dreams. We even have dreams during the day, when we're not asleep." Carol's mind's eye could see Prophet's wry grin.

"How does that happen?"

"When we think of something, it may be red or blue. It may be a man or a woman. The thing is, we don't just think it, we see it."

Carol leaned over the tape recorder once more. "But you know it isn't real, don't you? That it's a vision?" her metallic voice continued.

"Oh, no. It's real," he insisted. "And it isn't always bad; it can be good, too. Seeing things is proof that they exist."

"Proof?" She wondered what Prophet would make of Grandma's suspicions about the Wolfs and the Mattoxes.

"Yes, our people believe that if you can put a face and a figure to your thoughts, they're more real. It's just like talking to somebody, instead of trying to guess what they're thinking."

"But if the thoughts are just in your mind, and you can't explain them—"

"Lots of things can't be explained, Carol. Why, if life was just about the things you can see, taste and hear, it would be a pretty poor life. There's more inside here…" she could see him tapping his forehead "…than out there. Go with the flow. Don't pigeon-hole."

Suddenly, she yearned to talk more to Prophet about such things, now that she'd had the vision, and the pouch, she now believed, had caused her to have an accident. Suddenly, she needed to know about things like dreams and visions, not as an anthropologist, but as a human being. Despite her professionalism, she felt vulnerable.

Well, she'd have a chance to ask Prophet more when she got back to Arizona. She picked up the telephone to call Brian. After exchanging pleasantries and asking after everyone, then catching up with the latest news, she said, "I'm sorry, Brian, but I'd like to have a little more time here. My family—my parents—they're not in very good shape." *Nor am I,* she wanted to add.

"Take your time, Carol," he replied kindly, his Australian accent sounding stronger because she hadn't heard it for a while.

“That’s sweet of you. I just need a few more days. Maybe a week, tops. I’ll use vacation time, of course. I miss everybody there, and I’m anxious to finish what I was doing when I had to leave. I was just getting somewhere with Frankie.”

“The Nanjinas will be waiting for you.” Before she could reply, he added, “And so will I.”

It was open to interpretation. But she had little doubt about what he meant. And she dreaded another encounter like the last.

“I can’t do without my best researcher for long.” He cleared his throat. “I’ll be thinking of you. And I’d like to—”

Worried about what he might say, and wanting to spare his feelings, she broke in hastily. “Thanks. I’ll call and let you know what’s happening.” Then she offered a quick goodbye.

She couldn’t think of Brian as anything more than a professional colleague.

But then, she thought of every man like that. Except one. And she’d just seen him again after ten years, and it had all come back.

When somebody has saved your life, you never forget him.

CHAPTER NINETEEN

CHEROKEE NC, MAY 1999

The main floor of Winston Wolfe's law firm—his private office was upstairs—could easily hold thirty people. But on the night of the tribal election, he estimated that at least fifty of his closest friends and supporters were jammed into it.

A can of beer was hoisted high. "Here's to the new Principal Chief of the Eastern Band."

A sea of cans bobbed an answering salute as someone said, "Wow, that's quite a mouthful."

"I can't even figure out an acronym for that," said Winston's secretary, Susan Broadfoot. "We'll just have to call you Chief."

"That's all right unless we're in Oklahoma," somebody commented. "They've got another chief there."

"We're here because we didn't want to go to Oklahoma."

"We're here," Winston reminded them, "because Will Thomas persuaded the government to let some of us stay." He looked around. "His getting the Qualla Boundary recognized 'way back in 1837 led to us getting the casino now, more than a hundred and fifty years later." Land was one of his strongest interests. "You never know how some of these things will end up. Just shows—it always pays to get as much land as possible, as free and unencumbered as possible. It's important for the future," the lawyer in him advised. "Losing our land was how our troubles started, two hundred years ago."

"We lost it because there was gold on it," Harry Timson said sourly, "and everybody wanted that."

"Hey, Will Thomas is a distant cousin of mine," announced Patrick Yates, a tall, handsome young lawyer on Winston's staff.

"Well, he's one white man we can thank. Is that why you wanted to work for Winston?"

"No. Winston's the best, that's why," answered Patrick. "He's going places." Patrick was also Winston's political aide, in charge of helping him run for office—as far as Winston wanted to go.

Mark Owl returned to the subject of the Removal. "I don't know how people could have left here and gone to Oklahoma."

"They didn't have a choice, remember?" Winston's campaign manager sounded impatient.

"Let's not get into that argument again," Susan admonished them, snatching up a mug of pens that was about to be knocked off a desk. "It's done with."

But Winston told her firmly, "Nothing in the history of the world's ever done with. Everything leads to the future. That's why I'm focused on it; on the future of our people."

He could see Patrick winding up to throw him a question. "Okay, what's going to be your first job as Chief?"

Immediately Winston obliged. "We need more light industry; that will never change. But first we need to get some of our mountain land swapped for flat ground where factories can be built, not to mention a new school and hospital. I'm going to get very involved in that; it's right down my alley—environmental issues."

"Is anybody against swapping the land?"

When Winston hesitated, Patrick answered, "Not really. I think everybody agrees it ought to be done. But Senator Mattox has somehow failed to get it ratified by Congress. We need to make a new effort."

"Maybe get it re-introduced in the House?"

"Yeah, I think Charles Taylor could get it through."

"What else are you gonna do, Winston?"

"Well, I've been thinking..." his eyes swept the room, "we should study the Cherokee language in school a little longer."

"It's already in all the schools."

"The language is," he replied, "but we need to add cultural studies, our history and customs."

"Sounds good to me."

But Winston was nowhere near finished. "And we need another historical pageant to draw new tourists. 'Unto These Hills' is still great, but it's nearly fifty years old and everybody, even the tourists, has seen it a dozen times."

"That's a good idea. Why, with millions of people traveling through the Smokies every year, we could have two or three outdoor dramas, all of 'em about the Cherokees."

Before Winston could continue his wish-list, Wanda Running Bear insinuated herself between him and his friends. Smoothing down his dark, spiky hair with long fingers, she draped her slim, lithe body around him, snake-like, and pouted, "Now y'all are going to have to forget the rest of those boring old business things. The chief has more important things to think about than work."

Winston felt vaguely uncomfortable. "I do? There's hardly..."

She interrupted, with a smile. "He's got a wedding to go to."

"What?"

"When?"

"Whose?"

"Ours. Isn't that right, honey?" One slim arm swung from his shoulder as the room quieted.

Winston's insides flipped over, but he smiled, too, unwrapped his new fiancée, put an arm more loosely around her, and faced his loyal friends. "She's right."

"Hey, I thought this was an election party, but I reckon it's just turned into an engagement party."

"So, when's the wedding gonna be?" somebody repeated.

The new chief ran fingers through his hair, spiking it up again. He looked at

Wanda, whose dark eyes were shining. "It's up to you, honey," she cooed at him. But somehow, he thought, it wasn't the contented sound of a turtle dove.

He waved a hand as if trying to decide on a date. Then he flashed a chagrined smile. "Stay tuned, folks. You'll be the first to know."

CHAPTER TWENTY

"I want the wedding to be soon. In June." Wanda gazed at Winston from her white sofa. "The spirits say that's a good time."

"You've consulted the spirits?" Winston was surprised.

"Of course. It's important, for an occasion like this."

Despite believing the Cherokee culture should be preserved and celebrated, he didn't practice the old ways himself. But he respected them, and he knew Wanda's belief in them was strong. "Well, there's a problem with June. I'll have to spend most of the summer in Raleigh seeing about that land swap. I'll probably have to go to Washington, too."

Wanda's lower lip drooped. "You just don't want to get married," she flung at him.

"I have to admit, I haven't thought a lot about it."

"Whaaat?" She looked shocked. "But I told you that everybody expects us to. And you didn't say 'No.'"

"You said that about getting engaged," he pointed out. Try as he had, he couldn't remember deciding to get married.

"What's the difference between being engaged and getting married?" she asked, looking at him suspiciously.

"Well . . ." There were reasons. But he didn't care to examine them too closely.

She looked down at the floor, as if indescribably sad. "Don't you think engaged people are supposed to get married?"

He felt like a fool when she put it that way. "I just hadn't thought about taking the next step," he explained, lamely.

Now she looked like she was about to cry. "You made it sound like you agreed. You led me on."

"No. It's just that marriage . . ." He put out a hand, as though searching for a reason that would make sense.

"'It's just that,'" she mocked him. "You don't want to get married!" she accused again, and flounced off to her bedroom and slammed the door.

Was he supposed to follow her?

But he decided to stay where he was, in the big leather armchair in her living room.

Had he really agreed to get married?

He'd never thought much about any of those things. Through college and law school, then his early working years, he'd been too busy studying and sticking to his carefully-planned career path, to have much time to date. Much less have a relationship. Then he had returned to Cherokee, and discovered Wanda had grown up while he was gone. They went out a few times while he was establishing his law practice. And then they just seemed to become a couple.

It had all happened before he so unexpectedly met up with Carol Mattox in St. Joseph's Hospital last week.

And suddenly, he was face to face with those reasons he'd shied away from. He thought of another time, another girl. A totally different girl. She was small and pale-faced, with blonde hair that refused to do what it should and eyes the color of cornflowers. From the moment he had met her, all those years ago at Camp Hope, he had known there was something different about her. It was like he already knew her from somewhere else. He guessed that was what people meant by love at first sight, the kind everybody laughed at.

She was *hsing-ga-wa-la* to him: a 'little one' to love and protect, who needed him. Carol Mattox was the only woman he'd ever wanted badly enough to pursue. And where had that got him? He shuddered to think of that day, Carol's sixteenth birthday, when he'd visited the Mattox home in Asheville. Her parents had been downright rude to him. And they weren't the only ones who hadn't seemed to like him. Carol herself had sent his letters back, and never returned his phone calls.

All that was a long time ago. She was probably married by now, to her daddy's choice of husband. But he hadn't noticed a wedding ring. His heart raced. She had his card. Would she get in touch? And he still had her phone number.

But most likely she had someone. It didn't really matter, anyway. Even if he were free, she might still reject him. Her parents would feel the same about him, and he didn't want to go through that again.

Besides, he was engaged to Wanda. That much wasn't in question. Tonight had merely made it official. And as she'd said, marriage was the next step.

So he got up and said, through her closed bedroom door, "I do want to get married. We just have to be reasonable about the date, that's all." To make her feel better, he added, "Ask the spirits what they think about Thanksgiving."

CHAPTER TWENTY ONE

It was only the beginning of May, but the day was going to be a real scorcher, Carol realized, turning up the air conditioning as she exited the interstate and headed west on Highway 19.

Soon she was on the road that followed the Nantahala River through a twisting gorge so narrow it defied all efforts to widen it. A mileage sign said: 'Cherokee 21; Bryson City 34; Franklin 47; Murphy 64.' The place Isabelle's father had banished her to, as housekeeper for her brother at Fort Butler, was now the town of Murphy. Thinking of her aunt's forbidden love, Carol wondered again what Isabelle's life had been like. It must have been hard, nearly two centuries ago, to rebel against society. Even today it was hard.

And she should know. Often she'd thought her biggest problem was that she had inherited too much of her father's single-mindedness. Whatever the cause, her parents had been disappointed when she hadn't followed the accepted patterns for daughters of prominent families. She liked clothes and parties, but she had other things on her mind, too. Particularly, strange things from the past, like Aunt Isabelle's collection.

And then, of course, everything had changed, for the worse, after the summer she'd met Winston. Her parents had treated him badly, and then ... well, she still didn't like to think about what had happened.

After that, she'd refused to have a safe, and brief, career. Worst of all, she refused to make a marriage her parents deemed suitable, for it would have been loveless. She knew it wasn't what most girls would have done. And she had thought it was temporary. Slowly, though, it had become permanent. Most of the boys she knew, or met at college, were dismayed by her interest in anthropology. They guffawed, "Why don't you just learn how to cook?"

Why couldn't they understand that she wanted a home and children and a profession, especially one that might help people, even add to the world's store of knowledge? Except that she hadn't managed to achieve the first two. The only thing she'd got was a career. But she pushed that to the back of her mind. None of those boys had ever talked to her like Winston had, like she was an adult; about important things; about life; about what they were going to do with their lives. How to help others.

Finally, she'd simply turned off her emotions. It was easier that way, and she wouldn't get hurt again. She'd learned too early that love could never last. Winston had taught her that.

As she drove toward Cherokee—toward him—she wondered why she'd loved him so much that, even now, she found it hard to get interested in other men. It had started that summer at camp, when she was fifteen and had first met Winston.

She rounded a deep, horseshoe bend in the road, and gasped. It was the very bend of the river where Winston had pulled her out of the water and saved her life, and she couldn't stop the memories flooding back, starting with that day on the river.

CAMP HOPE NC, JULY 1988

The highlight of the final week at camp, at least for the senior campers, was white-water rafting down the Nantahala River. On a steep bank, Carol and her cabin-mates, five other teenaged girls, trampled the undergrowth for the best view of the water below. It buzzed with activity as the big rubber rafts were readied.

"Hey, watch it!" Carol yanked out the Walkman's earpieces as she slid a little way down the bank.

"This life jacket makes me seriously fat." Sharon sounded disgusted. "Just when Skip Barnett was starting to look at me."

"Aannd oraaange does nooothing for the complexion, my deahhh," Deirdre vamped. Deirdre wanted to be an actress.

Carol had kept quiet as her friends chattered. Now she stopped, suddenly still, as a massive shiver came over her. She had the strangest feeling that she had been in this place, done these things before.

Oh, well, she had read about how that happened. It was called déjà vu. It was eerie. Correction: it was dorky, because she'd never been here before.

She came back to earth when Alison asked, "Who d'ya reckon'll be lucky enough to go in Winston Wolfe's 'canoe'?" and rolled her eyes.

Carol bristled. "If that's a dig because he's Cherokee, you can shut it, please."

"Oooo, touchy, aren't we? Just because you're in *looove* with him—" The rest was lost in cascades of laughter.

"I am not," Carol retorted hotly.

But she spoke a lie, and she knew it. The first minute she'd seen him, she had felt there was something special about Winston Wolfe. He was easily the handsomest boy at camp. Correction: he was the handsomest boy she'd ever seen. Another Tom Cruise. Although it was more than just good looks. He looked at you like he was really seeing you.

Winston was the Outdoor Activities counselor because he was so good at everything: swimming, boating, hiking. And he was eighteen. Even if campers weren't officially off-limits to the counselors, he'd never be interested in a mere child of fifteen like her. Correction: sixteen in two weeks. Carol sighed, once again singling Winston out of the teeming activity on the water by his height.

Then he called out, "Okay, boys and girls, come down here and listen."

There was a scramble down the bank, worsened by unwieldy life jackets. But Carol managed to be in the front row as Winston slanted a commanding look around the group as he belted his own jacket. On him it looked good; but then he couldn't look dorky if he tried. He began, "Now, remember what I told you on the bus—you have to wear a helmet, and you have to hold on to the ropes on the sides of the boat, at all times."

"Can I paddle? I know how." It was an older boy, Carol noticed—Skip Barnett—and she heard Sharon's soft squeal.

"Are you sure?"

"Cross my heart," Skip answered.

"Okay," Winston agreed. "But you'll sit in the back." He looked at the group again. "I'm responsible for your safety, so just remember, whatever *I* say, *you* do."

A few of the older boys muttered "Heil, Hitler" under their breath. But except for the flicker of a muscle in his jaw, Winston ignored them, Carol noticed, impressed.

"Okay, now, grab a helmet over there. Six campers in each boat. Let's get started. You there, little one." Winston pointed to Carol. "Come with me. Now I need five more." Carol was almost as thrilled to hear her friends gasp as she was to be chosen for Winston's raft.

CHAPTER TWENTY TWO

CAMP HOPE NC, JULY 1988

With a few shoves from front and back, Winston's boat moved away from the safety of the bank and was caught immediately in the water's lithe movements. Suddenly, they were beyond the shore, beyond rescue, and Carol was beyond caring about anything but the moment.

The river moved them swiftly to a sharp bend. "Wwwhhooaahh," a boy yelled with glee, as they careened around its horseshoe shape to face a rushing torrent of white water dead ahead. "Left!" Winston ordered Skip. Then louder, and more urgently, "Left!" With a quick glance, Carol noticed Skip seemed frozen into inaction.

The raft began to buck and heave, just like a rodeo horse. Strangely, Carol felt no fear. With all his strength, Winston dug his oar into the raging torrent. Every muscle, every cord on his body, stood out. And then the raft's vicious motion wrenched Carol's hands from the ropes.

"Ooooohhh!" She yelled as she was thrown into the water. It was freezing, and the shock opened her mouth. Water rushed into it, then over her head, and pushed her under. She surfaced, sputtering. "Help!"

The rapids were strong. A violent force sucked her under again; she was in another world and powerless to fight it. Helmet and running shoes, even the life jacket, weighed her down, although she was glad of their protection against the boulders. When she surfaced, she felt as though she was on a water slide, with absolutely no control. She was crashing toward the next rapid, and taking in a lot of water.

Then Carol felt herself lifted, right out of the force of gravity. Winston had grabbed a strap on her life jacket. Trying to keep her head above water, she saw a bunch of huge rocks looming. Afraid of being smashed against them, she began to fight him. "No!"

"Don't!" he shouted, gripping her tighter. The raft rocketed along, dragging her with it, under water, over smaller rocks. The drenching went on and on and on, and water filled her nose and mouth. She fought to breathe. Just when she was wondering how much longer she—and Winston—could last, the boat shot off to one side. Mercifully, the water was quieter there. "Skip, keep us here, or I'll take it out of your hide," Winston threatened. To her he shouted, "Grab my paddle."

Her fingers were so numb that her first attempt failed. He repeated the instruction, this time in a kinder voice. "Come on, I've got you, Little One." Finally she grasped the oar, and he lifted her into the boat.

She didn't want to let go of him. "It's all right," he whispered, gently peeling her fingers off his arms. "Sit down here, where I can keep you safe." And he crouched over her, protectively.

They were the last boat to finish, at a shallow bend about a mile away, where the buses waited. Carol's legs were shaking so hard she couldn't climb out. "Let me help you," he insisted, practically carrying her through the water. "Are you all right now, *hsing-ga-wa-la*?" It sounded so nice that she nodded, although she wasn't.

Then he told her, "I'm sorry you got hurt. I shouldn't have let Skip paddle. I know how dangerous that horseshoe bend is. You know, my ancestors thought rivers lead to the other world."

She told another of her eerie feelings to go away. But the premonition that she'd felt—about the day having happened before, and somehow being important—returned.

CHAPTER TWENTY THREE

Carol came out of her reverie as she left the gorge and the exit to Cherokee approached. She noticed she was perspiring heavily, despite the car's air conditioning. It was, she thought, as though she'd just been carried out of the river, all those years ago.

As she took the exit and settled into the four-lane, she let the past claim her once more. She still hadn't found the answer to her question. Why had she loved Winston so much?

ASHEVILLE NC, AUGUST 1988

"Mother, can Winston come over next week?" Carol asked hopefully. Her parents had said they'd like to thank him for rescuing her.

"Oh, ho, who's Winston?" Phil asked in mock-girlish tones.

"None of your business." Carol grinned at her brother, swatting his arm. "Insect. Bug off!"

"Carol has a boyfriend, Carol has a boyfriend," he taunted.

Marcie Mattox said, "No, honey, Winston can't come over tomorrow; we have to go to Uncle Richard's funeral. You know that."

"Told you so."

Carol wailed, "But you said he could."

"He can, the day after tomorrow. That's soon enough after there's been a death in the family. Even then, I'm making an exception because it's your birthday." Marcie turned back to the stove, knocking open the door of a cabinet that had become lopsided with age. "Anyway, your father has made that decision. You know what that means."

"Yeah, no right of appeal."

"This house is not a democracy." Clearly, Phil was enjoying himself.

"Go away, pest! I'm trying to talk to Mama." Surprisingly, he did. Trailing behind her mother, Carol closed the cupboard door with a sharp blow, and protested her decision. "Winston's just in town for a few days. I didn't know Uncle Richard was suddenly going to die."

Marcie admonished her daughter, "None of us did."

"I could have told you he would." The voice from the doorway was harsh with grief. When they turned, Harriet Mattox stood there, her eyes large with unshed tears. She continued gloomily, "The oldest child in every generation of Mattoxes dies before their time, just like my Richard." The lines of grief in her face deepened. "It's the Mattox curse."

"Now, don't you go telling those old stories," Marcie gently reprimanded her mother-in-law. "Why, Carol might even believe some of the things you say."

"Why not? I speak the truth. And you know that. You just won't admit it." Harriet turned to leave.

"I don't know any such thing," Marcie denied to Harriet's disappearing back, as she returned to her cheese sauce. She waved the spoon with a manicured hand. "I declare! That woman! I love her to death, but honestly—"

Troubled, Carol inquired, "What's the Mattox curse?"

"Honey, don't pay any attention to her."

"But Uncle Richard wasn't sick," Carol pointed out.

"I know." Marcie paused for a moment before continuing briskly. "But accidents happen. Anyway, we can't blame Grandma; she's crazy with grief, poor darling. Now, what were we talking about?"

Still shocked by her grandmother's statement, Carol, nevertheless, quickly reminded her mother, "About Winston coming over."

"Oh, yes." Marcie poured milk into the pan and then looked for a place to set down the carton. "I declare, everything here is at least a century old. If your father doesn't let me fix up this old kitchen soon, I'm going to leave him."

Carol fidgeted at her mother's inattention. Finally Marcie continued firmly, "Honey, you have to be a little reasonable about this. If Winston can't come on Thursday, we just won't be able to thank him in person. I'll have to write him a letter or something. Where does he live, anyway?" Seeing Carol's disappointment, she peered more closely at her daughter. "You're sweet on this boy, aren't you?"

"I am not!" But, heading for the telephone, Carol crossed her fingers that Winston could stay in Asheville an extra day. She just had to see him again.

Correction: she would absolutely die if she didn't.

Carol had spent an hour prowling through the front hallway when at last the doorbell rang.

Winston's tall, rangy body was silhouetted in the shade of the deep veranda. Only his flashing smile lit his face. Carol's insides felt as though they were melting. "How are you, Little One? Been doing any drowning lately?"

"No, I'm okay," she grinned back, and relaxed. "My parents are in the parlor." She waved in its direction. "They said to excuse them if they aren't too perky, because my uncle died the other day."

"I'm very sorry to hear that. Are you sure it's okay for me to be here?"

"Yeah, yeah, sure. Come on in."

As Carol led him into the parlor, Marcie moved forward, hand extended. "We wanted to thank you for saving Carol's life."

"We're grateful to you, son," Stanley Mattox pumped Winston's hand, then flexed his fingers, giving the boy a second look. "And we wanted to say it in person."

"It's the least we could do." Her mother, Carol noticed, glanced several times from her to Winston.

"Glad I could, ma'am, Senator Mattox," Winston replied. "I'm sure it's going to be a life worth saving."

Flattered, and fascinated by such an idea, Carol asked, "How do you know?"

He turned to her. "Because I think when you've had a close shave like that, life becomes more valuable, and you treat it that way. You make it count."

Marcie was the first to recover, with the hostess's practiced gaiety.

"Geraldine has made us some iced tea," she gushed. "You'll have some, won't you? And, goodness, here we are all standing up; do sit down, Winston."

"Thank you, ma'am." He perched on the edge of the stiff horsehair sofa.

Stanley cleared his throat. "I believe you're off to college soon?"

"Yes, sir, in about a week. I'm going to UNC." He sipped from the tall, frosted glass he was handed.

Stanley's eyes widened. "Good choice. My alma mater, of course." He chose a comfortable chair near Winston. "What's your major?"

"Well," Winston was a little rueful, "I'd like to study history, but I'll probably do a business degree. Then stay on for law school, if I can get in," he smiled. "It's pretty tough these days."

"I'm sure you won't have any trouble," Marcie commented, pouring her glass of tea last. "Carol thinks you can do anything."

"Mama!" Carol had been anxiously following the conversation. So far, so good, she had thought. Correction: until her mother's dorky remark.

"Sorry, honey. I didn't mean to embarrass you. I just wanted to compliment Winston."

"That's quite an ambition you have there," Stanley commented.

"Yes, sir, I've planned it for a long time."

Stanley leaned back, puffing out his chest. "I like that in a young person. Well, son, just let me know if you need any help getting into Carolina Law. It'd be a pleasure for me to reciprocate what you've done for Carol. And," he grinned, "I do have some influence around the place."

"That's an understatement, Senator, and I thank you. Thanks, too, for letting me come over today. I understand you've had a tragedy in your family."

"Yes, my brother." Stanley's face saddened. "But we knew your time in town was limited." He burrowed further into his chair. "Law ... that was my profession, y'know, before I got elected to Washington. What kind of law are you interested in?"

"Land and environment."

"Oh." Her father's expression became guarded. "That's pretty contentious stuff, y'know. It's hard to please either side. You won't make friends with too many people."

"I know, but that's the best way to help my own people."

"Your people?" Stanley looked mystified.

"The Cherokees."

There was a lengthy silence. Carol watched in disbelief as her parents' faces froze, ever so slowly, in a parody of the warmth and gratitude they'd been expressing to Winston. She wanted to drop through the floor.

"What did you say your last name was again, Winston?" Marcie burbled into the silence, pulling at the crease in her white slacks.

"Wolfe. There's an 'e' on the end of it, ma'am."

But it was "Wolf" that Marcie heard and whispered back, gripping the arm of her chair and exchanging a frightened look with her husband. "Er, we didn't know you…"

"Were part-Indian? I am, and proud of it," Winston told them. "My family still lives in Cherokee, on the reservation." His gaze swept the parlor's portrait-lined walls. "Many of my ancestors were chiefs. To tell you the truth, I'm aiming to be chief some day myself."

"I see."

But Carol thought her mother's face looked shuttered to any further comprehension. The conversation certainly wasn't going the way she'd planned. Could her parents be prejudiced against Winston because he was part-Indian? It was hard to believe. Her mother was a pillar of the Episcopal Church. Her father was a lawmaker for the nation, an old-fashioned southern Democrat who, although wealthy himself, championed the less well off. And great-great (or was it great-great-great?) Aunt Isabelle had married an Indian.

But now her parents were sounding worse than her girlfriends at camp, who at least liked Winston for his good looks. "Mama, Daddy…" awkwardly she broke the silence "I think maybe Winston and I'll go out to the pool and swim. You brought your trunks?" She turned to him in mute appeal.

"Yeah," he smiled, setting down his glass very carefully.

CHAPTER TWENTY FOUR

For a long time neither Carol nor Winston spoke, as they raced each other several lengths of the Mattoxes' large pool. When they were resting, bare arms propped on the edge, she explained, panting for breath, "I'm sorry if my parents seemed, you know... about Indians, I mean." She was embarrassed, but determined to apologize.

He was barely out of breath. "Don't worry about it. You don't feel like that, do you?"

"Certainly not." The words rushed out.

"That's all that matters, then." He pulled himself out to sit on the edge.

"Why, one of my ancient aunts even married an Indian, a long time ago, according to family history."

"There you are, then. Maybe, as you said, they just weren't feeling too perky today."

Hoping he was right, she said shyly, "I admire what you want to do for your people." It made him different, more important.

"It's all I've ever thought about."

"You're making a big sacrifice, if you really want to study something else." She looked up at him through a sun-grin.

He leaned to one side to block the glare from her eyes. "Yeah, but it's worth it. I can always learn history. And I like the idea of being a lawyer."

"I'd like to help people, too." She climbed out and, toweling off, moved to a chaise lounge in the summer house.

He followed her. "That's great." When he flexed his shoulders, her eyes followed the ripple of his muscles. "Decided what you want to study yet?"

"What?" She blinked. "Oh. I'm thinking sociology, maybe anthropology. That aunt who married an Indian had a wonderful collection of stuff, and I used to love looking at it."

He brightened. "Could I see it?"

"My parents gave it all to the museum here in Asheville."

"Pity." He sat down on the edge of her chaise. If she put out her hand, she could touch him.

"I can't believe it. I won't believe it," Marcie told her husband as they stood at the wide bay window watching their daughter swimming and talking, much too seriously for a fifteen-year-old, with Winston Wolfe. "I declare, it's just like that old Aunt Isabelle of yours."

"I know, and it gives me the creeps."

"You think it's the same family?"

"They're probably related."

"Well, it's a pity; he seems a nice boy," sighed Marcie. "And you know she's at least halfway in love with him already."

"All the more reason to tell her she can't see him any more. We'd never hear the end of doom-saying from my mother."

Marcie hesitated, then asked, "Honey, how much truth is there in that story your mother keeps telling?"

"About the Mattox curse?" He threw back his head and laughed. "Don't tell me you believe in that."

"Well, your mother keeps saying Isabelle's Indian put a spell on the family when he couldn't marry her."

"They did marry, didn't they? Even if it was just an Indian ceremony. So there couldn't have been a spell. We have some kind of inherited vein problem. They didn't used to know how to treat it, but it isn't such a problem now. That's why so many of the family died, but it isn't serious."

Marcie thought for a moment. "Stanley, I know you don't want to hear this, but Richard didn't have vein trouble, and he was too young to die. You don't think—"

"Absolutely not, Marcie," her husband interrupted in his most aggressive tone, the one he used for making speeches in Congress. "It's damned sad, but Richard choked on a fish bone, and that's that." Stanley banged his fist on a table, causing an antique oil lamp to wobble.

Marcie rushed to grab it before it crashed to the Persian carpet and made another stain. "Well, if there's no truth to it, why don't you want Carol to see Winston?"

"It'll just keep all that old family gossip stirring around in Mother's mind. It'll encourage her to keep telling those stories, and talking about curses. She'll drive us crazy. I can't stand to hear all of that. And I'm going out there right now to tell Carol so." Stanley craned his neck. "I can't see them any more. What the—" He turned sharply and headed for the pool.

After a comfortable silence Winston asked Carol, "Do you ever get down to Chapel Hill?"

Her heart somersaulted. Correction: it nearly stopped, because he was saying he wanted to see her again. The University was in Chapel Hill. "I'll have to ask," she hedged, reluctant to admit she'd never be allowed to go to a college town alone. Then inspiration struck. "Maybe I could say I was visiting my brother. He's going to be in med school there. He wouldn't tell my parents; he's great about things like that."

"I wouldn't want to see you behind their backs. It isn't right."

She looked at him, then confessed, "I would lie for you. I wish I could."

"I know, *hsing-ga-wa-la*. That means 'little one'." He was quiet, then said, "As much as I'd like to see you again, I know your parents probably won't allow it."

It was hard to accept the idea. "Maybe they will."

"Not after that." He jerked his head toward the house.

She whispered, "I was hoping you could come over again."

"Thanks, but I think I'll have to wish you Happy Birthday and go," he smiled gently.

"I'm sorry about my parents," she burst out miserably. "They aren't usually like that." She thought for a moment. "You know, my grandmother says there's a curse on our family."

Winston laughed. "Then I'd better not come back. Wouldn't want to take the risk of associating with the accursed Mattoxes." He threw her a playful punch. "Don't worry about it." Then he got serious again. "Let's be positive. Can I at least write to you and call you when I'm back on semester breaks?"

"I'd be real mad if you didn't," she dimpled, feeling better.

He caught her chin in a big hand. "I've never saved anybody's life before. I may not be able to see much of you, but I'll never forget you. Will you remember that?" She nodded, not trusting herself to speak, as he gazed down at her. "You know, some people believe an old myth that says—when you save somebody's life, it belongs to you." His look became more penetrating, and he cupped her face in both hands. "Are you happy for your life to belong to me?"

She nodded again, finally whispering, "Yes."

He brought her face closer, and kissed her. His mouth tasted sweet, just like she'd expected. She sat up a little, to get closer to him. He caressed her bare shoulders, then pressed her backwards, following her, and they lay side by side on the chaise, still kissing. Winston's hands moved down to her breasts, and Carol was lost in a daze of longing when there was a loud exclamation.

"Just what do you think you're doing?" Stanley Mattox shouted.

They both jumped guiltily. Winston got to his feet. "I'm sorry, sir, I know what it must look like."

"Damn right!"

Winston replied, "I'd never do anything to hurt your daughter. I saved her life."

"Then this is a good place to stop, before you wreck it. You'd better go."

"Daddy, Winston wasn't doing anything I didn't want him to," Carol pleaded. "Don't make him go."

At her father's unrelenting glare, Winston picked up his towel and headed for the pool cabana.

Carol burst into tears. "Now look what you've done."

"I've done you a favor. I don't want you seeing him again."

determination, she told him, "But I must learn, and I will fulfill my duties. I thank you for your offer, but I'm fearful of you coming into the fort again. I will manage. And you must go away to Washington City."

"You want me to go away?"

She blushed again. "Of course not," she quickly answered, completely unsure of what she wanted at this point. "But I know you have to be going."

"Don't worry about Washington. I'll still go. But I can stay here a while longer, visiting with my mother's clan."

Her heart soared. To have the company of a friend—for sadly that is all he could be—as sympathetic as him from time to time in this desolate fort would be an answer to her prayers. But she was reminded of the consequences. "That isn't advisable. At last I know what Flapjack Foster meant about the danger to you from this fort. I don't wish another experience like yesterday. Several times I thought we were both dead." She shuddered.

His reply was quick. "I've been in far greater danger and doubtless will be again. Besides, your brother is not the one I wish to look at."

"You know what I mean." She could feel her face flaming up from the collar of James' shirt. "And now I'm sure you must go, afore we are seen."

He merely smiled again. "Do you wish me not to return?"

She was unable to stop the corners of her mouth lifting. "Yes," she replied firmly, forcing her lips into a straight line again to form the words. "That is exactly what I wish."

Had she but known, mind-reading was a particularly strong trait of the Cherokees. "Very well, then. I'll be back." He grinned cheerfully, turned, and disappeared into the trees.

CHAPTER THIRTY ONE

Walking slowly back to James' cabin, Isabelle was surprised to hear a female voice ask, "Hey, there. Are you Miss Mattox?"

She wheeled around and saw a woman climbing the hill, bent under a pile of bulging gunny sacks. "Yes. How-do?"

The woman could be her mother's age, Isabelle thought. Light brown hair threaded with grey was pulled straight back, but the bun at her neck was a loose one and tied into a crocheted snood. Her mouth was generous, her brown eyes lively. The woman wore a coarse homespun skirt, although her blue calico blouse was of good quality.

"Whew, that's some hill." She dropped her sacks to the ground and smiled. "I heard you were coming. I'm Elsie Hunter, wife of the Trading Post owner. It's that way," she nodded down the slope.

"I'm glad to meet you." Although wanting to cringe because of her outlandish clothes, Isabelle, nevertheless, felt her mood rising at the sight of another female.

Looking her up and down without the expected disapproval, Elsie gave Isabelle a hug which nearly toppled her. "Glad to have you in the settlement. It's called Huntington, after us," Elsie said proudly. "There isn't much goes on here we don't know about. And I come to the fort twice a week to sell vegetables to the cook. That's how I heard you were coming. There are other women here, too." Elsie rearranged her sacks. "My daughter Martha is betrothed to the army surgeon, Dr. Hitchcock. She's staying a while with our relatives in Atlanta, to be nearer her fiancé. He has to stay close to General Scott; we don't know when he's coming up here. But as soon as they're married, you'll have some female company right here in the fort. That's if you're staying a while."

"I don't know that myself."

"Well, come down and see us at the trading post. We sell lots of things—medicines like paregoric, food, salt and tobacco, shoes, champagne, suspenders…"

"Champagne?" Isabelle raised her eyebrows.

"…and we got some cloth. I can get it sewed up for you, unless you want to do it yourself?" Hastily Isabelle shook her head. Gesturing in the direction she had come, Elsie advised, "Just take that path there to the left, and follow the river."

"I'll see if I can get there. But I've got a lot to do, readying the captain's quarters." Isabelle felt dejected again. "And I've nothing to cook or to cook with."

"Oh, Lordy, haven't you got anything to eat?" Elsie's kind face was full of alarm. "Why, no, I reckon you don't, and you can't eat with them men." She took Isabelle's hand and urged, "Listen, you come along with me. We'll say howdy to the cook and get some food for you." She reached down for her sacks, but Isabelle grabbed the heaviest one. "That's mighty kind."

Elsie took up the other two, and they walked over the dusty parade ground, past half a dozen soldiers unloading a supply wagon, to a large, two-storied blockhouse. Inside was a huge, open fireplace filled with all the pots that James' lacked, and trestle tables and benches.

"This is the cook," Elsie muttered, marching straight up to a man with a grizzled beard as long as Flapjack's, a stained waistcoat over a collarless shirt, and the dirtiest, greasiest pair of army trousers Isabelle had ever seen. "Abner, meet the captain's sister."

Isabelle forced herself forward. "Thank you for sending me some breakfast."

Elsie showed no such reticence as she grabbed Abner's arm and marched him off to inspect her produce.

A tall, fair-haired soldier, sporting a handlebar moustache, ambled over. Isabelle was alarmed to recognize him as one of the soldiers who had nearly shot Wolf. Her unease returned even as he advised in a kindly manner, "Don't mind Cookie, Miss, he's always in a foul temper," and grinned. "We don't know whether his temper makes the food bad, or his cooking makes him bad tempered." At her nervous smile, he added, "We didn't have a proper meeting yesterday evenin'. I'm the quartermaster, ma'am, Sergeant Zebulon D. Hampton at your service, ma'am. You just come to me if you need anything. And call me Zeb."

Isabelle felt so desperate she decided to cast aside her apprehension. "Well, I do need lots of things. Our cupboard's bare," she sighed.

His look was sympathetic. "I know what the captain's quarters are like. I'll send you all the things I reckon you'll need. Stay right here a minute." And he dashed out.

She listened to Elsie haranguing Abner about the importance of fresh vegetables until Sergeant Hampton returned, his hands full of small sacks. "Here you are—salt, sugar and butter, flour and cornmeal." He slapped the sacks down on a table. "And before you go, I'll get the cook to dish up enough food to last you a day or two, 'til you find your feet."

Isabelle was so grateful she hardly dared ask. "Cooking pots?"

"Yes, ma'am."

"They'll fit our fireplace?"

"Righty, and ovens with lids. I'll send everything down."

"Ohhh." Her biggest worries were disappearing.

"Yep." As if pleased with himself, he rocked back on his heels, and this time gave her a slow once-over. "And tomorrow I'll send you some stewing beef; we just got some new supplies. Say, how'd you like your own cow? Might not have fresh milk if you don't."

Thinking of this morning's rancid offerings, Isabelle said regretfully, "I don't know how to milk."

"You must be a city girl." When she shrugged, he came to her rescue. "Aw, that's all right, I'll teach you myself. What about starting tomorrow?" At her cautious nod, he smiled. "And we're raising pigs; we'll be butchering soon's the weather gets cold. That way you can get some lard and bacon. Chittlings, too."

“Here, take some vegetables,” Elsie Hunter was back and offered Isabelle one of her sacks. “He wouldn’t.”

“Thank you. I insist on paying, as soon as I can get some money from James. And I have money of my own.” Isabelle followed Elsie out of the cookhouse.

“Aw,” Elsie waved her away, “pay me when you get around to it.” Once more she slung the sacks over her shoulders. But instead of departing, she looked at Isabelle as if trying to decide on something. Finally she said, “I have some advice for free, though. Don’t let anybody see you talking to the Indians—especially a man—like I seen this morning as I come up the hill.” She shifted onto her left foot. “Indians aren’t exactly popular around here right now. It could be dangerous for you.”

Isabelle promised, “I’ll remember.”

Once again she could only wonder how a man who’d saved her life could be dangerous.

CHAPTER THIRTY TWO

Next morning, Isabelle slept through the cock's crow and was awakened only by Reveille. She started out of bed but at once fell back, so severe was the soreness in her legs and arms. And the more the bugle insisted, the more her body resisted.

She lay on the rough mattress, shocked at the depth of her exhaustion. What could have caused such pain? Then she realized just how unaccustomed she was to the hard work she had done yesterday: cleaning many months' accumulation of dust in the cabin, then trying to scrub the heavy iron pots Sergeant Hampton had sent. And all of it had been mostly for nothing. The grease and food of a hundred meals had baked so thoroughly onto the pots that very little came off, and the cabin still looked dusty, even if she knew it wasn't. Her sigh was heavy with pain and frustration.

At last the sound of the front door scraping over the uneven threshold frightened her enough to propel her out of bed. Peering out between the slats, she saw her visitor was only James. But that was little consolation. A hand went to her mouth as she realized he had come for his breakfast. Not only had she overslept, she had cooked nothing.

Worse, the cabin was littered with her efforts. After the supper grudgingly provided by the cook, James had returned to barracks, and she had puzzled over the fireplace hooks and pulleys, then tried to hang the heavy iron pots. She hadn't succeeded and, exhausted, decided to leave them until the morning.

Now she looked at the disarray around the nearly dead fireplace. "I'm so sorry!" Her voice was deep with sleep and abject apology. "It'll just take me a few minutes to get breakfast started." But she realized the hopelessness of her good intentions even as she spoke them. Despite struggling with them to the point of exhaustion, she still had no real idea how to use the complicated hooks, pulleys and pots.

James looked her up and down, and she felt embarrassed, even if he was her brother. Now she wondered whether to take the time to put on clothes before trying to cook.

"Don't worry. I know you're probably not set up for cooking yet. Just thought I'd come down, you seem so determined to feed me." But his attempt to smooth matters over, she noticed, sounded a note of slight annoyance.

Hearing it, but grateful for even his glimmer of understanding, she leaned against the partition and wailed, "I haven't managed anything very handily. I fear I'm a failure, to both you and Father, and at my first tasks." With renewed determination but slowed by the ache in her limbs, she moved toward the fireplace. "Let me start breakfast; I'll figure out things as I go along."

His smile was thin as he turned back to the door. "I've no time to wait for it now. I can eat with the men, though they'll be nearly finished. I keep telling you, it's easier, anyway. And whatever you say, I'll take midday dinner with them. It means less time away from my duties. I'll still keep you company in the evening for supper."

"All right." But her head hung low.

"Would you like me to send the corporal with your breakfast again?"

"Oh, no," she insisted. "I know you all have work to do, you can't be looking after me. I'll fix you supper tonight, and make sure to have your breakfast ready tomorrow."

"Thank you, dear sister." He made a low bow.

Trying to be helpful, she noticed his hat and dark blue tunic hanging on the wall. "Don't you need those?"

"I won't bother with them 'til the weather cools off. Besides, 'til the rest of the garrison—and General Scott—arrive, a commanding officer in full dress isn't warranted."

"Speaking of clothes, James, dear, before you go, there's just one thing," she implored.

"What is it?"

"Could you fix me up a wash pot? In Asheville, Emily . . ."

This time he didn't bother to disguise his irritation, and stepped out of the cabin. "Isabelle, my job is to look after the army, not the washing. That's women's work." He turned his head briefly and threw his last words back over his shoulder. "By the way, I've had word that your trunk and boxes will be brought soon."

"Thanks be to the Almighty!" She clasped her hands.

When he had gone Isabelle felt, by turns, guilt-ridden and mildly resentful. Her sense of failure increased at the realization that she had forgotten to bring in water from the well. At the prospect of dressing again in her ridiculous clothes, this time without even a morning wash, she slumped onto the table and sought to get her bearings. Everything was so new and strange. And difficult. It was as though she had become someone else entirely, and almost overnight. Had her father intended her to struggle so? It seemed a harsh punishment for their quarrel, even for her disobedience.

Sighing, Isabelle rummaged through the remains of last night's supper and found a biscuit. And glory be! There was a slice of cured ham. The dough had hardened, but she chewed it gratefully, her glance idly traveling downhill toward the gate of the fort.

What was that movement? She craned her neck. It looked like a shadow, but she could swear she saw it move. Was it Wolf again? She was surprised by the quickening of her pulse, and told herself it was due to the hostility he might meet if he returned. Besides, surely he would be on his way to Washington by now. Although he had said he would return. Would he keep his word? And when?

His had been a promise filled with danger, and she couldn't decide whether she hoped he would—or hoped he wouldn't—keep it.

CHAPTER THIRTY THREE

Just as Isabelle had managed to dress once more in her makeshift clothes, Sergeant Hampton appeared, carrying a pail and looking especially tall, framed in the small doorway. "Ready for your milking lesson?" Without waiting for an invitation, he ducked his head and stepped inside.

"I'd forgotten that, too." She felt sheepish. "But I'll do it. Thank you for sending the pots." She decided not to mention their sad condition.

He looked at the disorder around the fireplace and grinned. "I see you ain't got the hang of 'em yet."

"Nay, but I'll have them working by end of this day," she promised, more to herself than to him.

"You're a spirited little thing," he observed. "I like that in a woman." Once more his glance lingered, as it had the previous day. She tried not to think about it. Being eyed by soldiers was something she'd have to get used to in an army fort, she feared. And he had done her many kindnesses.

As they walked to the cow shed, she felt her stiff muscles relaxing from the exercise. In the stall, he surprised her by taking both her hands in his. Before she could ask his reason, he rubbed them slowly down the heifer's smooth red-and-white flank. Somehow he made it a sensuous gesture and stood very close to explain, "When you're a stranger, it's best to soothe her a little, afore ye start." Though it sounded sensible, it added to Isabelle's discomfort.

Next he settled her on the milking stool, leaving his hands on her hips for a few unnecessary moments. But his look was bland and said he was merely instructing. “Now, this is the way ye sit.” There wasn’t much choice but to do as he said, so she tried to concentrate on her task. Squirming away from him, she discovered, only made him grasp her the harder.

Finally he knelt beside her. “Now, pull ’er tits down a few times afore ye start,” he demonstrated. Isabelle became rigid with embarrassment. This was almost as bad as the discovery of Preston McKeever, Jr. with his harlot. If only she could refuse to learn the milking. But it was part-and-parcel of feeding herself and James and meant she wouldn’t have to depend on the cook. For that alone, it was worth going through some mortification. She reminded herself about ‘sticks and stones’, bit her lip, and tried to concentrate not on what he was saying but on what she was learning.

At her first few tentative pulls, the heifer kicked. “You’re pinching ’er.” The sergeant’s voice had lowered to the consistency of molasses. “You gotta do it nice and slow, and always work the milk down into the tits a little afore ye start, and then pull down on ’em firm, but nice and slow.” He smiled again. “You need to be nice to her, and then she’ll be nice to you.”

Isabelle muttered under her breath, “And you need some manners.” But once again she forced herself not to think about his closeness or the feel of his hot breath on her neck. If only she had a dress to wear, it would remind him she was a lady.

Despite such difficulties, within a few minutes she had a goodly amount of milk in the pail. “You’re doing all right,” he leered. “You see, it ain’t difficult to get milk out of a cow. And that makes me wonder, now—just how hard would it be to get it outa you?” He made a dive for her breasts.

In a reflex, Isabelle squeezed the cow’s teat, so the heifer kicked again, at both the pain and the commotion, and in the tight confines kicked over the pail. The milk ran along a layer of straw and began to seep into the red earth. “Get away!” she cried in outrage, drawing back against the stall, trying to take his hand off her breast.

His breath came hot and heavy. “Come on, now, you know you want it. I can tell. Ain’t that why a woman past marrying age comes to an army fort all on her own?”

"You oaf! I'll tell my brother!" She beat at him with both fists.

"You cain't scare me," he grinned without a trace of remorse. "As I said, I like a spirited filly. Makes it more of a challenge. And that makes it more fun."

"You're disgraceful."

"Ain't I just." He reached for her again, easily catching her hands.

She freed one and managed to land her fist on his cheek. "Leave off me!"

The gleam in his eye remained strong, but the blow stopped him. He rubbed the spot, and gave a laconic shrug. "Don't matter. I'll keep trying. Some day you'll hafta want it. And I'll be watching and waiting. Just remember that."

"You'll be waiting a long time," she flung at him and fled.

He called after her, "All I done was be nice to you and feed you when you was starving. Anybody would think you'd be grateful. But if this is the thanks I get, I swear, I—"

Running back to the cabin, she slammed the door shut and bolted it home. In the darkness, she dropped to the cold, earthen floor, sobbing. *It's just like all the times Father told me not to worry about what a man was like. The only important thing was that he'd have me, not how he'd treat me.*

After a while, she sat up. In the dim glow of the fire, she gulped back her sobs, overwhelmed by utter misery. Only one thing she knew with certainty. Only the Indian, Wolf, had been truly kind to her. Even more than James, really.

Sighing, she gathered up the empty water bucket to take to the spring. Checking herself, with another sigh she turned back and picked up the chamber pot, holding it at arm's length as she left the cabin. Until yesterday, she'd never emptied a night jar.

As Isabelle knelt beside the clear, burbling spring, her wooden bucket tipped into its deepest part, she heard the unmistakable rustle of footsteps in the underbrush. Fearing it was Sergeant Hampton returning, she grabbed up the bucket, losing most of the water as she ran—straight into Tallaquoyah Wolf. "Oh! You startled me!"

"I didn't mean to," he apologized, adding, "I wouldn't make you unhappy for a moment," as they blotted water from their clothing.

The sight of Wolf was a mighty relief, and Isabelle longed to tell him how glad she was to see him, and not just because he wasn't Sergeant Hampton. But she couldn't admit to such feelings, nor that she was overjoyed he'd kept his word to return, and so soon.

"How are you adjusting to life at the fort?" His eyes held hers, making her feel intensely alive, a feeling that increased when he came closer.

"Not very well," she admitted ruefully, thinking of the past two days as she set down her bucket and rubbed her aching arm.

Wolf leaned down and started refilling her bucket. Doing so, his hands brushed hers. She jumped, but his touch was gentle. Again she pondered this stranger's kindness, although she still had trouble thinking of him entirely as a stranger.

There was something she'd been meaning to ask him. "How is it that you can come and go whenever you feel like it, around these parts, when it's so dangerous for Indians?"

"I'm careful, and it would be hard to find me in these woods. Besides, as yet they haven't started looking. Until then, I intend to live freely, as I want…"

It was almost better being an Indian, she thought, contemplating how she would have to dodge Sergeant Hampton without seeming to. But then he finished, unexpectedly, "…and what I want is to see you."

Confronted with such clear intent, she dropped her eyes. Of course, she could not acknowledge his meaning. Nor could she acknowledge what she felt for him. Already she'd gone too far. To mask the flutter in her breast, she reached for the bucket, now full. But he insisted, "No, let me," and lifted it easily with a quick movement.

She dared not look at him. Instead, she fussed in frustration, "You mustn't. I have to get back to the fort. And no matter how brave you are, it isn't safe for you to go there." And not safe for herself, remembering Elsie's warning.

He compromised, "I'll just take this to the gate for you."

It was tempting to let him. Dangerous or not, she didn't want to lose his company. And so she fell in behind him. An autumn wind was pushing leaves off the driest branches. His comment about coming to see her had pushed her thoughts and feelings strongly off their foundations.

As they reached a stand of poplars, he suddenly touched her shoulder, motioning toward the river, and put a finger to his lips.

She craned to see what he meant. "Oh!" She mouthed it silently. There was a young buck, standing stock-still and looking straight at them. "He's so beautiful!" Then she looked at Wolf. He was a mixture of hardness and softness, she thought. Granite and silk. He was also a fascinating mixture of white man and Indian. She never knew which one of these many sides he was going to show.

As they approached the gate, she looked around and whispered, "Now leave."

He returned her bucket, letting his hand rub against hers again. "I'll go, but I'll come back."

Something fluttered up her legs and settled, trembling, just beneath her belly. "Why ever for?" Thinking of a few reasons, she felt she shouldn't.

"Because even when I'm not with you, you're on my mind."

CHAPTER THIRTY FOUR

The daylight showing under the cabin door grew steadily brighter. "I'll get you blazing," Isabelle promised the fire, rubbing her arms against the chill advancing with September.

As the flames leapt, she put fragrant sassafras leaves into the teapot. Groaning with the effort, she swung the heavy iron cauldron out of the fireplace and dipped steaming hot water into the teapot, then into the pitcher for her morning wash, before swinging it back over the fire.

At the cock's repeated crow, she smiled. "I'm ahead of you today, mister smarty-pants." The rooster's voice added a staccato note to the bacon's steady sizzle as she set one end of the table. Stepping back, she looked at the table with pride, thinking how much her housekeeping had improved.

Whereupon James appeared, booted and in his uniform of collarless shirt and dark blue trousers. They were held up with thick straps crossed over the back and buttoned into the front of his waistband. "You aren't having breakfast?" He raised an eyebrow at the single place set.

Carefully she broke both eggs into the skillet, explaining, "I'll eat later; it's all I can do to get one breakfast ready on time, much less two, and mine can wait."

When she set the pewter plate before him, he fell to it. She opened the heavy iron door of the oven set into the hottest section of the fireplace coals, emerging triumphant with golden-crusted biscuits. "I'm not perfect at housekeeping yet, but I'm willing to work hard, and I'll improve. This morning, for instance, I hope you'll agree I've managed to give you a good breakfast."

"You have, sister, and I congratulate you." He took a biscuit, buttered it thickly, and returned to his plate.

As she poured the fragrant tea she remarked, "James, I've only one iron, when I need at least two, one to be heating in the fire, and one to use. And I would greatly appreciate your taking me to Brasstown."

He sipped tea and swallowed, staring at her. "To buy an iron?"

"To see some woodcarvings." She'd overheard a soldier talking about them.

James pushed back his empty plate. "Playthings."

She felt diminished. "No, handicrafts, to advance my knowledge and interest."

"Isabelle, I don't have time to gallivant all over the countryside with you. The survey has to be finished, and soon, before the Indians have time to get up a rebellion. More soldiers are arriving here every day. I must make provision for all of them, and build the new stockade." He gave her a perfunctory smile and scraped back his chair. "If you need things, go to the Trading Post. They keep an account for me. Just don't expect me to spend my time on frivolities."

Later, straining the heifer's fine red hairs out of the milk, she decided to take James' advice. She would try and find the Trading Post and see about some clothes. She had nothing suitable, even when her trunk and boxes arrived, for the life she was now living. She looked forward to seeing Elsie again, not to mention having the company of another woman.

Getting out would also take her mind off her keen interest in Wolf and the necessity, as strong, to deny it, and off the question of whether he was still here or gone to Washington. Relieved at coming to her decision, she felt more optimistic about life than she had in weeks.

CHAPTER THIRTY FIVE

Isabelle struggled along the deeply rutted track, looking for houses. But there seemed to be none, although the woods were so thick there might be a hundred, she realized, and she would not see them. At last there was a glimpse of the river, some way below.

Suddenly, she smelled something wonderful. Before long, she came across a patch of wild honeysuckle, surprised that it had found enough sunlight to spur an autumn flowering. Promising herself that next spring she would make a garden, she bent down to the honeysuckle, having neither seen nor smelled anything so beautiful since leaving Asheville.

As she rose up from the fragrant blossoms, she was once again staring into Wolf's handsome face.

"You should not always take me by such surprise," she remonstrated with him mildly.

"I can hardly come calling to your door," he pointed out reasonably.

She smiled in agreement. "How did you know where I was?" She hadn't herself known she was coming here until a few minutes ago.

"It's never hard to find people." He sounded complacent. "Besides, I told you I would return."

With some reluctance, she admitted, "I'm unused to men keeping their promises, at least so exactly."

He smiled again. "Then you must be keeping company with the wrong men." When she blushed, he broadened his smile, and even offered his arm.

After a moment she took it, as the path was so difficult. Leaning on it brought the remembrance of her body pressed against his during their ride to the fort, and she blushed again. As a distraction she remarked, "I see you haven't gone to Washington yet."

"Soon." He added, "I'll be sorry to leave you. I'm also sorry to leave my mother and sister, who have returned to live here because of the troubles in Georgia."

Surprised by his mention of family, she was suddenly intensely curious about them. "How much family do you have?"

"My son, my mother, two sisters. Sunnika is still in Georgia, with my brother."

His son. "You're married?" and despite its certainty, held her breath for his answer.

"Yes."

It was the reply she had expected. Yet she looked away, not wanting him to see her disappointment, not wanting to feel it herself, astonished at the intensity of her regret, the swift plummet of her heart.

As if from far away she heard him add, "That is, I was married, but my wife was killed, along with my father, by the Georgia militia. I have a fine son, Yaguska, who's looked after by my mother and sisters."

Immediately Isabelle's heart went out to him. He had lost part of his family and had to raise his son without a mother. Now he was in danger of losing his home and having to go to Oklahoma when he didn't want to. "All of that is a terrible sadness for you."

"Yes." Then he straightened his shoulders. "But I'm still alive, and so is my son, and I'm still on my own lands that I love. I still have my home, and most of my family, and their children. My home is a happy place; everyone is family. You would like it."

Isabelle thought how different was the fort. Not homely at all. Suddenly, she yearned for such close family happiness as he had, the kind she remembered from growing up with her brothers before their mother died. How different it had become since. After the rift with her father, she had hoped to find that closeness of family here with James. But it was proving elusive.

His hand caught hers, and he kissed it, all the while looking at her with emotions visible on his normally composed face. "I'd like you to meet my mother and sister. Would you like that, too?"

"Oh, I—" It was absurd; she hardly knew the man. Yet somehow, she felt she had known him forever.

He didn't wait for her to finish. "Good. Then it will be done. Although, unfortunately, not until I return from Washington." Quickly he drew her into the trees. His arms went around her, and a hand in the small of her back tilted her toward him.

Delicious sensations coursed down her legs, and she wanted to press herself even further into him. To stop this, she pushed a hand against his chest, but this only increased the feelings.

He caught her close and kissed her, his lips soft and warm. They lingered on hers until she took a breath, and he released her.

Slowly he traced his finger along her jawline, looking at her face as if memorizing it, she thought. His face came nearer, then nearer still. She looked, this time unflinching, into his dark eyes, feeling she might drown in their depths, as she had nearly drowned in the river before he saved her.

He reached for her again. This time she stayed in his arms. This time his lips told her how much he wanted her. And then, abruptly, they surrendered her. Her mouth felt wrenched from his, her lips heavy where the weight of his had been. Finally, she recovered herself. "You're going, then?"

He nodded. "Tomorrow. But I'll be back before long."

CHAPTER THIRTY SIX

ASHEVILLE NC, MAY 1999

Considering what Winston had done to her again, Carol felt like going back to Arizona immediately.

Caution had disappeared in an instant, as soon as she was in his arms. They'd come so close—so close!—to rekindling the love that had started long ago. For an instant, it had seemed possible, and she'd allowed herself to hope.

But now she was suffering for once again losing her head to Winston Wolfe. She should have known it wouldn't last. She was beginning to think that everything about Winston was bad news. Why hadn't she remembered that before she fell so hopelessly in love with him again?

Well, she'd learned her lesson about him, again. She couldn't wait to return to Arizona, and she'd do it as soon as she found out what was in that pouch. It would be almost comforting to return to her carefully cultivated emotional neutrality. Although that prospect wasn't great, either, now she'd tasted love again. Why, oh, why, she moaned to herself, was she unable to love someone as nice as Brian Keating?

No matter. Even stronger than her need to distance herself from Winston was her need to stay in Asheville and get to the bottom of the Mattox curse and things that had happened two hundred years ago. She was about to join her family in the living room, where she hoped to find out a little more about the secrets of the past. They would, she was sure, be useful for the future.

The living room was still called the parlor. It was high-ceilinged, large and airy. A triple bay window overlooked the elegant terrace and pool that, Carol knew, had once been a croquet lawn. Even now, an old-fashioned garden of hollyhocks and roses ringed the pool.

The room's furnishings, however, were mostly modern, and certainly comfortable, except for the Victorian horsehair settee that Grandma insisted on keeping. Squashy white sofas and armchairs stood against Wedgwood blue carpet and walls. Antique marble-topped tables and tall oil lamps indicated the room had a history, as did the large Persian rug with an ugly stain in one corner. Carol had always thought the carpet, although threadbare in places, glowed with the vibrant colors of another world, another time, and it was one of her favorite things.

The parlor held—outwardly, at least, Carol thought—a serene and happy family. Grandma was bent over a new piece of needlepoint. Down the long side of the room, her father practiced his golf putting with an iced tea glass. Marcie turned the pages of a new *Southern Living* magazine. When Carol settled near her, she smiled and said, with almost the first semblance of pleasantry since Phil's death, "We're glad you're staying on a while, honey."

Her words lit a tiny flame of hope in Carol. Except for the disapproval about her clothes, which had been expected, her parents had been mostly nonjudgmental since she'd arrived. Badly wanting to make peace with them, she felt encouraged by this. They might, indeed, tell her some things she needed to know. It might even be safe to confide in them a few important recent events, starting with the museum's proposal to move The Mattox Collection. She'd been waiting for a good time to tell them. That time seemed now.

When she had finished, Stanley aimed his putter, missed, and swore mildly, but not at the glass. "They have no right to move the collection," he fumed. "This is where we live, and we gave it to them because we want it here."

"I don't care where it is, as long as it isn't gathering dust in this house," Marcie said breezily.

But Harriet had dropped her needlework, and her thin shoulders jerked. "You mean they don't want it, either? What did I tell you?"

Carol sighed. This had been a bad idea. "They just think Cherokee can do more justice to it. I think so, too."

But Grandma wasn't convinced. "It shouldn't be moved. That might start all kinds of bad things! Why, if it gets closer to its ancestral home, the curse may get stronger. Did you see it? Did you see what put a curse on this family?"

Carol watched her father roll his eyes toward heaven before she admitted, "It—I'm talking to some people in Cherokee."

"So you did see something." Misshapen fingers holding the tapestry needle trembled.

Marcie propped bright-red-framed reading glasses atop her head, smoothed already-sleek blonde hair, put down her magazine, and asked, "Is that why you went to Cherokee?"

Carol tried not to rise to the bait. "I always like going over there."

Her mother frowned. "Did you see that boy again?"

The question infuriated Carol. " 'That boy,' as you call him, is now a man."

"That's why we thought you might be tempted to get involved with him again."

Carol said quietly, "You don't have to worry about that. He's getting married." For a moment, she remembered the pain of making that discovery.

Marcie looked happier, but kept on. "I know you've been talking to Grandma." She shot an aggrieved look at Harriet, who had resumed stitching. "I declare, I don't know how you can listen to things like that. And you with a PhD. Why, you're too smart to believe those old stories, especially about charms, or spells, or whatever you call them."

Carol said flatly, "My PhD is the reason I believe Grandma. In my profession, spells are part of what we call belief systems, and they are perfectly valid. The only question is which ones you believe in and how strongly you believe them." She thought of what Prophet had said on the tape.

Marcie remarked, more kindly, "You're just doing this because you're upset about Phil. It's natural to blame somebody, or something, else." She shot another look at Harriet, then wriggled her foot in Stanley's eye line.

Stanley changed the angle of his putter and obliged. "Carol, you and Grandma are going to drive yourselves —and us—crazy with this fixation on spells and curses. Accidents happen. Still do, as we know." His Adam's apple wobbled.

Carol spread her hands in an appeal to his reason. "Don't you think it's unnatural to have so many accidents in one family? That it's downright suspicious?"

"No more suspicious than your spell, or whatever it is you're trying to sell us on," he replied forcefully. "Your mama's right about one thing. Instead of living in the real world, you've spent too much time studying folklore. And as if our own hocus-pocus weren't enough, now you've learned everybody else's, too, right around the globe." At last the little white ball clunked into the oversized glass, hard enough to break it.

Carol retorted, "You just don't want me to see Winston. I found out how you and Mama kept us apart when we were teenagers."

Stanley huffed. "His family caused a lot of trouble in our family."

"Well, I've discovered that if there was a curse, and anybody's to blame, it was our family, because we killed one of the Wolfs."

"That's horse-shit!" Stanley exploded. "Who told you such nonsense? Our family could never have done any such thing."

"'Our family, ' Carol stressed to him, "has ruined my life."

Marcie broke in. "You've ruined your own life, not marrying any of those nice boys you met in college and insisting on studying something nobody can understand, including you! Living in a desert." Unhappily, she slammed down her magazine. "Why, I can't look my friends in the eye, because you aren't married."

Carol was stunned. Finally, she said, "I did all of that because I couldn't have Winston." She said it quietly, but it sounded like the crash of cymbals.

But that was just the sound of the telephone and answering it was her escape from the nightmare that had started again. How foolish she had been to think her parents had changed, or that they were any more accepting of her life than they'd ever been.

When Carol had gone, Harriet observed, "You'll be sorry if those two ever start keeping company again. You shouldn't allow it now, any more than you did then."

Marcie sighed. "Grandma, Carol is twenty-six years old. Nearly twenty-seven. We can't allow, or disallow, her anything."

But Harriet was unforgiving. "More's the pity. He'll ruin our family again. You wait and see." She gave her son a dark look. "Just like his old uncle did."

At the sound of Winston's voice on the telephone, so unexpected, Carol lost concentration, but tuned in as he was saying, "...then I gave that pouch to Dr. Raxter. He wants to talk to you about it; he just called me." Winston's manner was business-like.

"Did he say when? I don't want to make another wild goose chase over there." She was thinking of the futility of her last trip, not just because of not seeing Ralph Raxter.

He sounded chastened. "I'll give you his number; you can set it up yourself." There was another pause. "And, Carol, would you come by my office and let me know what he tells you?"

She hesitated. "Why?"

"Because that pouch concerns me, too. In fact, when you come right down to it, it belongs to the Wolfs, not the Mattoxes."

She wanted to keep as far away from him as possible, but she supposed he deserved to know. "I guess I can do that. After all, you're off-limits."

"About that..." he began.

"Don't," she interrupted. "There's nothing you can say that will make it any better."

CHAPTER THIRTY SEVEN

CHEROKEE NC, MAY 1999

"I've had a good look at this." Dr. Raxter held up Wolf's medicine bag. "But before we talk about it, let me apologize for missing you last week. I couldn't check my messages."

She noticed how quietly he spoke. "You don't need to; I took a chance, coming without an appointment. Anyway, I enjoyed the drive over, the mountains are always beautiful."

He beamed. "Then let me welcome you to the museum, Dr. Mattox, as a colleague."

Carol smiled back. "Please, call me Carol. And moving The Mattox Collection here hardly qualifies me as a colleague, although I'm flattered by the idea."

"What if there were a possibility of your being a real colleague?" He looked at her closely for a moment. "There will soon be a job opening here, and it's something you might like. Are you at all interested?"

She could feel herself gaping at the unexpected idea. "I have a job. But, sure, I'd like to hear what it is. I've always wanted to work here."

He smiled at that. "It wouldn't be anything as scholarly as I'm sure you've been doing. By now," he grinned, "the Cherokees have just about been studied to death. No, it's more on the education side than the academic. We're soon going to have an opening for an Education Director. Of course, you'd have to go through the selection process, same as everybody else, but I don't think that would be a problem, do you?"

Carol was sure her mouth fell open. It was a dream job. "I have to say I'm surprised." She was thinking furiously. She would be interested in such a job. However, she had vowed to stay away from Winston, which would be impossible if she worked here. Trying to buy time to sort out her feelings, she asked, "Why did you think of me?"

"Pamela Stewart recommended you, and that's all I need. Until I talked to her, I didn't know we had such talent right on our own doorstep. I can't tell you how glad I'd be to have you on our staff, especially you being a relative of Isabelle Mattox, and especially if her collection comes here. That woman did more to preserve Cherokee culture in her lifetime than all the politicians since the Revolution."

Carol confided, "She inspired me, too. I've always wanted to be like her. I'm trying to talk my family into moving the collection. Provided I get the okay, when are you thinking of bringing it?"

"Soon," he smiled, "and this medicine bag might become our star attraction." Shoving aside some paperwork, with careful movements he deposited the bag and its contents on his desk, then stepped back and gestured at them. "Those are all the things our ancestors once used to make somebody die."

Instantly, sweat beaded on Carol's upper lip, and her mouth trembled. But, needing to keep a professional manner in front of Dr. Raxter, she forced her voice to sound normal. "I know about some of those things, but not all."

He sat on the edge of his desk, his calmness belying his words and their effect on her. "To bring about a death, you needed to bury all these—the pebbles, and the root—plus some other things."

So Isabelle's husband had placed a curse on someone. Was it on the Mattoxes? That was still unclear, and Carol tried to stop quaking, stop the fear in her heart, as he continued. "To put a death spell on somebody was a very serious matter for the Cherokees. Although we made war on our enemies in the old days, we were never bloodthirsty people, and to lay a curse would have been a last resort, a consequence of being gravely wronged. But it could have happened. In fact, there's every sign here that it did."

Managing little more than a whisper, she asked, "You said—these things, plus others? If something's missing, could it still have been a death curse?"

"Well, the other things might be missing because they were used, for the curse. These may be just the leftovers." As he dashed her hope, Raxter stroked his chin with long, leathery fingers, each movement taking Carol closer to the brink of real fear. "The strongest indication that this bag contained at least the makings of a death curse is the root. It's wild horseradish, and this was the only thing it was used for, because it was poison."

Weakly, she made a final plea. "Since the bag is so intact, could it mean the curse was never put on?"

"Could," he agreed, "but we can't be sure."

To hide their shaking, Carol clasped her hands together. Even so, something that felt nasty crept along her neck. She contemplated the pouch, unwilling to touch its contents, and then felt irritated with herself. She had seen many things that were said to bring death upon people, and she hadn't been any the worse for it. Why did she feel this way now?

She knew it was because, from the day she'd seen it again, she'd had a feeling the pouch contained something evil. And now it seemed she had been right.

Finally, an even more important question tumbled out. "Do you think, if a curse was put on, it could still be in effect?"

"Now?" He whistled under his breath and thought for a while. Her nerves were shrieking before he said at last, "I wouldn't know about that. My area's identification, not interpretation."

Carol slumped. She was no closer to knowing the answers to other important questions. Had the curse been put on the Mattoxes? And was it still alive? Grandma was sure of it, and Phil had seen what seemed to be a deliberate attempt to kill him. Carol had seen something similar and had felt like a target herself since falling through the veranda floor.

Still, she couldn't, without a lot of reservations, believe in such a thing as an ancient curse.

Raxter gave her a considering look. "Why does this pouch concern you, above all the other things in The Mattox Collection?"

She thought of whatever had killed so many of her family since Tallaquoyah Wolf's day. How many more deaths, like that of her beloved Phil, would there be? There might even be her own: uncertain, unexpected, before her time. That was bad enough, but after her, who? Would it affect the children she might have? Would it continue to curse her family? Forever and ever? She didn't know what to believe any more. How could she find the answers to all her questions? Ralph Raxter offered the only way of finding out, and he was an expert. She gave in to the temptation to blurt out the whole story and waited for him to laugh.

He didn't. In fact, he sat very still until she finished, and then said thoughtfully, "I see why you came to me."

His very calm, and the seriousness of his answer, upset her more. "Can you tell me what's going on?"

He shook his head. "I'm afraid I can't. But I think visions can speak the truth. And often, the truth is decided just by how strongly you believe it."

It was almost what Prophet had said, she thought. But, whereas Prophet could be called superstitious, here was a distinguished academic saying the same thing. It couldn't be ignored. And it was terrifying.

"Yes, well ..." There was nothing left to say. Recovering her manners, she told him, "Anyway, I sure do thank you for looking at it and giving me your opinion."

"Not at all," Raxter said. "Glad to have been able to help you, although I'm not sure I have." To break the awkward moment, he said briskly, "Now, would you like to talk more about that job?"

It wasn't a good time. But this was a job she was qualified for, and she might enjoy the change it would bring. Just as she had followed her own instincts years ago, despite her parents' disapproval, she had to keep doing the right thing by herself now, even though it might put her near Winston. Surely, she was brave enough to work in the same town with him. In fact, it would be a good test of her resolve, not to mention get her used to him belonging to somebody else. And somehow, knowing about the pouch made her want to stay close to it; close to her family; even close to Winston, dangerous as it was. And it was still possible that he was behind the things that were happening.

As had become her habit by now, she told such an eerie feeling to go away. Taking a deep, shaky breath, she said to Ralph Raxter, "I'd love to hear more about the job."

CHAPTER THIRTY EIGHT

In Winston's office once more, a mass of conflicts whirled through Carol's mind. If only she could find quick solutions to her problems. But they seemed to be worsening. If only she were back in the orderly world of the research station.

Finally, she burst out with the lesser problem. "I've been encouraged to apply for a job at the museum."

For a second she saw Winston's eyes light up. Then she noticed that he carefully doused what might be interpreted as interest. "That's nice. What is it?"

"Education director."

He gestured. "It'll be a piece of cake for somebody like you."

"It won't be just anthropology, but that's one of the reasons I'm interested. Frankly, I'd be glad to get into education instead of the strictly academic. Then I could put all those studies—that anthropologists like me do—into language that can be understood by everybody, and get them into the community and the wider world, instead of just talking among ourselves." She realized she'd already worked up enthusiasm for the job.

"Are you going to take it, then?" He waited for her answer.

It was her turn to douse her feelings. "I have to apply, same as everybody else. And I haven't decided whether I'll do that, yet."

"What are you waiting for?" When she simply looked at him he went on, after what seemed a struggle to find the right words, "It'll be nice having you in Cherokee."

That's what worries me; it'll be too nice, or too dangerous, Carol thought. But she said, "At least I could keep an eye on The Mattox Collection."

He followed her change of subject. "So what did Dr. Raxter tell you about the medicine bag?"

"It seems our suspicions were right."

"Your suspicions," he reminded her. "I merely—"

"Yes, I forgot that you don't believe in 'museum pieces.'"

"All I said was that I concentrate on the present, not the past. And I don't practice superstitions."

Carol looked at him carefully. "Your ancestor, Tallaquoyah Wolf, did. Dr. Raxter says that what was in the pouch could definitely have put a death spell on somebody."

He seemed not to interpret it as an accusation. Gently, he laid a sympathetic hand on her arm. She stiffened, but reminding herself that it was just a friendly gesture, and comforting, she allowed it. At this, his other arm circled her shoulders, tucking her into his chest. She leaned into the strong body she remembered so well, that had been, and still was, forbidden to her. She could no longer bear the strain of suspecting him. Just as she had ten years ago, she once again needed his strength.

"Ssshhh, Little One," he whispered, just as he had done all those years ago. "Hush now, *hsing-ga-wa-la.* It all happened a long time ago."

"No," she gulped. "It's still happening, to my family."

He kissed the tears from her eyes, then from her mouth. And then his lips stayed there, warm and comforting, easing the hurt so much that she let them.

But after a moment she pushed him away. "You're practically a married man."

"I'm sorry, I just couldn't help it. It hurts me to see you upset. It makes me think of…" He didn't finish. Instead, his arms fell to his sides and he moved some distance away.

She felt bereft of his comforting touch, but she was glad he was out of easy reach. "Give me your honest opinion about this." She laid the medicine bag on his desk.

"'Honest?'" When she nodded, he thought for a while before saying, "I think that my old uncle—your aunt's husband—might, in those days, have tried to put on a spell, probably against your aunt's brother, James Mattox. After all, he was in charge of removing the Indians from around here, so it makes sense that he might have killed one of our family or been responsible for it. You don't have to be Sherlock Holmes to figure that out, and anyway, that story has been handed down in my family."

"And…?"

"Whether I believe in a curse, especially one that's been killing people for two hundred years, is another thing. Even if I did, from what I've heard our old people say, most of the time curses didn't work, however much you wanted them to. Just like medicine men weren't always effective. Not so different to doctors today, I guess."

"And yet something is causing people in my family to die before their time. What do you think it could be?"

He shrugged. "It could be anything. Sometimes, just hearing old stories can have a powerful psychological effect, and that seems to have happened in your family."

She looked up at him unhappily. "I've already been the victim of an accident." Then she told him about falling through the veranda floor. "And I know it had nothing to do with psychology."

He commented, "That wasn't fun. But after all, it is an old house. I'm sure there's nothing sinister, nothing to be afraid of."

"My grandmother says I may be the next one to die." She hugged herself and, despite a lot of effort, began to shake.

"You can't believe that." He was by her side in two long strides. He took her in his arms and started kissing her again. At first his mouth was soft and comforting, but soon it hardened, leaving her in no doubt of a feeling that went beyond sympathy.

It seemed to her that both of them had a need so strong it had existed forever; that each had been created just for the other, and just to be joined. Being together was so right it was, Carol felt, beyond the morality of his situation and beyond her sensibility.

She knew Winston was not hers to love. But that thought lasted only for a second. Despite the strong warning in her head, she gave in to her rush of feelings. She simply couldn't stop herself from responding with her own overpowering desire. This time, when his mouth demanded answers, she gave them. And each answer was "yes."

Their mouths clung together, and as their hands began to move, Carol felt the past unhappy years evaporate. Their bodies wrapped themselves around each others.' To get even closer and become truly one, they moved onto the leather Chesterfield that sat along one wall.

Tenderly he lowered her onto the warm animal skin. The light was back in his eyes, as brilliant as fireworks. One knee kept her away from the sofa's edge as he began to remove her clothes, and investigate her, ever so slowly.

Carol lay watching him, tender and compliant, happiness glowing through eyes that had so recently been drowning in sorrow.

First he opened her shirt. For a long time he simply looked at her. Her breasts thrust themselves at him, yearning to be free. He released them, his eyes watching them spread, warm and wanting. Reverently, he cupped them before bending his head.

Taking one in his mouth, he ran his tongue around and around the nipple's edge. Carol moaned as it stood up, begging for more, and she raised up to get it closer to his lips. Then, just beyond Winston's shoulder, the doorknob turned.

She clasped her shirt together, struggling against him in warning, but this merely seemed to fan his desire. Looking surprised, and pleased, he bent closer to her, hand on his belt buckle.

Then the door opened wide, and a tall young woman with long, straight black hair stood gazing at them.

"I was feeling faint," Carol told her loudly, not altogether untruthfully.

Winston turned, slowly, toward the doorway. This time, he thought, Wanda's normal sullen look had become dangerous. Her mouth was a thin, hard line; her eyes shone with malice. For a moment he felt she was a totally different person, perhaps not even a person at all, but an evil spirit. "Wanda?" Almost, he was asking if it were really she.

But Wanda, having flicked a cold glance over him, and without even seeming to see Carol, made no reply and, slowly, shut the door again.

In a tone that was embarrassed, but not unduly concerned, Carol asked, "Was that your secretary?"

Winston thought for a moment before replying. "That was my fiancée, Wanda."

"Oh, no!" Carol struggled free, and their moment was lost again, as it had been lost so many times.

CHAPTER THIRTY NINE

That evening Wanda asked Winston, "And what was that disgusting scene in your office all about?" Standing in her living room, refusing to sit, she tapped her foot.

He was as stung as she by his betrayal but recoiled from her description. "Please don't just walk into my office like that."

Incredulous, she mocked, "Oh, so you can make out with all your women on the couch!"

"No!" He fought to maintain his dignity and his right to at least professional privacy. "Like today, I could be meeting with an important client."

"Meeting with?" She sneered. "Don't you mean sleeping with?"

Because it had been Carol—who was special—he couldn't admit to cheating. And they hadn't actually done anything. Not that they wouldn't have, if Wanda hadn't interrupted them. "You're completely wrong. Like she said, she's a client, we were talking, and she started feeling faint. I suggested she lie down." He hated the sound of his own words, the bitter taste of the lie. So logical, so false. He'd never lied to anyone, and didn't enjoy it.

"Hmph," Wanda snorted, walking up and down in front of the window in her severely white room. "Most of your clients are men." When he decided to refuse that bait, she tried a more direct route. "What's her name?"

"You don't know her."

"Try me."

He sighed. "Her name is Carol Mattox. And she is a client. Or, rather, her father is. He's a business associate, an important one. He's Senator Mattox, and I'm chasing him about that land swap. That was the reason we postponed the wedding, so you ought to remember, you were so mad about it. Maybe now you'll believe me." And if she didn't, he was ready to call everything off. He just couldn't lie any more.

But Wanda suddenly said, "I'm sorry. I guess I've just got wedding jitters," and even smiled at him.

He unclenched his hands. "That's all right. It happens." But he felt a curious lack of relief.

Wanda knew it wasn't all right. But she also knew she was willing to put up with whatever it took to be Mrs. Winston Wolfe. So determined was she to marry the chief of the Cherokees, jealousy was a luxury she simply couldn't afford. She had wanted to make him feel bad, wanted him to know that she was no fool. She felt better for it. But in the end, it was smarter to keep silent.

Someday, she would get revenge on Miss Carol High-and-Mighty Mattox. She knew just how to do this. And when her revenge came, it would be all the sweeter for today's affront.

CHAPTER FORTY

WASHINGTON DC, OCTOBER 1837

John Ross glanced up as Wolf entered the library. When Ross, principal chief of the Cherokee Nation, was in the town that had become the capitol of the white man's country, the Cavendish Hotel was his headquarters, this room his unofficial office.

"You're just in time to hear my latest submission to the president," Ross told Wolf, crisply stacking papers on a gleaming mahogany desk.

"I'm sorry, but I can't stay. I came to remind you that I'm speaking to the Senate committee this morning, as arranged by Daniel Webster."

Ross looked up at Wolf from beneath deeply arched eyebrows. "He failed to stop ratification of the removal treaty."

"True, but he remains our friend and staunchly against removal, and agrees with me there's still a chance of avoiding it, through my plan for citizenship."

Ross folded thick fingers over his papers and spoke slowly. "Your fight for citizenship is good, but it alone will not stop removal."

"I disagree."

"Well, we will see. I wish you luck, my friend. Let us proceed in every way we can, for our very survival is at stake. I'll be there, of course."

Wolf paused in his speech and looked around the oak-paneled room in the Capitol building. It held the large group of influential senators—nearly fifty, he judged—that Daniel Webster had persuaded to attend, who believed there was room for both natives and newcomers in this huge, empty country.

For the past half-hour, Wolf had spoken eloquently and from his deepest convictions. In closing, he had one last chance to urge a practical measure: a law giving citizenship to Indians.

He took a deep breath. "The Cherokee are the proudest tribe of all. We have always been free men, able to do as we wish and need. But new customs have eroded our freedom in recent years. Now we also need to be free men of another nation, that of the United States."

"Hear! Hear!"

He acknowledged their support with a raised hand. His vision was strong with purpose; his deep voice thundered more powerfully than ever. "It is our dream—more than a dream, a necessity—that the Cherokee become citizens of the United States of America. Then we will be truly free men, with the same rights as every other citizen. This government should respect our desire for that. England treated you badly, and I would remind you that's why you fought the War of Independence."

Several senators, led by Webster, spoke through the applause.

"You're right, by gad."

"This is just what we need to stop removal."

"We pride ourselves on being free and fair, and we'll do whatever we can."

"Thank you, gentlemen," Wolf responded, encouraged.

CHAPTER FORTY ONE

FORT BUTLER NC, OCTOBER 1837

Isabelle opened her trunk. "*Ooooh,*" was her involuntary reaction to seeing its contents after so long.

Even full of wrinkles, and water-marked from the river, the clothes were a fine sight. There was the silk taffeta afternoon dress of blue and yellow plaid, her most flattering shades. Beneath it, a smart dark gabardine riding dress. Where were the day dresses? There they were, near the bottom.

Closely following such pleasurable sensations was a despair that rocked her back on the heels of her ungainly new boots. How wonderful was the memory of wearing such beautiful clothes. It felt to her, almost, as if it had happened to another person.

With that thought, she marveled that she had brought such clothes to a remote army post. She should have brought Emily's clothes; they would have been far more suitable for her life as James' housekeeper, although that was too fine a title for her daily drudgery.

She delved further into her finery. Discovery of the white kid-leather pumps with buttons down the sides brought a sob. They had been her very best and the envy of her friends. On impulse, she removed her heavy boots and, finding a pair of silk stockings at the bottom of a hosiery box, put on the soft shoes. On an equally wild impulse, she cast off her coarse homemade clothes and slipped into the plaid taffeta dress. Almost in a frenzy now, she lifted from her hat box the blue velvet bonnet trimmed with a large blue taffeta bow.

"Oohh." Silk and velvet felt wonderful after so long wearing homespun, although her work-roughened fingers caught on the luxurious material.

She stood up on the high heels, parading awkwardly across the dirt floor. But she slowed, not just from its unevenness. After two months of hard work and hobnailed boots, the lovely leather shoes pinched and were very uncomfortable. Trying to regain the knack of wearing them, up and down the small room she teetered. If only she had a looking glass, she could see herself in her city clothes, one last time. It might sustain her on darkest days.

Ferreting out the small dressing table mirror, she propped it on the kitchen table. But instead of admiring her clothes, she was shocked at the change in her appearance. No longer was her complexion pale and smooth, but browned from sun and dried from wind, and totally without artifice. *What has become of me?* she wondered as she stared at the stranger reflected in the mirror.

Eventually, from the sheer delight of being beautifully dressed once more, she began to pirouette before the little glass. She found herself singing a tune remembered from the last ball she'd attended in Asheville. Round and round she went, remembering the flutter of candlelight, the hot night on the Smathers' veranda, the heavy sweetness of magnolias in full flower, her golden curls shining, not unkempt as they were now. The party seemed like something out of a dream, the memory encouraging her to twirl faster and faster, trying to dance as gracefully as she had on that night.

Until she turned her ankle and fell to earth. Sprawled there, not bothering to collect herself, she began laughing so hard she was soon in tears.

After a while Isabelle stirred, and wiped her eyes and face. With longing and regret, the white kid shoes were put aside. Slowly, smoothing her hands once more over the fine fabrics, she removed the clothes and, even more slowly, packed everything back into the trunk. It would stay there until that longed-for day when she returned to Asheville and what was left of her former life.

With her face on her fists and elbows on the table, she gazed into the mirror, letting herself remember that fateful day on the riverbank of the

Nantahala. It had been many weeks since Wolf had gone to Washington, and as many since she had had stimulating company, and she had been lonely.

She picked up her hair brush and tried to put it through curls that hadn't been combed for months, but it fell from her hand. Smoothing out so many knots and tangles would require patience and time.

CHAPTER FORTY TWO

WASHINGTON DC, OCTOBER 1837

Wolf took a moment to survey the glittering scene in the Cavendish Hotel ballroom. It was a lavish party for the visiting Indian delegation. Such entertainment was by now a time-honored custom.

From a podium at one end of the large, rectangular room, an orchestra played waltzes, interspersed with reels. The pale green room had long swags of velvet drapery at tall windows that overlooked Pennsylvania Avenue and the imposing Capitol building. The walls had recently been paneled in the latest London style and were softly lit by hundreds of white candles, which also gave off the exotic smell of beeswax. The ballroom, Wolf saw, was filled with beautiful women and handsome men, all luxuriously dressed in the latest fashion.

He also saw, with satisfaction, that the Cherokee delegation was there to a man. Most of them were resplendent in white tie and tails. Wolf himself wore a new set made especially for this occasion.

A few of the Indians, however, had taken the opportunity to wear more colorful dress. Some wore plaid sashes, blanket-style, over the shoulders of their tuxedos. There was also the occasional bit of fancy dress. Chief Walking Stick from east Tennessee predictably wore his blue sash and turban. Even more common were the guests in elaborate buckskins, such as Wolf had loaned to Isabelle, their glossy black hair laced extravagantly with feathers for the gala occasion.

Miss Lavinia Moore escaped her circle of admirers and headed for him, her smile wide. Her smooth, gleaming chestnut hair was piled high atop her soft-looking, milky-white neck. "Are you ready to dance with me, Mr. Reid?" She fluttered an exotic sandalwood fan, scenting the air.

"I'm at your service, Miss Moore."

The fan waved faster as she pouted prettily. "You make it sound like a duty, sir."

"I assure you it isn't." Lavinia Moore, the daughter of the prominent Senator Burke Moore, was this season's most sought-after debutante. Last week the senator himself had left no doubt in Wolf's mind that a suit to Miss Moore would be favorably received.

But a totally different woman was in Wolf's thoughts—a small woman, with tousled blonde hair and eyes of cornflower blue. He had thought much about Isabelle while he had been away. He was worried that because the negotiations were taking so long, she might be gone by the time he returned south. That wasn't too much of a problem; he knew where to find her. No, the worse problem, by far, was her family. Her brother had tried to kill him once, and might do so again. The rest of her family couldn't be much different.

Thus, enticed by the senator and, on the whole, tempted with such a beautiful woman as Lavinia, and a favorable family situation—beyond a man's ability to refuse—he had told the senator he looked forward to dancing with Miss Moore at the ball.

Now he moved her into the throng of dancers, feeling her warmth under the soft, silken gown. Round and round they went, her long curls dangling down the back of her head as she nodded seductive assent each time her head moved, which was often. She was aware of their effect.

Nevertheless, he soon noticed that she danced rather woodenly. Under his hand, she felt more like an oak tree than a sapling. When he had kissed Isabelle goodbye in the woods, she had felt as pliant as a young maple. Suddenly Lavinia's heavy, exotic perfume nearly overwhelmed him, and his step faltered.

He held Lavinia closer, trying to recapture what had seemed so promising. Alas, by the time they'd danced several lengths of the room, he had realized the futility of his attempts to return the Moores' encouragements. Nothing moved within him when he looked at the beautiful, elegantly-dressed, wealthy and available Miss Lavinia Moore. His loins, as well as his soul, stirred when he looked upon the unavailable Miss Isabelle Mattox, even in her disarray, and this had been so from the first moment he'd seen her, helpless in the river.

At the end of their dance, he allowed Lavinia, despite a whispered appeal, to be enthusiastically claimed by her next partner. Seeking cooler air to calm his thoughts, Wolf strolled onto the balustraded stone balcony. There he came upon Daniel Webster who, smiling as he lit a cheroot, observed, "I see you've been dancing with the belle of the ball. Are you enjoying yourself, my friend?"

Wolf considered telling Daniel about the woman who filled his mind, instead of the one who had merely filled his arms, but instead asked, "Has there been any word from the Senate committee?"

Webster's mouth drew thin as he exhaled. "I don't have good news for you on that subject, I'm afraid. The committee has deferred the matter to the next session of Congress."

"The next session!" Wolf repeated numbly. "But that won't be until after Christmas! By then it will be too late!" He gripped the balustrade.

"Don't despair," Webster soothed. "If we get it through in January, it could be law by Easter."

Wolf looked closely at his comrade. "You're saying we're not going to get citizenship, aren't you?"

Webster drew hard on his cheroot before saying gently, "I'm afraid that is so."

"But what happened?" Wolf cried.

Webster hesitated but finally confided, "As I'm not officially on the committee, I can't be sure. But I heard that your leader told the head of the committee that the Cherokee wouldn't press for it. If true, that would have doomed it. No one is going to put up a strong fight for something that's not even wanted."

Not wanted? His dream—his life's work—not wanted? "But that cannot be! John Ross is our leader, yes, but our way is to have many chiefs, not just one. Why didn't they listen to me?"

"Because our way is to have only one leader. And Ross is senior to you."

Wolf bowed his head and remained silent for a long time. Then he clenched his fists and straightened. Excusing himself from Webster, he strode back into the ballroom. Lavinia Moore was waltzing now in the arms of the President of the United States, but he barely noticed her.

Wolf drew John Ross behind a pillar before grabbing the lapel of his tail coat. "I demand to know what you told the Senate committee." The smaller, older man was silent. Wolf was so angry he nearly shook his leader. "Do I have to bring the chairman over to verify it?"

Ross became voluble. "Citizenship was never going to be given. They were just leading us on, trying to spin things out until the removal date neared."

So it was true. Wolf's life's work had just been scuttled by his own leader, a man he trusted. "That wasn't your judgment to make," he seethed.

"You're wrong there, too. We're getting more people daily to see things our way, to stop the removal."

"We're getting closer daily to the date the president has set for removal," Wolf corrected him, pacing the polished floor. "And daily the situation in Georgia is worsening. My entire estates are listed for the new lottery, which means they will be given to some white man. The only question is when," he said bitterly.

"My home's in Georgia, too," Ross reminded him, "yet I'm still confident that things will work out for the best, for all of us."

Wolf turned away, to hide his pain and sorrow at his closest friend's betrayal.

Ross moved to confront him. "I've written a new proposal and I'd like you to hear it."

"You've served our nation well for a long time," Wolf said through clenched teeth, "but the time for writing proposals, even making new agreements, has passed," he said quietly. He suspected they were seldom or never read.

With a raised eyebrow Ross said, "Bitterness and quarreling among ourselves has always brought harm to our cause, almost more than the white man has. We need to keep a unified front."

But Wolf's heart was sore and heavy. Grimly he said, "I, too, have spent many years in the service of the Cherokee Nation, but now I need to worry about myself. I need to get home and see to my estates, before they are taken over by the settlers."

And besides the matter of his lands, tonight he'd discovered he had another matter to deal with. Although different, it was also a matter of the heart.

CHAPTER FORTY THREE

FORT BUTLER NC, OCTOBER 1837

Bill and Barbara Hughes' new barn had been built in a single day by the men of Huntington while the ladies made quilts for the approaching winter. Now that the work was done, it was time for dancing. Saw-horses became trestles for tables of food the ladies were loading with their finest offerings.

John Duncan picked up his banjo and played a note for his wife and son, who tuned their fiddles to it. The Duncans' beautiful, black-haired daughter Pearl, long curls let down to her waist for the evening's party, played the tub, a round zinc bath mounted on a wooden pole with strings that she plucked, just like a bass fiddle.

The smell of fresh-sawn pine invigorated Isabelle, heightening her happy mood. The musicians' first, tinkling notes, not even a song yet, set her feet to dancing. She'd worn her leather slippers, cast aside these past months, and the lightness of them brought a memory of her old self. But tonight it was going to be as much fun to dance in a barn as it had been to dance in the mansions in Asheville.

Her rabbit stew had kept warm over Barbara Hughes' hearth fire during the quilting, and now Isabelle added it to the food being set out. Everybody had worked up a good appetite. First the children, then their fathers, crowded around the tables before the ladies had them properly set out.

"Now, Joe Luckett," a woman told her twelve-year-old, "you stop that," as he grabbed a pone of cornbread as soon as it went on the table.

"Daddy's done got his!" Young Joe was pained by the injustice of it.

"I declare, where are your manners, you men?"

"We lost them, building this barn," Joe's father Henry piped up, and everybody laughed.

"Well, you can just wait 'til we say the blessing!"

Despite the pause, the dishes were soon empty. "Why, there isn't enough left to feed a hound dog," pronounced Elsie with satisfaction, helping Isabelle and the other ladies clear up so the dancing could begin. "Except for Sarah Allen's pickled beans." She shared a quiet chuckle with Isabelle. "They're as sour as she is, an' she's made her husband Dave the same way." They set a large pan of Sally-Kate Stiles' gingerbread, and a jug of her husband's apple cider, on a small table where the dancers could help themselves. "Ah, Lordy, isn't it great to see people eating and enjoying themselves!"

Dale and JoNell Barton had walked nearly two miles for the rare entertainment. Dale commented, "This is prob'ly the last time we can have anything this year, it'll be getting too cold soon."

Just then, the Duncan family started playing square-dance music. It rippled out of their mellow instruments and rang against the new rafters. Dale's cousin Grant began beating time with his foot.

Willy-nilly, twenty or thirty people rushed to find a partner. Children danced with their parents. Isabelle found herself dancing with Mrs. Hughes's daughter Deborah. The Bartons' son Tyler danced with his little sister Rebekah. Tyler was about Deborah Hughes's age, fourteen, and Isabelle could tell they were sweet on each other by the way they scrupulously avoided each other.

"Aw-right, now," Grant called out in time to the music. "Circle going left." The dancers obeyed. "Circle going right!" There was laughter and stumbling as people followed the change. "Now grab your partner…" his face creased with pleasure "and do-si-do!"

In high spirits, Isabelle hooked arms with Deborah. Around and around they went.

Several other men arrived. "Most of 'em's soldiers from the fort," confided Elsie, casting a speculative eye at the tall figure pushing through the crowd.

What was Sergeant Hampton doing here? Isabelle was vexed at encountering him on her first carefree evening.

"Awright, now, folks, this is the Virginia Reel," announced Grant. The musicians began a more sedate tune, and dancers lined up opposite each other.

Sergeant Hampton sidled over to Isabelle. "I want this dance with you."

She flinched from the odor of strong liquor on his breath but replied calmly, "As you can see, I already have a partner." She turned away, dipping a deep curtsey to Tyler.

Hampton guffawed. "You need a real man."

"Thank you, Sergeant, for that advice. It seems to be all you think about. You won't mind, I hope, if I don't take it."

"You should take it while you can get it," he leered, then grabbed at her shoulder.

"Leave her alone." Tallaquoyah Wolf stood in the open barn gate. Isabelle gasped, feeling blood rush to her head. She'd been waiting for him for such a long time.

"What the . . ." Sergeant Hampton cursed.

"It's a Injun, who asked him?"

"Anyway, he's welcome."

"No, he ain't."

While the music continued, Wolf walked calmly up to Isabelle, took her hand, and kissed it. Then, holding it close, he asked, "May I have this dance, Miss Mattox?"

She drank in his strength, his handsome, chiseled features. As always, he was dressed in a fine black suit, with a soft, expensive white shirt, and made all the other men look shabby.

"Thank you." She accepted his offer, and they moved into each others' arms. The Duncans began playing a slow, throbbing waltz. Isabelle recognized it as a Strauss waltz. The other dancers fell away and gave them the floor. She and Wolf, their eyes only for each other, moved to their own music.

After a few minutes, Sergeant Hampton walked up to Wolf and tapped him on the shoulder. "You won't mind if I cut in, will you?" he sneered. "I've been trying to dance with this lady all evening. I thought she was just being particular about who she danced with, 'til you showed up."

Wolf looked at him levelly. "I do mind. I've come a long way to dance with her, myself." He looked back at Isabelle. "I've ridden almost all the way from Washington City, to tell her something of great importance."

She smiled with such happiness she was unaware she lit up the whole barn.

"You'd better tell me what you've got to say," the sergeant said.

Wolf asked, "Why? Are you her guardian?"

"No, but her brother is, and I'm his second-in-command."

"Maybe at the fort, but not here," Wolf dismissed Hampton's claim. Turning again to Isabelle, he murmured, "It's crowded in here; let's go outside," and waltzed her out of the barn and into the cold, crisp, starry October night.

Once there, he stopped and held her close. In the light of a huge golden harvest moon, he whispered, "You see, I've come back."

"I'm glad, for I didn't know if you would."

"And now that I'm back, I never want to leave you again."

"I don't want you to, either. But…"

He put a strong finger over her mouth and softly, gently, moved it around and around, stirring her senses. "We'll think about realities later," he advised. "Right now…" he replaced his finger with his mouth.

Isabelle could feel his lips gathering hers into a sensuous knot that might unravel, uncontrollably, in a hundred delicious ways.

Instead, the next thing she felt was the force of a heavy blow, and Wolf was lying face down in the muddy pasture.

Zeb Hampton stood over him, a two-by-four still raised high.

CHAPTER FORTY FOUR

At the sight of Wolf sprawled unconscious, Isabelle screamed as though she was the wounded one. She dropped to his side, horrified by the splash of scarlet blood on his white shirt. Failing to rouse him, she felt for his pulse. When it proved steady, she sighed with relief, and called out for help.

Her call went mostly unheard. The music continued. No one helped Wolf, although several men swarmed around his prone body. No one held Zeb Hampton back, and he stood, wild-eyed and menacing, bare-fisted now but looking, Isabelle feared, like he might hit Wolf again.

Finally Dave Allen reached down and yanked Wolf up by his collar. Isabelle scrambled to her feet, protesting, as Dave shook the inert body. Two other men stood Wolf upright—his eyes dazed, his limbs rubbery—in front of Zeb Hampton, who hit him again with a sickening smack.

"No! Help! Help him!" she screamed.

One of the soldiers crowed sarcastically, "What a coward—he don't even defend hisself."

Isabelle wailed, "How can he, when he was king-hit from behind by a real coward." She glowered at Hampton.

Elsie Hunter shoved through the men and, gathering a weeping Isabelle into her arms, flung at them. "What kind of skunks are you, to hit a man when he's already down? That isn't the way we do things around here."

In answer Hampton raised his fist again. But the men had fallen back a little at Elsie's intervention. Hampton settled for pushing out his chest. "Ah, well, hittin's too good for him, anyway. We need to teach him a good lesson for insulting a white woman. Who else thinks that?"

His fellow soldiers muttered agreement. Then the dozen or so other men chorused, "Yeah," as the cheerful notes of square dance music floated crazily out of the barn.

Hampton shouted, "I say we lynch him."

"Yeah," the others agreed again, and Hampton shot Isabelle a look of triumph.

At this Isabelle recovered her spirit, pushing out of the comfort of Elsie's arms. "How dare you talk like that?"

"Because you've disgraced yourself with this mongrel," he spat at her. "Wouldn't dance with decent men, but you danced with him."

"He's more decent than you'll ever be!"

"Insulting me will get him lynched before you can say Jack Rabbit, for sure."

"My brother will have something to say about that." She grasped at the thought of James like a lifeline.

"Remember the day you arrived at the fort? Your brother will help me lynch a Indian. We should of done it then. But let's not miss this chance to get rid of a trouble-maker." Hampton grabbed a coil of heavy rope from the side of the barn. "We got a good place to do it; they's strong new rafters on this barn," he said with menace, uncoiling the rope and throwing one end over a piece of raw wood. He tied the other end around Wolf's neck, knotting it firmly. Standing back to admire his handiwork, he frowned when Wolf began to open his eyes and make a few feeble movements.

"Quick, afore he comes to," said Dave Allen who, with the sergeant, dragged a now defensive Wolf up to the rafter.

Seeing the return of Wolf's fine senses was like a knife blade stuck into Isabelle's heart. Somehow it was worse if he knew what was happening. It might as well have been she herself dragged to the slaughter. This man had saved her life. And it wasn't just that. She loved him, and she had known it for a long time.

The time for denying that love was over. Meeting death called for honesty, for her best efforts. As the soldiers began to hoist Wolf's body upwards, she let out a cry of rage. "Aaarrrggghh." Then she flew into the circle of men, beating, tearing at them with her hands, trying to drag them away so she could release Wolf. Helped by surprise that a mere female would dare to cross them, she succeeded in reaching him. Her body shielding Wolf's, she turned to face his tormentors, her eyes ablaze with an unearthly light. "Leave him be!"

"Isabelle, honey, don't—" Elsie began.

"Aw, get her outa the way."

When large, rough hands reached out, Isabelle screamed, "Then you'll have to lynch me, too!" Her body sheltered Wolf's while she lashed out with every insult she could muster, hoping one would find its mark. "If you kill both of us, you'll be a disgrace to this town that you have to live in," she panted, looking at the townsmen, then at the soldiers. "And you'll be a disgrace to this fort and the country you've sworn to serve." They had quieted, and her resolve gathered momentum. "I can promise you, you'll answer for it. And if not to my brother, there is an even higher power." She looked to heaven and spoke her final words very clearly. "God himself will punish you."

At this the men shrank back, staring at this woman who dared to cross not just one but many men, and them in a lynching mood. The music had stopped. She could see other men, inside the barn, standing on tiptoe to see what was happening. Dave Allen recovered himself first and replied sourly, "We'll do our own answerin' to God," and reached again for Wolf, who by this time had put his arms protectively around Isabelle.

"It's pretty clear you don't even talk to God!" Elsie cried out. "Archie, come out here and talk some sense into these animals!"

Archibald Hunter appeared at his wife's calling. "What's all the commotion about?" When he saw the rope around Wolf's neck, he said quietly, "Put him down, men."

"Aw, Archie, you're just protectin' your trade with the Injuns," protested a soldier.

"I'm protecting the law of the land and justice to our fellow human beings," Hunter said sternly. "We're a civilized country now; we don't take matters into our own hands. Take that rope off him."

Sergeant Hampton moved toward Wolf. But with a defiant sneer, he tightened the noose instead. Isabelle's blood boiled, and she flew at him. "Take that thing off!"

While Hampton was busy holding her at bay, avoiding her fists and the feet kicking his shins, Archie Hunter loosened the noose, and then removed it. Quietly, he asked the injured man, "Can you walk to the trading post?"

Wolf nodded and, leaning on Archie, moved away. Elsie put her arm around Isabelle and carried her off too. "We'll go home and give him a shot of whiskey—that'll fix him up," she assured Isabelle, whose defiance had begun to weaken now the worst of the danger had passed. Sobbing, she clung to Elsie.

"Matter of fact," Elsie said, hugging her closer, "we might have one ourselves."

CHAPTER FORTY FIVE

Before he left the trading post, Wolf said to Isabelle, "Thank you for your help."

Her concern had not lessened. "It was no more than you did for me. Not even as much."

"We could argue about that, but we won't, for I intend to finish what I started telling you before all this happened. I came back because I learned something in Washington City. I missed you." He took her in his arms, holding her close. "I learned that I love you. And I think, maybe, you would not offer to die for someone you didn't care for."

"You're right." She shivered at the memory, and this caused him to clasp her closer. Her heart was filled with passion, but there was also relief at unburdening the secret she'd kept so long, even from herself. "I love you, too."

This time their kiss was not interrupted. It was long and slow, and sweeter than the previous, urgent one. In the hour in between, their lives had hung in the balance. This kiss was better, she thought, for the more considered feel of it, and because of the rough rope that had laced Wolf's neck. And then she blotted out everything but the feel of his mouth that said he'd never let her go.

When finally he stopped kissing her, he kept her close and murmured, "I'm aware of the difficulties this makes for you."

"And for you."

As usual he waved a big hand dismissing the danger to himself. "We have to keep in touch, somehow, for I couldn't bear it if I couldn't see you. Especially not now." He held her tighter.

"You suffer less than I do, I assure you," she whispered, "for you're all I have. At least you have the love of your family," she said bitterly, "while mine is—"

"I wish it weren't so, and that I didn't have to go back to Georgia and see about business. Our mission to Washington failed to change anything."

"I'm so sorry," she murmured, her lips against his hand.

"You couldn't possibly be as sorry as I am." The pain of losing his fight was still raw. "But I don't have time to mourn. We must be practical now, my dearest. How will we see each other? After tonight, it will be nearly impossible. Will you make a pact with me?"

"Of course." Her reply came without hesitation.

"When you hear the call of the whippoorwill, take the path that goes behind the fort away from the trading post, and I'll meet you."

"Where?"

"I will find you. But first I must find a place where no one can find us."

Isabelle had been summoned by Corporal Fowler, who had escorted her to James' office. Now she stood before him as, seated at his desk, he wrote in a large, thick book. She hadn't been asked to sit; indeed there was no chair to sit in. She stood first on one foot, then the other, like a guilty subordinate, and stopped when that thought came to her.

James finally threw down his quill and looked up at her with a severe set to his face. "What's the meaning of your behavior last night?"

"You should be asking that question of the men who nearly lynched Wolf!" Her temper flashed. "I was trying to save his life, as he'd once saved mine," she reminded him tartly.

"He may have saved it once, but now he's about to get you killed," James observed, his mouth thinning under the broad mustache.

She stood her ground, and spread her hands in appeal. "We were merely dancing."

"Dancing." James looked down at his papers. "You were dancing with an Indian, in front of soldiers and the whole settlement, and you didn't think that was anything that could have got you killed?"

"It shouldn't have been," she persisted. "Nothing would have happened if certain people had left it at that."

Now he leaned back and looked at her. "You don't seem to understand how provocative your behavior was."

"Provocative?" She sputtered with indignation. "How can you blame me, when Sergeant Hampton caused all the trouble? That's terribly unfair."

"It's the way of the world."

"I don't accept that."

"Nevertheless, Sergeant Hampton was just doing what any other man would have done in the circumstances."

"Pshaw. He was drunk." Putting her hands on his desk, she leaned closer. "And let me tell you that Sergeant Hampton is far from the golden-haired boy you think him. At first I let myself be persuaded that he was being kind, giving me supplies when I was desperate for them, to look after you. But I soon saw it was not my welfare he cared about, but his own desires. And I can assure you they are not honorable. He molested me."

But James replied, "This is an army fort, after all, and men are apt to—" he shrugged. "You provoked him, he says deliberately."

She held out her hands. "Then tie me up and throw me in jail."

He sighed. "I would, if you were one of my soldiers. Just don't see the Indians again. Especially Tallaquoyah Wolf. Or Gordon Reid, or whatever he calls himself. And that's an order," he added. "The Indians are our enemies."

"You said I'm not one of your soldiers, to be ordered about." She tossed her head.

With a movement so quick she didn't see it coming, he rose and slammed his hand onto her shoulder, gripping it hard. "You're right, you're not. You're my sister. You belong to me. Therefore, you will do as I say."

Isabelle gasped from the pain of both his hand and his words. Did he truly think of her as one of his possessions? If so, she would have to show him he was wrong.

I'll find a way, she told herself. *Or Wolf will.*

CHAPTER FORTY SIX

RALEIGH NC, JUNE 1999

Winston opened the door of Senator Mattox's office in the state capitol and did a double-take. "I didn't know you'd be here," he said when he saw Carol.

"Same here," she said, feeling as uneasy as he sounded. "I thought I might catch up with my parents. They were here in Raleigh last weekend. It's been a while since I've seen them and, believe it or not, I've missed them. Daddy has been in D.C. most of this month, and my mother's been with him—important parties to give, don'tcha know. That's left me alone with Grandma for a few weeks. Much as I love her, she isn't a barrel of laughs." She stopped, realizing nervousness was making her prattle. She shrugged and confided, "The truth is, he's working extra hard because he hasn't got anywhere with the dam authorities about the day Phil was drowned."

Winston's silence seemed sympathetic. Then he asked, "He's still here?"

"No." She couldn't help sounding slightly exasperated. "I've just found out they went back to D.C. this morning. I was going to tell them about getting the museum job. And thank him because, to my astonishment, he's agreed to move The Mattox Collection."

Winston said quickly, "I heard you got the job. Now it's my turn to congratulate you. How's it going?"

"Great, thank you." She relaxed a little. "Everybody has made me welcome. I feel like I've really come home again."

"And what did they have to say about it in Arizona?"

She remembered her last conversation with Brian. "They were very understanding," she said. "I think they realized that I want to stay at home. You know, now that I'm here, it isn't such a bad place." She grinned. "My boss even said I could go back to my old job if I ever wanted to. How's that for a reference?" And he hadn't even tried to say anything personal. He'd just said, "I wish you luck. If there's ever anything I can do for you, you've only to ask."

"Definitely the kind of reference to have," Winston agreed.

She shouldered her handbag. "Well, I'd better get going. There's a museum conference over at the university. Why are you in town? If it's to see my father, I'm afraid you're out of luck, as much as I am."

"That isn't news." He sighed. "I've been trying to meet with your father for months, about a land swap we need. He won't even see me in Asheville, keeps giving me the runaround, making me come down here to talk to his constituent affairs guy—I'm sure you know Bob La Bruto—who claims to lack the authority to make a decision about such things. I've had to make a lot of trips down here, which takes up time. Then, in the end, it's useless. Only your father can really commit to the deal we're after, and he spends most of his time in D.C." He sighed again. "I'm just getting tossed back and forth like a football."

Carol had listened quietly, and now set her handbag back down. "Maybe I can help. Would you like me to put in a good word for you? Not that he'll listen to me, but at least I can hit him with it when he's least expecting it." She grinned. "That's if I ever see him again."

"If you could do that, I'd be very grateful." In a reflex motion, he put his hands on her arms, as though to seal their bargain with a kiss.

Carol summoned up the courage to move away from him. "Uh-oh, let's not go there again."

"Look, I want to apologize about that day."

"Save it. I knew it was a huge mistake to go to your office. But I didn't think—I was so embarrassed when—"

"I know, and I'm sorry." Suddenly he looked as though kissing her was the furthest thing from his mind. He moved to face her and gave her a look that was as solemn as his voice. "I promise you..."

When he hesitated, she prompted, "What?"

He dropped his hands. "I'll tell you, when I'm sure I can keep the promise."

When Winston returned to Cherokee, he called Wanda and asked if he could drop in after work.

"Are we eating?" she asked.

"I don't think I'll have time," he fobbed her off. "I've just got back from Raleigh, and I have several hours' more work to do at the office." This was met with the silence that, he realized, had become normal between them.

When he arrived at her condo, he took his time working out how to tell her. He looked at her ultra-modern, all-white living room, wishing at least one thing were out of place. But even the curtains were crisp, standing at attention rather than gracing the windows. Although she couldn't afford it, she refused to have a roommate, who'd surely be too messy, she'd said.

He still couldn't think of a good way to begin, so he just plunged in. "There's something I have to tell you." Squaring his shoulders, he began to pace up and down the room. He noticed that, sitting on the sofa, she had angled her legs in a most attractive way. Was she thinking that he wouldn't be able to resist her?

Wanda was thinking that it never hurt to display herself well. You never know when it could be an advantage, and it usually worked on men. She replied, seductively, "And what is it?" For good measure, she rubbed her hands slowly down her long, slender thighs.

Winston focused on the wall over her shoulder. "I need to tell you something, and I don't know how to say it without hurting you. So—" he took a deep breath and then looked squarely at her, "here it is. I've met somebody else."

Wanda's hands stopped abruptly. But, though sounding a little forced, she asked sweetly, "Her name wouldn't be Carol Mattox, would it?" He knew he looked surprised as she continued, in her usual laconic tone, "Well, just because you've met somebody, it doesn't mean anything."

He wanted no compromises—could not, would not—so he broke in quickly. "No. You don't understand. I want to be with her."

Wanda considered. "For how long?"

"Forever."

"Forever?" She began to shout. "How can you be with her forever when you're going to be with me?"

"I want to marry Carol, not you."

She bolted off the sofa. "Oh, no, you can't pull that one on me again. Our wedding date's been set! It's been announced."

"I know, and I'm sorry." He raked both hands through his hair. "I never expected this to happen, in a million years. I sure didn't plan it."

"Well, just stop it from happening. I'm willing to turn a blind eye to some things, but I won't do it forever."

"Believe me, I've tried. But I can't stop it. And the truth is, I don't want to."

Her eyes were blazing. "I'll never give you up. You're mine."

"Not any more."

Desperately, she cast about for sweet words she could say to make everything all right again. But all she tasted was vinegar. "If you keep seeing this other woman—this woman who's not even one of us, one of our people—I'll make sure everyone knows what a cheater you are. It could ruin your career. You'll be sorry to the end of your days. That I can promise you." Her eyes became narrow slits.

Winston confronted her. "Wanda, let's be honest, you and I never had a great passion, anyway. I should have said it long before now. I have that passion with Carol, and what's more, it's been there for a long time." He sighed, just thinking about how long. "It feels like it's been there forever. And I've been as truthful as I can be, at least give me credit for that."

"Truthful! You've been seeing another woman behind my back! I, at least, have a great passion for you." She flung the lie at him.

Her admission pained him. "You know there's never been anyone else but you. I've never been unfaithful to you. I still haven't. I'm breaking it off before I get to that point. And Carol is not just 'another woman.' We knew each other when we were younger." He went back to pacing the room. "There's even more to it. Our ancestors were married to each other. Somehow, somehow that even we can't understand, we just belong together. I met her again by accident. I would never have sought her out, or tried to meet anybody else. But now I can't deny somebody who's been part of me for so long." When Wanda remained impassive, he finished, "Please forgive me."

Wanda opened her eyes and stared at him, her dark eyes unwavering. "I'll see you in hell before I'll forgive you. And the same goes for Carol Mattox. You speak of ancestors, but in our ancestors' day, the blood laws would demand revenge for a sin as serious as this."

"Well, it's a good thing we're completely civilized now, isn't it?" He turned to leave.

Her eyes followed him. "Are you so sure we are?"

Desolation deadening her toes and fingers, Wanda sat down again after Winston left. Although she had known something was going on, after finding them together in his office, his confession had been worse than expected.

She remained very still, her eyes closed. She could see nothing through them anyway, just the color of blood, so warm in contrast to the coldness that gripped her heart. The July day suddenly felt as cold as December.

Some might have said she wasn't even conscious. Only her eyelids moved, blinking rapidly in rhythm with her thoughts. And those thoughts were directed at Carol. 'I'll see **you** in hell, too. You won't get away with this. Somehow, I'll make sure you don't. The laws of the ancients demand that you be punished for what you've done, maybe through those very ancestors who started all this. For my spirit guide is even older than they.'

And immediately, she set about contacting her guiding spirit, the one who had always helped her, who had made sure she got engaged to the new chief. Her trance deepened, and as had happened more and more lately, she entered that other world she lived in. She spent the next hour talking, then listening, to someone there. It was a world far, far away; a world as old as time. But it wasn't this world.

CHAPTER FORTY SEVEN

CHEROKEE NC, JULY 1999

Passing Dr. Ralph Raxter in the hallway of the museum, Carol said, "Good morning."

"How are you settling into your job?" he asked pleasantly.

"It's great. I love it," she replied with enthusiasm.

"Not bothered by those things we talked about?"

"No," she said happily. She hadn't thought much about the Mattox curse for a while. Since Dr. Raxter had exploded his bombshell, she had made an effort to put the mystery on the back burner before she drove herself crazy thinking about it, just as her father had suggested. Then, too, she'd been busy first getting, and then starting, her new job.

Just this fleeting thought about the curse, though, sent ripples of alarm through her again. She marveled at how, in only a few months, she had changed from a skilled, professional observer who dealt with myths and legends matter-of-factly on a daily basis to being a frightened woman on the receiving end of them. The two worlds were very different, she'd discovered.

Passing the museum's auditorium, Carol saw that the daily story-telling session was in progress. Officially, it fell under her responsibilities as education director. But in practice Harry Wolfe, a venerable elder—and Winston's great-uncle—who had been the storyteller since the museum opened, needed no input from her or anyone else. He was an expert at holding an audience spellbound. And what Harry didn't know about his people and their customs, Carol had discovered, simply wasn't important.

She wondered how much Harry knew about Tallaquoyah Wolf and about removing curses.

Glancing into the story-telling room, she saw that Harry was talking to a large group of children—fifth graders, she judged—sitting in a semi-circle at his feet. It gladdened her heart to see them so entranced.

"And have you heard the story about why the mole lives underground?" Harry asked them.

Most chorused, "No!" But one small boy said, "I know! There was a big blast that made a hole—" he swooped his arms up in the air, "and the mole—and the mole—" Then his imagination petered out.

Harry considered this very seriously for a moment. "That's a pretty good guess. But do you want to know what the Indians say?" He put his head on one side.

"Yes!"

"Yes!"

By now Carol, as interested as the children, decided to eavesdrop.

"Well, there was this boy who was sweet on a real pretty girl." Harry looked around the group. "I guess you're too young to know about that stuff."

"No!"

"You mean, like my mommy and daddy," revealed a little girl with long blonde hair.

Harry grinned at her. "Just like that. Well, the girl, she wasn't at all interested in the boy. She wouldn't even talk to him."

"He tried everything. He went to the conjurors and asked them to put a spell on her that would make her fall in love with him." He looked at the little boy with the big imagination. "But they couldn't do it either."

"He didn't know what to do. And then the little mole—you know what a mole looks like?" Harry spread his hands about six inches apart.

"Yes!" they asserted.

"Well, that little mole, he waited 'til that pretty girl was asleep, and then he went and stole her heart. And then he took it back to the boy."

"The next day she woke up and said, 'I had the strangest dream.'" She went to the boy and said, "'I think I dreamed I gave you my heart. I think I'm in love with you.'"

"Oh, no," said the imaginative little boy.

"Oh, wow," said the little blonde girl.

Harry Wolfe winked at them. "Well! That boy was so happy he could have died. He asked her to marry him, and she said yes."

"But when the conjurors heard about the wedding, they got mad at that mole, 'cause his magic was stronger than theirs. So they chased him around, trying to kill him."

"The only place he could go was down a big, dark hole. And you know, even today, he still lives there, 'cause he's too scared to come out."

The children laughed.

But Carol didn't. All she heard was how the conjuring men had worked their spell. Something like that had caused the Mattox curse. She wondered what more Harry Wolfe might know about conjuring. Could he tell Winston about the old ways? Could he help her?

Still thinking about this when the storytelling was over, Carol didn't notice the woman who stood just inside the glass entrance doors. Noisily and jostling each other, the children left the auditorium and spilled out into the big foyer. The teachers began to shepherd them to a different part of the museum. Carol was headed back upstairs to her office when the woman stepped directly in front of her. For the second time, Carol looked into the face of Winston's fiancée, the woman who had opened the door of his office.

The woman stared intensely at her. Carol's hands felt clammy. Wanda was extremely attractive, Carol thought, suddenly conscious of being short and blonde in vivid contrast to the tall, willowy brunette before her.

"I won't waste time. I know who you are." Wanda flung the words at her.

Carol asked politely, "Can I do something for you?"

"Haven't you've done enough already?" Wanda bit out. "You're a homewrecker."

"Now just a minute—" Carol began.

But Wanda interrupted, looking her up and down. "He's left me for you."

"He hasn't left you. We're not—"

At her protests, Wanda became even angrier. "Phhaahh." She spat, and the wet, slimy mucous landed on Carol's blouse.

Carol watched it sliding downward, and for a moment, she was unable to move or speak. "Yyykkk!" Only a superhuman effort kept her from ripping off her shirt, right in the middle of the museum. Then her temper rose, fast. "There's no call for you to be so rude. Nothing happened between Winston and me that day—and I'll be honest, I wanted it to! Winston and I are just friends."

Hearing those words, Wanda knew Carol was lying. That meant she had lied about everything. They'd probably even fucked in his office that day.

That meant Winston had lied, too. In a fury now, Wanda tossed her hair. "Yeah, that's what everybody says, isn't it? Well, I know better. I know you're lying. And I've come to tell you that you'll be sorry. I'm going to make sure you'll never be happy with him." Turning on her heel, she stalked away, her body stiff with hurt and anger.

As she went, Wanda decided that because Carol had lied to her so shamefully, she would ask her guiding spirit for an even harsher punishment, for both of them, but especially for Carol.

A few days later Winston propped himself in the doorway of Carol's office at quitting time. "Are you going home now?"

She was getting ready to leave but stopped and answered, warily, "Why do you ask?"

"Because I want you to come take a ride with me."

Remembering Wanda and the slime that had slid down her shirt, Carol retorted firmly, "No way. You are bad news."

"Why the attitude?"

Carol told him, commenting wryly, "Now I feel like there are two evils against me; Wanda *and* the Mattox curse."

He shook his head. "That's why I need you to take a ride with me," he repeated.

"It involves Wanda?" she asked incredulously.

He waved away the idea. "No, no." Then he pleaded, "Please?"

He looked so unhappy that she weakened long enough to ask, "Where are we going?"

"I'll tell you when we get there."

It wasn't a good idea to take a ride with an engaged man, especially to an unknown destination. But he had behaved honorably as far as she was concerned, and if Wanda didn't understand that, she was crazy. After all, it wasn't the Dark Ages, no matter what Wanda thought.

They walked out into a bright, sunny mid-summer's evening, cooler than the fierce heat of the day but not yet the shivery night air the Appalachians were famous for.

Winston drove his black Jeep a little way out of town and onto the Soco Road. He stopped at a small white wooden house surrounded by a tidy lawn leading to a burbling stream. Carol counted seven huge oak trees behind the house before Winston commented, "This land has been in my family since the Qualla boundary was established."

"I can't go to your home," she said quickly. No telling what Wanda might do if someone saw them together at his house.

"You can," he assured her, "because you've got nothing more to fear from Wanda. I've broken off my engagement to her."

The reason for Wanda's visit became obvious a few moments after his words sank in, and Carol turned to him, incredulous. "You mean—?"

His face came very close to hers. "I mean we're free to be together at last."

Carol felt giddy. As his lips reached hers, her only thought was, *it's been worth the wait.*

They had both nearly forgotten their long prelude to this moment, reveling in the sudden freedom to acknowledge their love at last.

He had taken her to his big, warm bed. At first she was skittish, as though not believing they were finally together. So he gentled her, stroking her arms, rubbing her thighs, caressing her breasts, until he felt her body relax under his hands. Then he returned to what he had started nearly two months earlier—no, ten years earlier—and to what they both wanted now more than ever.

All the years of wanting disappeared in the intensity of long deprivation.

Pent-up emotion and the sudden freedom to release it was a heady mix. Their joy, as well as their passion, knew no bounds.

He removed her skirt, bringing her panties down with it, revealing the coppery threads that protected her soft mound, which in turn protected her hard, swollen nub.

With a deft motion he shed his pants, and it was her turn simply to look.

When she had seen her fill, and had answers for all the questions she'd asked in years of midnight dreams, she began to touch him, and he closed his eyes. Finally, groaning, he stopped her, then ran his fingers slowly through her wiry wisps of hair, and then through them, around and through, over and over stroking the special place underneath them until she shuddered, as if from electric shocks, and cried out, "Please! Oh, please!" And he obeyed.

For a long time they made the kind of love they'd both been dreaming about. Enough to fill the last decade. Even to fill the last two centuries.

CHAPTER FORTY EIGHT

ASHEVILLE NC, JULY 1999

When the doorbell rang at the Mattox home, Carol felt as excited as she had all those years ago when she had waited for Winston to visit after camp.

This time they were going to Shindig on the Green in the Asheville town square. The real purpose of the evening was to get Winston in the same room with her father and give Winston the chance to state his case on the land swap. It had taken weeks to find the right moment because the senator had been visiting all his electoral offices.

On the way to the parlor, Winston whispered, mischievously, "I see the ancestral portraits are still here. Which ones were ours?"

"I don't think our ancestors ever got hung," she grinned back at him, "unless it was from a stockade." Her mother had looked terrified when Carol told her Winston was coming over.

Bringing him in, she watched her parents cautiously. "Mama, Daddy, you remember Winston Wolfe?"

Marcie looked at her husband. They both looked like they'd swallowed cockroaches.

"Sure, sure." Stanley didn't spend much time on a welcome.

"I'm glad to finally meet you, Senator," Winston said politely, but pointedly.

"The Appropriations Committee keeps me busy," Stanley huffed.

Carol knew he was furious over her springing Winston on him without warning. Trying to put him on more familiar ground, she remarked, "Daddy, aren't you going to congratulate Winston on being elected chief?"

"O' course, o' course," Stanley obliged. "Did you have a strong opponent?"

"Yes. But I liked the challenge. Even the rough-and-tumble of politics gives me a buzz."

Narrowing his eyes, Stanley queried, "You like politics?"

"Yes. I like practicing law, but there's something about making laws that appeals to me. I guess I like to feel I'm helping as many people as possible, and convincing them of something I believe in. You understand that, sir, I know."

"O' course, o' course," Stanley repeated, and Carol knew he was flattered.

Winston continued, "You know, that land swap we want will bring more people into Cherokee to work—and vote. I think you might like to hear more about it."

Stanley gave Winston a long and considering look. "I'm going to be in Raleigh next Tuesday. Can you come down and see me?"

"Sure thing," Winston grinned.

Winston propped his elbow on an outsized pillow. "Are you still worried that my ancient uncle put a curse on the Mattoxes?" He put on a fierce expression and went nose-to-nose with her. "Aren't you worried I'll... hex you?"

Carol felt the familiar stab of worry that occurred every time she thought about the Mattox curse. It was no laughing matter, but she forced herself to match his playful mood. "You've sure put a spell on me, all right." She snuggled closer to him in his big, comfortable bed. "Maybe that's why I'm getting so cold."

He grinned. "No, it's just the first day of real autumn weather. But hey, whatever, as long as it forces me to keep you warm." He gave an exaggerated sigh as he dived under the plump covers and gathered her closer. "Is this what's cold?" He moved his hands. "Or is it this?"

Carol giggled, protesting. "That's not what I meant."

His hands kept moving.

After a while she whispered, close to his ear, "I'm so happy. It *is* going to last this time, isn't it?"

"It sure is," he replied sleepily.

"You won't dump me again, will you?"

He came wide awake. "I'll never leave you, and I didn't dump you then, remember?"

"Okay." A niggle of worry persisted but, content for the moment, Carol rolled a few inches away from him and asked, "Does knowing that Wolf and Isabelle were in love make you more—or less—in love with me?"

"More. What about you?"

"More . . . because I have this feeling that I've loved you, not just for the last few years, I've loved you for centuries." This time she was going to hang onto him and never, ever let him go. Every day she felt like pinching herself to make sure she was living the dream she'd had for so long, that had finally come true: she and Winston were together. This time nothing could keep them apart, not even the threat of an ancient curse. Or the modern threat that Wanda had promised.

With the joy of pure possession, she ran her fingers through his dark hair, spiking it up. "Now you look like a fierce Cherokee Indian chief," she laughed.

He caught her hands and pressed them to his heart. "Maybe I look like those stereotypes in the movies. But in reality, many of our chiefs had long, wavy hair."

"How come?"

"They had a lot of Scottish blood, from the traders. Even Tallaquoyah was better known by his Scottish name, Gordon Reid."

"It seems there's a lot I don't know about Tallaquoyah Wolf," she said with irony. "But do go on." Her hands still in his, she rubbed his chest.

"Indian mothers wanted to marry their daughters to important, wealthy men. That way, the daughters would always be taken care of. As daughters inherited their mothers' houses, the traders were enthusiastic." He grinned. "Anyway, it caused a lot of wavy-haired children."

Carol took one hand out of his clasp and moved it downwards. Then she started rubbing the inside of his hard thigh. It was incredibly warm. Still unused to being in bed with another person, she marveled at how much heat a man's body put out. "Nothing's changed; mothers still try to get rich husbands for their daughters." She was thinking of all the dates with dull-but-good prospects she'd endured, many of them at her mother's insistence.

He shifted the leg she was rubbing, guiding her hand to another, better spot, a softer spot, at least for right now. "Will you demand that for our daughter?"

Carol took a sharp breath before assuring him, "I want our daughter to marry the man she loves, no matter whether he's rich or—"

"—has wavy hair?" he interrupted, tickling his hair against her face.

Nose twitching, she laughed. "You got it. But what I think is even more important…"

A little breathlessly, for parts of him were moving now under her hand, he asked, "Yeah?"

"… is that you're talking about having babies." And she began to stroke him.

"That's part of the deal. And it'll happen pretty soon if you keep doing that." He reached for her.

CHAPTER FORTY NINE

FORT BUTLER NC, NOVEMBER 1837

When Isabelle heard the call of the whippoorwill, she hurried out the gate of the fort. Where was he? He'd said he'd find her. The small movement of a pine bough caught her attention. When the bird call sounded again, nearby, she walked toward the tree. Closer now, she could see Wolf's outline behind its feathery branches. She smiled, and he gave her a mischievous look. "Come, I have something to show you."

Pulling her shawl closer, she followed him past the pine tree to a thick stand of mountain laurel. He bent down and crawled through a gap in the big leaves, motioning for her to follow. "Come just a little further."

The long green leaves caught at her clothes. "Oooohh!" she cried in exasperation, which quickly became a sigh of admiration as she saw the expanse that opened up inside the circle of tall, thick shrubs.

"I cut away the inside branches," he explained, "and made this special place for us. Do you like it?"

She was wide-eyed. "I love it." It felt very secure and special, away from the rest of the world and its problems. Knowing he'd prepared it just for them made her indescribably happy. She was no longer alone. She was now connected to another human being.

Wolf spread a blanket and drew her down. "We'll meet here from now on. No one can see us, and no one will come through such a thicket just by chance." He moved her closer, and began to kiss her. A warm glow seeped through her body. She'd come to know that his lips tasted sweet. But now they began to pulse on hers—gathering her mouth, then letting it go, then starting over. The warm glow inside her turned into a raging fire, and she moved even closer to him. It felt so natural, so right, like they had been kissing each other forever.

When he finally stopped, her mouth felt so bereft that she eagerly sought his lips again. And when she did, he laid her back on the blanket, whispering to her, running his hands up and down her limbs. Then he put a hand on her breast.

She knew she should stop him, but she wanted him to keep on kissing her, holding her, touching her, feeling her. And there was a strange dampness between her legs. She trailed a hand down his arm, and then put it on his broad chest.

He had just started to undo a button at her throat when a branch snapped in the forest, quite close. Wolf's fingers stopped; his head shot up, and he tried to locate the sound. Then he put his finger on her lips as they heard the thud of boots and the shouts of soldiers.

"Where d'ya reckon they could be?"

"Danged if I know. We hafta look for them, the captain said. Although blessed if I can see where they are, or how they could be anywhere in these thick trees."

"Maybe we can flush them out." There was thrashing, and a stick poked through the hedge about an inch away from Isabelle's head.

She was terrified, but Wolf kept still, and kept his finger on her mouth.

"What's she want with a Indian, anyhow?" The soldier's question came from a safer six feet away.

The reply was more distant still. "Danged if I know. I'm just following orders."

When they had gone, Wolf gathered her back into his arms. This time, when he held her close, it was to stop her shaking. And his kiss was a promise 'til the next time.

'MIMOSA,' NEW ECHOTA GA, DECEMBER 1837

"There's a bunch of men riding up the road," said Wolf's sister, Sunnika. His house was set in a grove of graceful mimosa trees which gave it its name. Quickly Wolf moved to the large window. "Who are they?"

"I can't tell, but they're white, and they're armed," she said meaningfully.

He grunted. Several times he had seen men lurking in the trees surrounding his estate. The Georgia Militia. The same bunch who'd killed his father and his wife, Dunaki.

Before the riders could dismount Wolf went out to meet them. Standing on his veranda, he demanded, "What do you want?"

"We've come to claim my new land," said a man whose felt hat was full of holes. As if staking his claim, he spat out a stream of tobacco. "I won it in the lottery."

A chill like none he'd ever had coursed through Wolf. "The lottery was illegal."

"Tell the bastard, Fred," the new owner said to one of the armed men.

"Orville's right," the soldier leered. "The governor's just okayed it. Thinking you Injuns'll maybe cause us more trouble, we've come along with our friend here to carry out the orders."

Indians cause trouble? Wolf thought of the night his father and Dunaki were killed, doing nothing but walking up to the house. Wolf said sarcastically, "Well, as there's no justice in Georgia, I'll take my case to the Supreme Court."

"Won't do ye no good," said the soldier.

"But," Orville grinned through tobacco-stained teeth, "I tell you what I'll do, seeing as I'm such a nice man and all. I'll give you 'til Christmas to get off my land. Now what could be fairer than that?" He guffawed, and his friends joined in.

"I'll never give up my land," Wolf told him coldly.

"You ain't got no choice no more."

CHAPTER FIFTY

Despite their previous close call, the laurel thicket was the only place Wolf and Isabelle felt safe. It was the only place Isabelle felt happy. When the whippoorwill called, her life began, and the oppressive days in between were forgotten.

Now she sat beside him, fanning herself with the straw bonnet he'd once rescued. For, even though it was December, the day was as warm and sunny as June, especially inside the thick bushes.

He watched her. "You're looking peaked today. Of course you're still beautiful, but your cheeks are fairly caving in."

She tried to dismiss his concern. "It's all the work I do, I expect."

"Is everything all right at the fort?"

A tear started down her cheek. "It's hard to get food."

He was surprised. "Hard for everyone outside the fort, but that's the one place where food is abundant. The soldiers won't starve."

She pointed out, "I'm not a soldier."

He pushed fair hair off her face and studied it, concerned. "And so you're not eating?"

"And so I have less and less to eat each week." She didn't tell him Sergeant Hampton had severely rationed her food supplies since the night of the lynching. James had so many problems that she couldn't burden him further, and she made sure he didn't suffer the quartermaster's deprivations. This meant even less for her to eat.

But Wolf seemed to know these reasons without being told, and his teeth clenched. "If only—" he smote his palm with his fist and then grasped her by the arm. "Come. Come with me."

"You know it isn't safe out there," she protested.

Wolf looked into the forest for some time. "I don't see or hear anyone." Then he motioned urgently. "Come quickly, while it's still all right."

But she had another excuse. "No, it's too hot. I can't."

"You must," he insisted, and before she could protest further, pulled her out of the thicket. "We're going to see my mother's family."

"Why didn't you say so?" Then, more quietly, fearing they might be heard, she asked, "How far is it?"

"Not far. It's at a place called Kiowa, near the trading post," he explained. "These woods run close to it, and there's a place to cross the Hiwassee River."

"At the fording place? But we'll be seen."

"We'll cross below the ford; there's a place almost as shallow."

Wolf kept alert as they threaded through the bare, winter forest. Dry leaves crackled as they went down the slope and finally reached the river.

She removed her boots and stockings, tying them around her neck. Holding up her skirt and petticoat, she splashed across the river with Wolf's help. The cold water even felt good on such a warm day, but she couldn't help commenting, "I'm glad it isn't deep enough to drown me."

At this Wolf circled her, threatening a serious splashing before they dropped, laughing, onto the opposite bank. He reached over and kissed her, then let his hand slide over her breasts until, reluctantly, he pulled her to her feet again.

As they walked, more sedately, Isabelle smelled smoke from fires she could not see. "We're getting close to Kiowa," he told her. And then they stepped into a clearing that had several log cabins. Smoke billowed from bark cappings on the roofs. The first four circled a wide expanse of hard-packed earth where two women stood. The older one smiled at Isabelle, came forward and put out her hand, while the younger one hung back.

"This is my mother, Naomi," Wolf said with pride. "And my sister, Noquisi."

"We wish you welcome." Naomi's English was halting and careful. "It is our pleasure."

Charmed by her friendliness, Isabelle replied, "It's kind of you to let me come to your home. I hope we're not disturbing you."

Beaming, patting Isabelle's hand, Naomi told her son something in their own language, finishing with, "*Sge!*"

"I'll leave that to your imagination," he smiled at Isabelle. "Suffice it to say she approves." Turning back to his mother, Wolf explained, "The lady would like to see Noquisi's baskets," and added, again in their own tongue, that the lady also needed food.

Several children peeked out from behind Naomi's long skirt as she motioned her guests inside. But when Isabelle smiled at them, they giggled and ran away.

Wolf explained, "These are some of my sisters' and brother's children. My brother, Kwahala, lives on my property in Georgia, and this is Tusquittee, his son, and Noquisi's children. My other sister, Sunnika, lives at my home in Georgia with her children. And there are more nieces and nephews somewhere in the forest," he smiled, moving aside the huge black bear skin that protected his mother's doorway.

In the dim interior light, Isabelle could just make out the cabin's contents, as sparse as James': a seat built into the wall, a sleeping platform with log bed-ends. When her eyes became more accustomed to the darkness, she saw the bright colors of several rugs on the earthen floor and exclaimed, "These are beautiful." She noticed Naomi putting into a woven cloth some of the pumpkin flesh that had been strung up to dry behind the fireplace. Then Isabelle's attention was captured by a circle resembling a spider's web, hanging on a wall, that was so beautiful it took her breath away. She could see something of how it had been made, of hide and feathers.

"It's very beautiful. Would you make me one?" But her question was greeted by silence.

Naomi looked perplexed, and there was some discussion in Cherokee before Wolf told Isabelle, "She could never make one for anyone else or to give away. It is very personal because, according to your thoughts when you make it, it receives its magic power."

Isabelle was as impressed as she was crestfallen. She had thought that if she could hang such a beautiful thing in James' cabin, her life there might be more bearable.

Noquisi spoke, and Wolf translated, "She wants you to come to her house."

Inside were her baskets. Striking geometric patterns in red, brown, and black were finely woven from the natural river cane. There was also beautiful pottery, stamped with similar designs. They were works of art, no question about it, Isabelle realized. "I've no money with me, but I want to buy that cup as a Christmas present for James."

"The cup will be yours, without money, as is this package my mother has gathered for you." It was the woven cloth.

Isabelle protested, "I can't take your food. It's for your family."

He framed her gaunt cheeks with big hands. "There's more where this came from. We won't starve, whereas you might. Come, now, to my house." He guided her to the last house in the compound.

His floor was also covered with rugs, their patterns reflecting the colors of the earth. Her attention, however, was caught by one, which was different, that hung on the wall. It was pale, and showed a river and forest, with a bright sun overhead. It was as beautiful as a landscape painting. "That's my favorite. My mother made it, and I'll take it home to Georgia, where it will bring me luck."

Her hand in his, she was on the point of leaving when she saw, sitting in a corner, a small boy of five or six. He looked so much like Wolf that her heart stopped. "Hello, what's your name?"

"I am Wolf," he said in a solemn voice so like his father's that Isabelle's smile spread.

She bent. "Are you Yaguska Wolf?" When he nodded, she said, "My name is Isabelle."

"Isssble." She couldn't resist reaching out, putting her hand on the dark hair so like Wolf's and soft, but not as curly. Wolf's dark brown eyes, too, glowed back at her. But instead of the adult's hard-planed cheeks, Yaguska's little face was round. He wore a homespun shirt, a small breech-cloth, and tiny deerskin moccasins on plump, crossed legs. He was the most adorable little boy Isabelle had ever seen. "Isssbel," he repeated, without improvement, and smiled at her. And this time held out his arms.

"Ohhh." She clasped him close. "I'm going to like getting to know you," she told him, catching Wolf's eye over Yaguska's head.

Wolf put his arms around them both. "You make me very happy."

She, too, was happy, despite knowing that she should have fallen in love with anyone except Tallaquoyah Wolf. And his son Yaguska. For the feeling between them was not only against convention, it was also against sensibility.

Yet she knew she would love Wolf for the rest of her life. She might even love him forever.

CHAPTER FIFTY ONE

When the shooting began, Isabelle bolted upright out of a sound sleep. Outside there was great commotion, and men were running through the fort.

Someone shouted, "It's Indians!" She felt a stab of fright. It was the Indian uprising James had been expecting!

"Where are they?" she heard James demand, as she lifted her woolen robe from its peg.

"They're in the grain store!" was the reply. "They're attackin' our food supplies!"

"They'll be in the ammunition next!"

James' voice was clipped. "Keep them out of there, for God's sake!"

Another volley of shots rang out. After a few minutes Isabelle opened the door, summoning the courage to peer outside. She saw James charging through the compound, pulling up his suspenders and checking his musket as he went. "James? What's happening?"

"Stay where you are, Isabelle!" he shouted. "And keep your door shut!"

With fear in her heart—for exactly whom she could not say—she pressed herself against the wall, shivering but otherwise motionless in the January night, listening to running footsteps, gunshots, and cries in the night. Was Wolf out there? Was he wounded? Or worse, dying? Could she help him?

After what seemed several hours, but was probably much less, she thought, there was quiet. The frantic calls lessened. There were fewer shots, and they were further away, although it could just be a lull in the fighting. Unable to bear the suspense any longer and determined to help, she finally defied her brother's order and crept outside.

There was no moon, and hardly any star shine, but she saw soldiers lined up on the ramparts, shooting long muskets into the dark. She saw no battalion of axe-wielding Indians scaling the palisade. None with guns, either. The only Indians in sight were three lying on the parade ground, wounded, or dead, and she could see no injured soldiers.

When one of the Indians tried to crawl away, a soldier hit him with the stock of his musket. The Indian let out a groan and crumpled back to the ground. Without hesitation, Isabelle ran to him. Then she checked the others, satisfying herself that none of them was Wolf.

As she was inspecting the Indians' wounds, James materialized out of the dark night. Desperate for news, she asked, "Are we under attack?"

"No, don't worry."

"Then what is happening?" She drew her robe closer.

"Some damned Indians tried to get into the food stores."

She thought of the generosity of Wolf's family in giving her their own sparse food. They had also taken to leaving food for her in the laurel thicket. "There's a lot of starvation among the Indians."

"Ah, you'd know about that, wouldn't you? I've had reports that you've been seeing them again, behind my back." James' sneer became a snarl. "Well, this was just plain looting."

"Or desperation." She sat back on her haunches. "Why not give them some food?" James snorted in disbelief but she rushed on. "We have plenty, and can always get more from the Army."

His jaw dropped. "That food belongs to the government, to the soldiers, not the damned Indians."

"But—"

"Isabelle, I'm not going to feed the Cherokee Nation. They knew how to grow food long before we even got here. Now let them look after themselves like the rest of us do."

"But under threat of removal, they haven't known whether to plant their crops. That's if their lands haven't already been taken."

James stalked off.

Distraught, Isabelle called after him, "Will you please give me your knife?"

He whipped back around. "Only if you're going to scalp that Indian."

Her reply ignored his unseemly humor. "I'm going to bind his wounds with strips of my dressing gown."

"What on earth for?"

"Because he's a human being, he's hurt, and he needs help."

James raised his musket. "This is all the help he needs."

Eyes full of terror, the wounded Indian called out in a hoarse voice and tried to crawl away. Isabelle shouted, "No!" and tried to shield his wounded body with her own.

James said harshly, "Isabelle, I will shoot if you don't get out of the way."

Looking into the black barrel of James' firearm, Isabelle knew true terror and despair, at the hands of her own brother. "God, deliver me," she whispered, then slowly said aloud, "Yes, I think you would shoot your own sister. What I can't believe is that you're my brother."

The gun was unwavering. "Don't say I didn't warn you." Isabelle shut her eyes. And then he fired.

As the Indian went limp, Isabelle realized she was still alive and threw herself across his inert body.

Despite their injuries, the other two Indians tried to move away. James called for two more muskets. "No, James, don't," she cried, but he shot both men. She covered her face and eyes to the sight of three dead bodies, to the sight of her brother. But she knew it was too late; she had already seen too much, too much that she would never forget.

She rocked back on her heels, keening. "How could you? He wasn't badly wounded. I could have healed him." As the bodies were carried away, she turned from the sight. Looking at James did not calm her heart. She wondered whether his gun barrel had veered away from her even at the last instant, or whether he'd simply missed.

"Do not interfere!" he shouted. "The more Indians that starve, and the more I kill, the fewer I have to worry about taking to Oklahoma."

She felt as if James himself had been killed. In a way, he had, and she mourned his loss. "You are my brother, and until this moment I would have said you could not do or say such terrible things."

"And I would never have thought I had an Indian-lover for a sister. You should never have come here. Ever since you arrived, you've tried to tell me what to do about matters that are none of your concern. This is men's work. You are an infernal, meddling woman." He paced a few steps, then wheeled back. "And you can tell that to Father, in person."

She shivered, more from a new sound in his voice than from the freezing night. "What do you mean?"

"I'm sending you back to Asheville, back to Father."

The enormity of his words hit her like his fist. Once she would have been glad to leave this life of unrelenting drudgery, but leaving Wolf was another matter. The memory of him and Yaguska and the family at the settlement flashed through her mind. "No, please, James." It was her turn to beg.

"I won't deal with you any more. You'll return to Asheville as soon as I can make the arrangements."

"Please don't send me back."

She nearly added, *You might as well shoot me, too.*

CHAPTER FIFTY TWO

But on the following morning, James repeated his decision to send Isabelle home.

Over and over she asked herself, *What am I to do?*

Even though her love for Wolf could never be acknowledged, it sustained her, and she had hoped to keep him and his family in her life somehow. At the thought of losing them forever, her heart began to break. Never again see Yaguska's trusting smile? She had not heard the call of the whippoorwill for weeks now. She might be gone before she could even explain to Wolf what had happened, and that thought was almost worse than the leaving itself.

Paralyzed by anguish, for once she was glad so many chores filled her day. There wasn't much time for moping. Or packing. She delayed making a start on leaving. But, complaining at her inaction, James had her belongings rounded up, her trunk and boxes fetched from the storeroom, and ordered her to begin filling them.

Busy as he was, he kept an eye on her progress. He also gave up all pretense of living in harmony. Every meal was now taken with his men. It made her life more lonely, but it had one consolation: there was more for her to eat, until the quartermaster figured out that her rations no longer included James'. She rarely saw her brother, except when he hurled an order at her. It was like living under an armed truce.

After nearly a week of such strain, 'whip-poor-will! whip-poor-will!' cascaded through the forest.

With haste she made for their secret bower. "You're here at last!" She flew into Wolf's arms and clung to him.

Finally, she leaned out of his embrace, smiling. "I'm a lot warmer now."

But he refused to release her. "Then I'll keep you that way. I'd like to keep my arms around you forever." His kiss was gentle.

After a while he told her, "I couldn't come before this; there were many soldiers in the forest after the raid." He felt her body as if searching for wounds. "You weren't hurt?"

She shook her head. Wolf's hands were like flames licking at her. In the bittersweet knowledge that she would never see him again, she gave in to the sensations they were causing.

This time he kissed her until, remembering her sad news for him, she pulled away. "Tell me honestly, are the Indians going to stage an uprising?"

Wolf's laugh was mirthless. "The Indians don't even have food, much less muskets. Far from caring about politics, they are simply hungry. I wish those braves had come to me instead of trying to steal the fort's grain. If they had, they would still be alive."

The memory of their horrible deaths made Isabelle hang her head in shame. "I am so sorry." She wanted to repent for the whole Mattox family. Her head hung lower. Still she could not bring herself to tell him about leaving.

"There's no reason for you to apologize."

But there was, and she pressed Wolf's hand to her lips. "If only I could help you."

"What is it, *hsing-ga-wa-la?* You look so worried today. And even thinner."

"I am worried, because I may not be here much longer."

He jerked, as if he'd been shot. "Why do you say that?"

"My brother is sending me home."

"To Asheville?" At her despairing nod Wolf slumped. "But you can't leave. Don't leave me, Little One. And what about Yaguska?"

She covered her face with her hands. "I don't want to! But I don't have a choice. James will force me to go, just like he'll force the Indians to leave." She looked at him with a new realization. "I'm just like you; I'm being removed against my will."

"He can't." Wolf tried to pace, but the laurel thicket was too confined.

Isabelle told him sadly, "He'll imprison me if necessary, I know it now. Why, he nearly shot me during the raid." She shuddered to recall the black infinity of his musket. "He'll stop at nothing to get his way."

"Isabelle, for such a wrong as your brother has done you, Cherokee custom allows—even demands—that I avenge it."

"I know, so would our customs too, probably. But revenge isn't the answer. My dearest, I don't want you to harm James, because if you do, there will be even more reason for the soldiers to hunt and punish you." She kissed him. "I don't want anything to happen to you."

Wolf put his arms around her but stood thinking for a few minutes. "You know that I love you?" His kiss was tender.

She nodded. "I love you, too."

"Then we can never be parted."

"But I have to leave. James—"

"Never mind about him. Isabelle, will you marry me?"

At once she knew her answer. And at once she gave it. "Yes."

CHAPTER FIFTY THREE

Isabelle kept to her normal routine. But she moved through her duties—made more difficult by the freezing January weather—as if in a dream. Indeed, she spent the next days dreaming about her new life. Shortly, she would be done with her miserable existence, her unloving brother, the hardships of frontier housekeeping, the fort with its cruelty and death; and be a married woman living with her true love in a life she knew would satisfy her like none other. They would love each other and be happy. It made her think of the verse from Matthew: 'What profiteth a man, if he should gain the whole world, and have not love?'

She would have a husband and a family, live in harmony with nature and all its creatures; be able to create beautiful handicrafts with things that came out of the earth and would someday go back into it the way everything was supposed to be.

Coming after so long and difficult a time, when she had despaired of finding such love, the future was almost beyond joy, and she hugged her secret close, lest it escape before she did.

They would not risk leaving their escape too long. They planned to elope as soon as the moon was favorable. Wolf had said he would come for her as soon as it had fully waned, so that darkness could hide them.

Now that their plans had been laid, she made a show of packing her trunk, thinking it might satisfy James' orders and slow his efforts to arrange her transport. And despite being increasingly lonely, she was grateful for James' absence and their estrangement.

The irony was that she put into her traveling trunk things she intended to leave behind. Everything else, ostensibly for disposal, she put into a pile which she would take with her, bundled in a cot sheet. Knowing she should keep this light, she couldn't, nevertheless, resist adding a lace-trimmed white cotton nightgown. *It's the closest I'll get to a wedding dress,* she thought, and grew excited at the prospect of being next to Wolf with only a thin layer of cotton between them.

Within a few days she was ready. Once more, she awaited the sound of the whippoorwill, smiling nostalgically to think it would be for the last time. Though the moon was still full, every night she listened hard, so anxious was she to begin her new life.

But the call did not come. She knew that everything in Georgia was uncertain. She didn't know when the moon would wane and feared to ask in case it aroused suspicion. The suspense was excruciating, but cocooned her in a more pleasant place than reality.

By a Sunday night in early February, the full moon had been finished for two nights, and Isabelle had been on tenterhooks through each. Even the pale new moon was growing brighter and, worried, she drew a shawl closer as she kept her vigil.

And suddenly, 'whip-poor-will'. Then there was a pause. Had she only thought she'd heard it? Then, unmistakably, came 'whip-poor-will', and from the direction of the watch tower. Overcome with anxiety, nevertheless she made herself move calmly. Although her hands trembled, she bundled her clothes, and her Bible, into the sheet and walked out of the house where she had been so discontented, toward the bird's call and happiness.

There was no one in the tower. Dismayed, she started to return to the cabin. Then she heard a rustle, and Wolf stood in front of her. "I've come for you, as I said I would." His eyes were grave and pinned her as he held her at arms' length. "Are you ready?" he asked, as if he half-expected her to have given up their plan.

If only he knew that she had been thinking of nothing else but their life together. "Yes." She tilted her chin at him, a fierce courage strengthening her now that she was with him. "How are we going to get out?"

"Just follow me, and don't think too much about what we're doing. If I explain, it might frighten you. Anyway, the less we talk the better." With that said, he took her bundle and began to climb over the palisade. Seeing her hesitate, he beckoned. She took a deep breath. 'Whither thou goest …' She remembered the words from the Bible and hitched up her skirt.

Wolf had placed, on the other side of the fence, a strong ladder of saplings bound together with deer hide. Once down it, they started along the dark path they had so recently followed on a warm winter's day.

Suddenly a voice demanded, "Stand! Who are ye?"

Isabelle froze, clutching her swag, as Wolf, in silence and camouflaged by the trees, began to circle behind the soldier whose long firearm was trained on her.

She drew on all the strength she possessed. "Put your musket away. I am the captain's sister."

"Ar, and what are ye doin' out this time of night?"

"That's none of your business, but if you must know, I'm going to the springhouse."

"That's not a bucket in yer hand, I'll warrant." Suspicious now, he peered at her through the darkness. "I've heard ye're trouble. Ye ain't up to none of yer tricks now, are ye?" The gun remained pointed.

Just then Wolf's arm slid around the soldier's throat and yanked upward. There was a soft groan as the soldier slumped to the ground. Wolf gave a short, sharp whistle, and Weenook appeared. Wolf helped Isabelle up, then leaped astride, and urged the paint into a trot, even through the forest.

"We can't go to Kiowa now. We'll have to ride all the way to Georgia. They won't follow us there."

This time, as Isabelle put her arms around him, she vowed she would never let him go.

They alighted at the foot of the wide steps that led up to the deep verandas of Mimosa. "Why are we stopping here?" Isabelle asked. "Shouldn't we get safely to your house first?"

"This house is as safe as anywhere. And it *is* my house. Mimosa is your home too, now."

Open-mouthed, Isabelle looked up at the large and gracious plantation house. Thick, two-story-high white pillars glowed against the brick as if the moon were at its fullest, not smallest. Shutters along the verandas, both upstairs and downstairs, were closed tight against the night. As she stepped onto the brick floor, Wolf swept her up in his arms and carried her into the wide hallway and up a gracefully curving staircase.

Upstairs, he carried her into a spacious bedchamber. Spread on the tall, four-poster bed was Naomi's beautiful rug, with its scene of the river, and she knew she was in her bridal chamber.

"Welcome to our home." His voice was soft, his touch light and reassuring. "We'll be happy here."

"Yes." Isabelle had never felt things were so right until this moment when, according to everyone else, she was making the biggest mistake of her life.

Wolf stood close to remove her bonnet and coat.

"I brought a special nightgown just for tonight," she said shyly.

"Tonight neither of us will wear any clothes," he told her, letting down her long, golden hair before taking off her dress.

When she was completely naked, he touched her in many different places. Then he laid her on the rug. "It's where I want you to become mine."

His lips touched hers, and then left them. Then they returned with a force that made her gasp. He took her breasts in both his hands and kissed them before he licked, then sucked, her nipples.

She was yearning for him as his mouth moved down to her navel, which he thoroughly licked. Just as she relaxed and began to think about how she should be caressing him, she felt his hand between her legs. Suddenly, it thrust inside her, and this time she cried out.

But not from fear; it felt exciting. And after his hand continued just a little more stroking, when he seemed sure she was ready, he parted her legs and put himself inside her.

To her surprise, her wetness guided him in, although he was bigger than she had expected. Then she felt pain, and cried out again. She thought the pain would sharpen, but instead, it disappeared as he thrust further into her. Harder, faster. It was the most wonderful feeling she'd ever experienced.

Now she was truly his. No, she thought; now they truly belonged to each other.

CHAPTER FIFTY FOUR

Isabelle woke to sunlight and birdsong, disappointed that Wolf had already risen. Imagine having a window again! And it was warmer here in Georgia. The sun slanted through small-paned windows onto the big bed where she had just spent her wedding night. She smiled again and stretched, thinking about it.

Hastily she put on her clothes and, following the smell of strong coffee, went downstairs.

"Why, if it isn't Miss Mattox." The woman was middle-aged and slight, Isabelle noticed. And she was a Negro.

"Good morning," Isabelle replied.

"I'm Posy, Mister Reid's housekeeper," the woman went on. "If there's anythin', anythin' at all, I can get you, you only got to ask." Shyly she added, "We're glad the Mister's got a new wife. We been worried about him. It isn't right for people to live alone."

Occasionally, Isabelle wondered about James. Had he been furious to find her gone? Would he make trouble? Perhaps he was merely relieved. How she wished her family knew of her happiness! Surely, even her father would relent his disapproval for such a joyous reason?

Despite such worrisome thoughts, the days continued happily, each one bringing a new revelation about a life she could only have imagined. Her heart was warmed by love and renewed by nature in the approaching springtime.

"And have you had a happy day?" Wolf greeted her with a kiss on his return from seeing to business, seating himself in an elegant wing chair covered with yellow silk damask.

"Yes, today and every day I've been here." She kissed him back. The servants giggled at how often they kissed, but they paid no heed. "Only one thing would make our life better."

"And what's that?"

"I miss the children, now that Sunnika has returned to Kiowa."

"She thought you'd want to be mistress of your own home."

"I do. I also want to be a mother to my own son. Can't Yaguska come to live with us?"

He beamed. "He can, and in time for our marriage."

"Our marriage?" She barely breathed the word.

"I've been arranging it."

"That makes me happy, but I consider myself already married." Now that she had disobeyed her family and flaunted society, she'd stopped worrying about what others might think. She had sealed her fate, and accepted it.

"Then you'll have to be a bigamist," he smiled at her, "for you're getting married again. It will take place the day after tomorrow."

"Does it take long?"

"No, but longer than your kind of ceremony."

"What do I need to do?"

"Nothing, just be there."

"Try to keep me away."

The elders had conferred. Clearly, many things about this wedding would be contrary to tradition, so they had agreed that, instead of the council house, Wolf's own house should be used for the ceremony.

The men filed into the living room but, instead of sitting on the gilded chairs or sofas, they crouched against one wall. The last of them was a white man, in somber clothes, who stood. Then the women came in and stood against the other wall. Isabelle came into the salon, in her white cotton nightgown. Wolf had been the first to enter.

Wolf's mother had come and now, according to tradition, presented him with a venison roast and a blanket, so that he would forever be fed and clothed. Sunnika stood in for Isabelle's mother, bringing her an ear of corn and a blanket. Wolf's brother, Kwahala, conducted the ceremony, and bid them greet each other and exchange their gifts.

Wolf grinned at her. "My brother says we may now exchange the blankets. This is the most important part." Solemnly, he took Isabelle's blanket and folded it into his, looking at her with a love that was almost tangible. "The blankets are joined. Now we're married," he smiled, and kissed her. "And now that we are, I have another surprise for you." He beckoned to the white man. "This is the Reverend Michael Shuford from Ellijay. I've asked him to marry us again, this time your way, because I thought it would make you happy."

Isabelle was wide-eyed. "I'm already happy, but I must admit to even greater happiness for this gift, and not least because you thought of it." She kissed her husband, then hugged Yaguska. "I must get my Bible, that's part of our custom."

"We're both part of each others' traditions now."

"And they'll both be better for the combining."

When Isabelle awoke the next morning, she wore her white nightgown, and was encased in silken bed sheets. For an instant, she wondered why she felt so happy. This time Wolf slept beside her, his hand on her breast. Then she remembered their wedding—both of their weddings—and she was filled with peace.

At the beginning of March, Wolf asked her, "Do you hear that?" pointing to the ground.

"What is it?"

He smiled. "All those things down there are starting to grow. They're pushing through the sleepy earth, telling it to wake up. They're very loud."

She smiled back. "Then it's true that Indians can hear better than white people," she teased, "for I don't hear any of those things."

"You must learn. You're an Indian too, now. Can't you smell the earth waking up?"

She sniffed once, then again. “Oh, you mean the oak leaves rotting from the winter rain and the fresh horse manure?”

Wolf grabbed her. “Those things, too, smell wonderful.” He kissed the breath from her until she felt dizzy. She thought she would burst with desire for him, longing for his strong body inside her. He carried her into the house, where he made passionate love to her on their special rug.

As she moved through the estate over the next few days, she was sure she heard the mimosas stirring after their long sleep. It was as though they were all saying, ‘Good morning,’ as she passed.

Or was it just the sound of happiness?

CHAPTER FIFTY FIVE

CHEROKEE NC, AUGUST 1999

Carol spoke into the telephone on her desk. "Yes, I'll make sure your new book gets into all the shops on the main street and that there are plenty here at the museum. We'll put them in the book shop and on our information desk, too."

Intent on carrying out this mission immediately, she stood, picking up a stack of *Cherokee Heritage Trails* from her desk and headed downstairs to the bookshop. The pile was so large it came nearly up to her chin.

The next thing she knew, she had landed heavily on the hard, polished wooden floor of her office. The books spilled, and her right arm felt like it had been caught in a vise that was slowly tightening. Grasping it where she felt the pain, she cried, "Ow! Ohhhh. OooohH! Help me! Help!"

There was the silence of emptiness from the only office near hers. She sat for a moment, hoping the shock and pain would lessen, trying to gather her thoughts that had scattered like the books. The first thing she needed to do was get up. The second was to call somebody downstairs for help. She could put no pressure on her right arm to help lever herself off the floor. Just letting it hang was painful, too. She found that holding her fingertips hurt a little less and, gingerly, hands together, got up.

Once on her feet, she looked around to see what had caused her fall. The bottom drawer of her desk was open, and she had tripped over it. It hadn't been open when she had stood to pick up the books. It hadn't been opened since she'd buried Wolf's medicine bag deep in the back of it.

Her thoughts raced as fast as her heart. The desk was made of wood. So was the floor. Wood was an element of nature.

With a shaky left hand, she lay her injured arm on her thigh and awkwardly gripped her telephone.

"It isn't broken in two; it's just a fracture," said Dr. Edwin Saunooke as he stuck Carol's X-ray on the light box.

She waited for him to elaborate but when he didn't, she asked anxiously, "That's better, then?"

He nodded. "Definitely better. Nevertheless, I'm going to put a cast on it."

"Oh, no," she moaned. "I have to carry a lot of stuff around, books and papers. A cast will be bad for my work."

"Looks like it."

"And I won't be able to drive! I have to drive over two hours a day, between here and Asheville."

Sighing, he agreed, "You won't be driving for a while."

Whatever would she do? "If it isn't broken, won't it just knit back together if I keep still? Couldn't I just keep it in a sling?"

He rounded on her. "You couldn't drive then, either, and it will hurt more. Besides, I couldn't guarantee it'll heal as well as it will in plaster." Sounding annoyed, he delivered his ultimatum. "So, it boils down to whether you want the full use of your arm again, or not."

Suddenly realizing her lack of patient skills, she said guiltily, "I'm sorry, it's just that this has thrown me a curve ball."

"You can't think a broken arm won't make any difference to your life," he scolded.

"I know. You win," she sighed, as he called in his nurse.

CHAPTER FIFTY SIX

Winston picked Carol up from Dr. Saunooke's office. "Patrick took your car to my house. And now I'm taking you there, too." When his concerned once-over registered that she was intact except for the cast from elbow to wrist, his glance turned mischievous. "You can't get far with that. Guess I'm going to have a house guest for a while, yes?"

She gave him an answering smile. "Whether you want one or not, looks like."

"I want, I want," he assured her, grinning from ear to ear.

Needing courage for what she was about to say, she waited a moment trying to gather it. "Hon-ee, I had a long time to think while they worked on my arm, and I started wondering—" She trailed off as her determination lessened.

Winston prompted her. "Wondering what?"

She took a deep breath. "Is there anybody who might know anything about a curse? How it could be taken off, somehow? Maybe somebody who knows how to do the old magic?" She held her breath.

Winston raised an eyebrow. "Are you talking about an exorcism?"

She felt uncomfortable. "Not really. But, well, I don't know what to call it. Just something that will stop these accidents."

"It's possible, I guess. Things still go on. But I don't know a soul who'd do anything like that."

"What about Ralph Raxter?" she interrupted. "At least he knows about those things."

"I doubt if he could do anything about it. I doubt if anyone could do anything about it. Or would, even if they could. This is the twenty-first century, after all, and curses and spells just—" He shook his head.

"Well," she said, "I'm beginning to think the curse is real. This is the second accident I've had. I think that, somehow, the medicine bag caused me to fall, both times. It was there, both times. I don't know how, or why, these things are happening, unless it *is* Grandma's curse. And you said the story is told by your family, too." Suddenly she burst out with what was really bothering her. "Do you realize I'm the next in line to die if there is a curse on the Mattoxes?"

"Whaaatt?" As he jerked the wheel by reflex, the Jeep ran off the shoulder of the road. Bringing it back onto the blacktop, he groaned, "Aw, honey, you can't think that."

"This broken arm—and before that, almost a broken leg—makes me think that," she said harshly. Then she took a deep breath. "You said your grandfather knew about the old magic, that he'd taught you the old ways."

Slowly, as though he were trying to figure out her meaning, he said, "Well, yes, but just legends and stuff—stuff about our heritage, to be proud of, but nothing that would ever be used."

"It's a pity he isn't still alive, because he could help us."

"Help us do what?" he asked suspiciously.

"Remove the Mattox curse."

He gave her a look that suggested she might still be in shock. "He wouldn't. Especially, he wouldn't do any of the old conjuring."

"Did your great-uncle know about the old magic too?"

He glanced at her. "Well, yes. Most people did, back then."

She felt desperate. "Maybe nobody's ever needed to use the knowledge again, until now. At least the older generation saw some of the old magic being used and heard the old stories. Your uncle tells them at the museum. If only we could find out, a little more exactly, if there is a curse."

He shrugged. "I don't see how we can do that," and gave her another wary look. "Sometimes I think you believe in the power of curses more than an Indian would."

"I believe in their power because I work with such things, and because I'm having accidents, and because it's my life that's at stake."

When that brought a concerned look from him, she pressed a little more, feeling even more distressed. "Could you at least ask your uncle whether he knows any more about Tallaquoyah Wolf? Especially, what happened to him? I just feel that if we could find out why the curse was put on, it would be easier to do something about it."

Winston hesitated, watching a pickup truck that threatened to come out of a side road. "Of course I'll ask him, but don't hold your breath for an answer."

"Not even one that would help his future in-law?" She reached over and put her good hand on the back of Winston's neck. "I think you'd believe in the curse, too, if you let yourself."

"No way."

She began to rub his neck. "You saved my life once. Now you may have to do it again." As his silence persisted, so did she. "Once you told me I should make my life count for something. Well, I want to make it count for you. It's all I've ever wanted." She rubbed more softly. "Couldn't you at least ask your uncle Jerry about it?"

When Winston finally spoke it was very quietly. "I can tell you now that he will say not to dabble in conjuring, even if you think you know what you're doing. It isn't something that should be done lightly. Magic really exists. Remember that both Tallaquoyah and your great uncle, who may have started this, died very young."

She, too, was silent for a moment before remarking, "But not as young as I am."

His jaw softened. "Okay. I'll ask him."

Wanda sat on the edge of her bed and swallowed the sleeping pill she'd had to take every night since Winston had dumped her for Carol. At first she'd resented the white oval pill but soon realized it had an advantage. Having a regular, dependable period of half-consciousness made it easier to put herself into the trance required for the ritual she also practiced every night. Transiting from the conscious to the unconscious was the best time for getting your wishes answered. She had proved this over and over.

And now Carol Mattox had had an accident.

But in a way, Carol's accident had only made things worse. Carol's living in Winston's house, something Wanda had never been invited to do, strengthened her already-steely desire for revenge.

"*Sge!* My spirit guide, I ask you to help me again! I need more revenge on the white woman—on him, too, but mostly on her. And now, as you asked, I have given you first-hand knowledge of the woman." Her voice turned scornful. "She is small, and pale, and should be easy to deal with."

There was no answer, but Wanda didn't expect one. She knew the spirit was listening. "You can see her car at his house every day, so you know they're living together, too, and only a few months after he broke his sacred and binding promise to me."

As she slid under the white coverlet, she felt the tears start, something else that happened every night. "I need your help. Please find a way to scare off the white woman so I can have him back. He belongs to me."

CHAPTER FIFTY SEVEN

Several days later, while they were having dinner, Winston broke a bread stick and told Carol, "My uncle said exactly what I thought he would; that anybody who delves into magic, whether it's good or bad magic, is playing with fire."

His reference to one of the four elements stung her to retort, "Fire is playing with us," and nodded at her arm in its plaster cast. She tried to lift it a little, and winced. Then she went back to struggling to eat with her left hand.

"Well, let's hope nothing else happens, and let's be positive." He sounded relieved as he reached for another bread stick.

Carol thought for a moment. "That leaves one last person I can ask for help."

Surprised, he looked up. "Who? We agreed that Harry was the only possibility."

She looked at him levelly and spoke slowly. "Your grandfather taught you all he knew."

He stared at her. "Oh, no, you can't think—"

"But I do. I need to think about every possibility."

"I just know the textbook stuff, nothing about doing it, and I would never—"

She pushed back her plate, which was still half-full. "You've told me you practice some of the old customs. You consulted the spirits about your wedding date with Wanda."

He looked uncomfortable. "Aw, she did that. What I used to do was just ordinary, everyday stuff, like burning the tobacco. I don't mean to disparage the old ways, but it was just for fun, like reading the horoscope in the daily newspaper. It was more of a habit than anything else, and it was a long time ago when I was a kid."

"Couldn't you practice up and do it again?"

"No." He was adamant. "I won't do anything like that any more."

"Not even for me?" she appealed to him.

He paused. "I'd do anything for you."

"Then—"

"Because it wouldn't work, that's why," he interrupted. "Maybe you think it's like a crystal ball, or a ouija board."

"You know I don't think it's anything like that. I respect peoples' beliefs as much, or more, than you do."

"What you're asking is—well, it's about contacting the spirit world, and that's really hard."

"But it can be done. I've known many different kinds of people who've done it and described it afterwards, perfectly clearly."

"Well, theoretically, maybe. Actually doing it is something else."

"It isn't all that different to talking to God, is it? Who hasn't talked to God and felt we got an answer?"

He stared at her. "I've never done anything really serious, like you're talking about. I agree with my great-uncle: people shouldn't dabble with conjuring." He gave her a plaintive look. "And whatever you call it, you're talking about an exorcism!"

Carol slumped. "I just want to stop the dying. I know the secret lies in the past. Secrets always do. I want to find out what happened. I'd just like to talk to Isabelle, that's all. Or Wolf."

He was quiet for a moment before saying, "If I did anything as crazy as you're suggesting, and somebody found out, I'd be a laughing-stock. My career would be ruined. Nobody would hire a lawyer, or want a politician, who practices voodoo instead of the law. Even my position as chief could be affected." His fork clattered onto his plate.

Carol thought once more of the man in the red cap bound with gold that

Phil had seen as he lay dying. She'd always wondered if it might somehow be Winston. Right now Winston was doing the equivalent of opening the flood gate; except that, this time, it was she who might die. She jumped up, a little lopsided, and started trying to clear the table with her one good hand.

"Here, let me help do that." Picking up the plates, Winston said, "Honey, I'm sorry."

"You're not nearly as sorry as I am," she replied sadly. Would she have to leave him now, just as they had found each other again? To save her life?

Some weeks later, Carol climbed into Winston's Jeep in front of the doctor's office.

"How'd it go?" he asked, and waited for her answer before switching on the ignition. When she didn't reply, he joked, "They didn't cut off your arm with the saw?" When she remained silent, he peered at her. "Oh, come on, it couldn't have been that bad. Even my joke wasn't that bad."

She squelched the fear that had grown in the last hour. "Nothing is bad. Everything is good," she finally said with a smile, thinking of the extra examination Dr. Saunooke had given her when she asked him about her other symptoms. "But there is one problem."

"What?" he yelped.

Her smile grew. "We're going to have to move to a bigger house." At his startled look, she laughed. "Or maybe we can just build on a couple of new rooms. Because from now on, there's going to be three of us—Daddy."

He slumped over the steering wheel, setting off the horn. As if liking its celebratory note, he hit it a couple more times, then kept his hand on it for what seemed five minutes, just sitting there in the parking lot, grinning, blaring his joy to the world.

Then he started the engine and drove her to what had become their home. As they approached the front door, he suddenly picked her up in his arms. "What the—" she cried, protecting her injured arm as he carried her over the threshold. "Hey, you didn't do this when I moved in with you."

"I'm doing it now. And I'll do it again after the wedding."

"After the wedding, we'll be in the Bahamas." She draped her good arm around his neck.

They kissed through the living room, through the hallway, and into their bedroom. He lay her down. "I want to keep on kissing you forever," he told her.

"And I want you to." The fear had dissolved.

Then, carefully, so as not to disturb the child they had conceived—which one of the many times? — when their passion had burst into streams of hot liquid rich with life, he showed her not how much he wanted her, but how much she meant to him.

CHAPTER FIFTY EIGHT

'MIMOSA,' NEW ECHOTA GA, MARCH 1838

"What was that noise?" Isabelle had started up the stairway with her candle.

Wolf, who had been following her closely, leapt to the front door and looked through its side panels for some time. Finally he told her, "Wake up Yaguska, gather some food and clothes, all you can manage, and meet me behind the smokehouse."

"But why?" Fear clutched at her. "What's happening?"

"The people who have come to steal my land have arrived. They gave me until Christmas, and that's past. It seems I've outstayed my welcome in my own home," he finished bitterly.

"Then—?" She couldn't bring herself to finish the question.

He did it for her. "If we want to continue living, we must flee. And I want us all to live."

She looked around the beautiful entrance hall with its polished wooden floor and curved balustrade. "How can you stand to leave Mimosa?"

Grimly he replied, "I would never do it by choice. But I'm one man against many."

"What about the servants?"

"They'll be all right, they'll be useful to the new owners; it's us they want out. Now you must do as I asked, and please be quick about it." He set his mouth in a hard line and dashed out the front door.

Isabelle glimpsed lamps bobbing along the avenue that led to the house. There were over two dozen men, she estimated, advancing on foot, having left their horses just out of earshot.

Yaguska woke quickly. Helping him dress, she confided, "Your father says we need to travel."

"Where?"

"Probably back to Huntington."

"Good. I can see my grandmother again, and Tusquittee." He followed her without complaining as she gathered warm clothes from the bedrooms, bundling them into Wolf's special rug and a sheet she tied around her shoulders. Yaguska could bear the lighter load of food.

"Let's go, now." She took one last look around the bedroom where they'd been so happy.

"Yes, Mother." The word made her heart soar, even amid such sadness.

Yaguska's sturdy little legs bounded down the long stairway. In the pantry, she grabbed the remains of their supper—bread, sausage, a few pieces of chicken, an apple pie that Posy had baked—from a wire meat safe and wrapped it in a dishcloth that she tied around her son's waist.

Shepherding Yaguska, she ran toward the smokehouse. The lanterns had nearly encircled Mimosa. Wolf held two horses. And two muskets. "Get up, quickly, and take Yaguska on your saddle." Then he handed her one of the firearms and a bag of lead balls.

"What am I to do with these?"

"Leave all the shooting to me, but it's better to have it than not, especially if we get separated. If we do, head north for the Blue Ridge, and then east for Huntington, to my mother's settlement. Near there we have some land hidden in a cove." She took a tighter grip on the saddle horn as he pointed to the far corner of the estate. "There's a trail just there, by the big pine tree, that I made in secret. It'll lead us to the highway."

"But we'll have to go through that line of men!" Their lights were closer now.

He replied grimly, "They're walking, we're riding. I hope we'll have the advantage over them. If not—" He leaned over, Yaguska between them, and kissed her. Atop Yaguska's warm little body she clung to her husband. "Are you ready? Then may God go with you." It was the first time she had ever heard him use the name of God. This, too, pleased her, despite the circumstances.

Wolf touched Weenook's sides and urged him into a gallop. Her horse, Honi, thinking it was the game they frequently played, followed. Both horses aimed straight for the men. The line didn't move. The horses didn't stop. Isabelle wanted to shut her eyes but knew she couldn't. This was life or death, for her and her family. There could be no resiling.

Wolf felled a man with the butt of his musket. A lantern spilled and started a fire in the grass. From the other side, a man rushed at Weenook, but Wolf shot him.

"Give me your musket, and ride quickly!" he called to Isabelle. "I've made a gap."

As they thundered through the line, shots rang out. Isabelle hunched lower over Yaguska, praying. "Watch out, my darling!" she shouted to Wolf as a firearm was aimed at his retreating back. Deftly Wolf swerved, the shot went past him, and he turned and fired back. As he did, a shot came out of nowhere and she saw her husband flinch, moan, and grasp his left thigh. But he kept riding.

Finally they were out of firing range, and had found the path to the road. "Are you wounded?"

"It's nothing," he said, pressing his leg.

"Let me see."

"There's no time." As they turned their horses north, a huge flame shot into the night sky. They turned to see their front door flattened and the gracious hallway alight, flames licking along the staircase.

Isabelle put a hand to her mouth. "Who could be so cruel?"

"They just want to scare us off. They'll put out the fire, for they want the house for themselves," Wolf counseled in a choked voice, pressing on his leg.

Isabelle wondered which pain was greater—his wound or being forced to flee his beloved home.

CHAPTER FIFTY NINE

TOMOTLA NC, APRIL 1838

"It's beautiful here!" Isabelle circled Honi in the clearing surrounded by high mountains.

After fleeing Georgia, they had spent several weeks in Kiowa. Now, Wolf had insisted they move further into the mountains, to his mother's land at Tomotla. It had been a difficult journey through thickly forested woods, with no trail to follow except that one cleared by his instincts.

He seemed pleased at Isabelle's delight. "I thought it wise to come here when the notices went up. Tomotla is so deep in the mountains hardly anyone knows it's here, and the soldiers would know even less how to find this cove. I only wish there had been time to build you a better house. I wanted to build you a house like Mimosa." But the sweep of his arm encompassed a humble, wooden lean-to covered with hides.

"This will do fine."

"I'm glad you're happy."

"And you've brought our special rug."

"I've brought these, too." Her eyes widened at the sight of a pile of gold nuggets in his red cap. "If we need anything, we can take one to Elsie at the trading post. But I didn't build this hut even to last the winter. We'll stay here through the summer, until the soldiers leave for Oklahoma. Then we'll go back to Kiowa."

She looked apprehensive. "Won't we be captured?"

"Once the soldiers have gone, I don't think they'll come back," he said confidently.

"And what about the rest of your family?"

"They'll hide in the mountains."

As she pounded corn for their meager diet, Isabelle wondered about the rumor Wolf had heard before they left Kiowa. Had James really told her father to disown her? She imagined her name being crossed out of the big family Bible and felt a sadness heavier than the pounding-stick. Would she ever see any of her family again?

Wolf had noticed her mood. "Are you sad?"

She smiled at him. "Yes, but only about my family. And I miss your family—your sisters and your mother. It was such pleasure to be in their company while we were in Kiowa, even if I couldn't speak their language."

"We'll see them again, when we go back. Who knows, after this trouble has passed, I might be able to help my people again. Even citizenship is still possible, if I fight for it."

She knew his dream stuck in his heart like a cocklebur. "That would be wonderful."

"Why, I might even get my lands and estates back."

She joined in his enthusiasm. "Wonderful things might happen; why, even the removal date might pass without action." She looked at the now unmistakable signs of spring. The leaves on the oak trees were the size of dandelions, and her heart was full. "I love it here; it's even more peaceful than the settlement. It's like all the world belongs to us alone." She took an excited breath. "Guess what else I've been doing today?"

"Making corn husk dolls?" He recalled her most recent pastime.

"No, though I've made six. No, today I started teaching Yaguska how to read English."

"How?"

"With my Bible."

"Let's hear your first lesson, my son."

Yaguska squared his small shoulders and read, 'In … the … be … gin … n ing …" but Wolf could not wait to hear any more before embracing his son, he was so overcome with pride.

Joyfully, Isabelle hugged them both. "I hope we'll soon have another child."

"Nothing would please me more."

"I'm just sorry it hasn't happened yet." But even as she spoke her hands moved to her stomach. Lately its usual flatness had rounded a little. There were other changes in her body, too. But it was a little early to be sure.

"The old folks would say there's been too much bad magic. It can be hard to turn bad magic into good," he grinned, "but I'll make new magic, good magic, and then it will happen."

"Of course," she suggested mischievously, "there's something else we could try, too. It's also magical."

He glanced at Yaguska. "Perhaps our son could practice his reading out by the apple tree."

In his headquarters, General Winfield Scott faced Major Jason Smith. "Is everything in order? You've read my instructions?"

"Yes, sir."

"Then you'll know—and tell Mattox and every officer in charge of a fort—that the Indians are to be treated with respect. No cruelty, no brutality. And they'll be fed well. I've given my word to the president."

"I've already passed on your orders, sir."

"They'll have a slow journey at first. They'll have to walk to the Cumberland River." He turned. "But after that they'll travel by boat, down the Mississippi to Oklahoma Territory."

"All is ready, sir."

"Good. The removal deadline set by Congress is not far away."

"Talla-quoy-yah! Talla-quoy-yah!" The voice, low but urgent, came from beyond the deer hides that formed their lean-to. Wolf and Isabelle, startled to hear another voice in their perfect, but perfectly silent, world, realized it was Naomi.

"What brings you on such a dangerous journey, my mother? Has something happened in Kiowa?"

"Kwahala has been captured by the soldiers. They've jailed his whole family, too, for nothing more than visiting his wife's relatives. You must help them. You must get them out of the fort. You know how; you got Isabelle out. Then we'll go into the mountain caves."

Wolf thought for a long time. Getting into the fort would be more difficult now. And they had built a new stockade. "Maybe he can escape by himself."

"It is doubtful. They say Indians in the fort are not being fed, and that he is too weak to escape."

"I'll think about it. If I decide I can do it, then I'll make a plan."

While he stoked the cook fire, deep in thought, Naomi whispered to Isabelle, "You are with child?"

Surprised, Isabelle asked, "How do you know? I'm not even sure myself."

"*I* am sure."

Wolf returned to them. "All right," he declared. "I'll try to find Kwahala and Powlina and their children."

Naomi looked questioningly at her daughter-in-law, but Isabelle, although feeling enormous happiness, shook her head. If her husband was going on such a dangerous mission, he might be hindered by knowing about her condition. She would tell him the wonderful news when he returned.

CHAPTER SIXTY

FORT BUTLER NC, JUNE 18, 1838

"Aaarrright, you bastards, you'll be glad to hear this—we're gonna let you go." Wolf watched Sergeant Hampton push his way into the fort's small jail, stepping on whatever part—a leg, an arm, a spine, or a face—of those Indians unlucky enough to be in his way. And there were many, for the prison overflowed. "Come on, come on, you've wanted to be free all these months, haven't you? Well, now, here's yer chance."

Some inmates looked up, eyes dulled by deprivation and humiliation, yet showing a flicker of interest. But Wolf felt only caution. This sergeant had once tried to kill him; it might happen again.

"What's keeping ye? Get a move on!" The savage boots kicked out.

And so the Cherokees closest to the door stumbled to their feet and started outside, slowly. The sergeant grinned, and Wolf's caution turned to concern. Only the prospect of worsening the Indians' plight could have caused that bastard's happiness, and Wolf knew then that something was wrong.

More prisoners crowded through the low, narrow door. Wolf, too, was pushed along by the tide of those who glimpsed freedom. He had been imprisoned a long time, himself. For nearly a month he had lain squashed in the dark, fetid air, worrying about his wife. How would she know what had happened to him? He missed her with an endless ache.

He hadn't found his brother Kwahala, nor any of his brother's family. That rankled him as much as getting captured.

There had been nothing to do in the stifling prison but listen, and for some time now there had been increasing movement outside. Every day he could hear numbers of people arriving, soft-shod, so they weren't soldiers. In the stockade itself, men and horses tramped in and out. And he could hear the sounds of wagons. Many wagons. The fort was full. The new arrivals were Indians. The soldiers were going somewhere. But where? And what would happen to the prisoners?

Forced now out into the bright June sunlight, Wolf blinked first at the smells and then at the sights. Instead of the orderly, familiar activities of the garrison, he saw a confusing mass of bodies, both human and animal, swirling, turning, like the wooden tops Isabelle carved for the children. Heat and dust consumed everything. The misery of the Indians mixed with the determination of the soldiers. He saw, too late, that the men from the jail were being herded into a pen.

Then, suddenly, he felt the hope he had earlier spurned. For already in the pen, mostly lying on the ground, were many Indians, scores of them, and families—women and children too. There! There, in the middle, was his sister-in-law, Powlina, kneeling over Kwahala, holding up his head.

Not caring what the sergeant or even Captain Mattox might do, Wolf leapt to his brother's side.

CHAPTER SIXTY ONE

"Powlina! Powlina! At last! How's my brother?"

"Very sick," she said sadly. "I'm afraid."

"Don't be; I'll help you." Gently Wolf moved Tusquittee aside and knelt on the dusty red soil to gather up his brother. Ohhh, he felt so frail. Kwahala opened his eyes, but they held only a faint spark of life.

Slinging Kwahala's medicine bag around his own neck, Wolf opened it to see if it contained anything that might help. Wolf was so occupied with this that at first he barely heard Captain Mattox's announcement. "You've been gathered up to go to your new hunting grounds in Oklahoma. I know you've all been looking forward to it." His tone was so sarcastic that Wolf began to pay attention. "Well, today we're going to take you. Gather all your belongings. We leave within the hour."

Wolf sat back on his heels. Then it had come to pass. The removal. Awed, his thoughts raced to Isabelle. How would she, and the rest of their family, survive without him and his brother? As quickly, he mourned the son of Isabelle's he might never have.

Mattox rode over. "Well, if it isn't my brother-in-law!" he snarled. "It'll be a real pleasure to take you to Oklahoma." For emphasis he spat at Wolf, who adroitly avoided it, and the vile missile landed in the dust. Wolf felt only contempt for such an action; he was spitting out his soul. It was dangerous, for someone could capture it.

The Captain motioned to Kwahala and shouted an order to one of the soldiers. "Get this lazy, shiftless Indian on his feet. He has to walk a thousand miles to Oklahoma." He laughed at his own cruel joke.

Kwahala tried to struggle to his feet, but he stumbled and fell down again. His wife cried out; his children cringed at the pitiful sight.

"On second thought, throw this dog's turd into the woods; he'll never make it to Oklahoma," James amended his order.

Slanting the captain and the soldier a defiant look, Wolf gathered up his brother and whispered, "Don't worry, I'll look after you."

"I think not," James replied, reining in his horse so tightly it reared above the grief-stricken family, forcing them to cower lower. Two soldiers restrained Wolf. A third wrenched Kwahala's thin body from his grasp and started for the gate.

"No! I'll carry him."

But the captain only gave a curt shake of his head. "You'll get no favors from me, even that."

Wolf heard his own desperation. "Don't let him die alone in the woods! At least have the decency to shoot him! And he must be buried!" When Mattox remained silent, Wolf let out a roar of agony, straining against his guards. "Let me shoot him, then! At least I can bury him."

The captain wheeled his horse. "You're a fine one to beg for decency, after what you did to my sister."

Wolf glared. "I married your sister, and I'll love and take care of her as long as I live." At this Mattox raised his stick, and poised it to strike. The guards moved away but Wolf straightened, as if inviting attack. "You treated her no better than a house slave, and made her father disown her." Head raised with pride, he growled, slowly, "Yet you call us savages."

As the blow descended, there was a shout from the other side of the stockade. Wolf felt a sharp pain, but the stick had lost some of its power before it struck and hit the ground, splintering. "There'll be plenty of time to take care of you." Reluctantly Mattox rode off.

Wolf wanted to die, too. But first he wanted to kill the man who had mistreated Isabelle and ordered that his brother die alone, so painfully, without dignity, without even burial.

The blood laws demanded revenge for his brother as well as his wife. He had promised Isabelle he wouldn't harm her brother. But now, Mattox's treatment of Kwahala had surely broken that promise.

Wolf looked again at James' spittle still glistening in the dust. Killing could be done in different ways. It could be slow and made to hurt as much as the captain's own actions.

A cloud veiled the sun. It would be a deserved curse—a just one, Wolf thought, and more powerful because of the ties of blood and flesh.

Starting the spell would take only a minute now, and he could finish it later. Quickly Wolf bent down and, using two splinters from the captain's stick, gathered up the spittle. Wrapping it in a leaf, he put it carefully in Kwahala's medicine bag. He hung back, looking to see whether anyone watched. No one seemed to; there was too much movement and confusion. Good. He would find the other essentials for the curse that would kill the captain—the pebbles and rock, the right kind of tree—as they walked. As for the necessary fasting, he'd had so little to eat in the past month, it could be considered to have already started.

The Captain shouted, "Keep in line, now. All right, start moving 'em out."

Soldiers shoved Wolf toward a milling knot of people. The day grew darker. Seeing this, Wolf smiled to himself. It was a good sign. The gods were angry. There was a crack of thunder. Wolf looked up at the sharp-peaked mountains. A jagged flash was followed by another ear-bursting clap of thunder. He knew then that the mountains themselves were encouraging him in his decision.

Finally, prodded by a musket in his back, Wolf began to move. With hate in his heart—as much hate for her brother as he had love for Isabelle—he reluctantly headed, with hundreds of others, north toward Tennessee and the Ohio turnpike which would lead them west.

The wise men taught that death lay in the west.

CHAPTER SIXTY TWO

ON 'THE TRAIL OF TEARS,' JUNE 18, 1838

Hundreds of people walked silently, throwing up a mile-long cloud of dust.

Being among so many people had its advantage, Wolf decided. He worked his way to the edge of the column. There he found a patch of wild parsnip, poisonous and powerful. While digging it up, he also found three of the seven earthworms he needed. Squashing the worms was necessary to start the magic.

The spirits are treating me well, he thought with satisfaction, depositing his booty in the medicine bag inside his shirt.

Through the hot afternoon, he managed to collect most of the other items he needed. He found many more worms and a flat rock close to the yellow color required. But the pebbles were also yellow, not the preferred black.

Just as they made camp for the night, he saw the young oak tree—not that its type mattered—which had been struck by lightning. Its jagged trunk had weathered, so the strike hadn't been too recent. Good. Quickly he picked off some of the splinters.

He worked the spittle, the crushed earthworms, and the splinters together and, with a small stick, stuffed the mixture into a hollow he had carved in the biggest knob of parsnip, putting the leftovers in the medicine bag.

Everything was ready, except for the pebbles. Yellow was acceptable, but should he wait, in the hope of finding black ones? Making substitutes could cause the spell to go wrong, make it easier for the victim to conjure up a new curse to turn the bad magic back. On the other hand, the spell must be done while the spittle was still moist, and it might dry out while he looked for black pebbles. He decided to complete the ritual. The spittle was all-important. Substituting yellow for black was acceptable, and better than nothing. This was an emergency. He was sure the spirits would agree.

He dug a hole at the base of the tree. Down went the flat rock, the filled parsnip root on top, then the pebbles. "*Sge! Na'gwa tsudanta'gi tegu' yatawa' ilateli' ga. Tsuwatsi'la elawi'ni tsida'histani'ga.*" Next, all was covered with earth and, borrowing coals from a nearby cook fire, he lit dry twigs he had mounded. The ancestors thought fire obscured the freshly-dug earth, so no one would suspect a curse might lurk beneath, and thus counter it. In this case, traveling on the next day would provide even more camouflage. No one would ever find the curse. It would lie undisturbed, working its magic, forever.

Finally, after several weeks, the ragged band—exhausted, footsore, stomachs upset from the unaccustomed diet of white man's food—arrived at Fort Cass. It was, Wolf knew, in eastern Tennessee near the Cumberland River.

"We'll rest here a spell," Captain Mattox announced, "while we organize the boats that will take us from here to the Mississippi."

Wolf noticed that James' strength had paled like his face.

One never knew when the curse would work. Only that it would.

CHAPTER SIXTY THREE

TOMOTLA NC, AUGUST, 1838

The moment Isabelle had seen Weenook gallop, riderless, into the yard, she knew something terrible had happened to Wolf. "God in Heaven, what do I do now?"

She had many problems, but food was the biggest one. Soothing her swollen belly—ironically so empty of food—Isabelle worried not about herself but about her unborn baby. And about Yaguska.

As killing animals for meat was beyond their capability, they subsisted on corn mush and bean bread, made from the supplies they had brought to Tomotla in April. But both were getting low. Fortunately, Wolf had planted new crops before he left to look for Kwahala. She and Yaguska had kept the corn hoed, an exertion that got harder by the day and made her ankles swell. Still, the new crops had to be brought to harvest. Could she do it, with only a child to help, and a baby about to be born?

In case she did not survive, one day she urged Yaguska, "You must continue the Wolf family tradition of helping your people; this should forever be a Wolf trait. The Cherokees must have citizenship. Remember that word: citizenship. It's all-important." Wearily she added, "And now we must hoe the corn."

As they walked to the cornfield, she heard the warning rattle. "Ccbbrrrr! Ccbbrrrr!"

"Stop where you are, and don't move," she urged her son, who did as he was told.

In the long grass, Isabelle could see the snake, the rattles on the end of its tail sticking out of a mound of coils, its head reared up. It was poised to strike.

With her right hand behind her skirt to camouflage the movement, she began to raise the hoe over her head. In one swift action, faster than she had thought herself capable, she brought it down with both hands, putting every ounce of her strength into the blow.

The snake's head was only partly cut, and the flat beads still sang their warning. "Run! It might still strike," she told Yaguska. Sure enough, she felt a sting on her left leg. It was painful, but again and again she brought down the hoe until the rattler's head, eyes now closed in defeat, rolled into the grass. Only then did she sink onto the ground, with both fear and relief, clutching a frightened Yaguska close before she looked at her leg. There were two puncture marks around a rapidly swelling red patch. She tried to bend her mouth to her leg, but the bulk of her stomach prevented it.

"My darling, you must suck out the poison, and spit it out of your mouth." As he obeyed, she prayed he would get it all.

When he had finished, Yaguska looked at the snake's long coil. "What will we do with it?"

She looked at him solemnly, hardly believing the thought had even occurred to her. "We're going to eat him."

CHAPTER SIXTY FOUR

ON 'THE TRAIL OF TEARS,' OCTOBER, 1838

"Fort Cass is a terrible place, so many people are sick and dying. Why have we been here so long?" Tusquittee asked Wolf. There were funeral services every day. The ablest men, Indians and soldiers alike, spent hours digging graves.

"For the same reason that the well has run dry, and the river's too low to use the boats. There's been no rain," Wolf replied as he fried their daily ration of bacon.

"Are we going back home?" When Wolf shook his head, Tusquittee wondered, "What will happen to us, then?"

"I'm not sure, but we'll be told soon, I think. If not boats, they'll probably take us in wagons." Wolf paused. *Surely they won't make us walk all the way to Oklahoma Territory.* He picked up a wooden bucket. "Watch the bacon; I'll fetch some water."

On his way back from the stream, he met James, whose face had yellowed and become haggard.

"Ah, brother-in-law," James said. "You've given me the chance I've been waiting for." Weaving drunkenly, he made a show of unsheathing his knife. It was long and had several nicks on the sharp edge. "There's nobody to see us, nobody to know you didn't attack me."

Wolf stood where he was and gave James a wary look. There was no smell of alcohol. James' condition clearly was due to the death spell. It was working, even considering all the substitutes he'd had to make. The magic was powerful. "I'll know," he replied. "But weak as I am, you're even less fit for a fight, and I'd never take advantage of you. You'll die soon, anyhow."

James' laugh was a sick grimace. "You think I can't kill you?" The knife came closer.

Wolf put down his pail, but he wasn't fast enough, and the knife slashed his arm. As blood ran out of Wolf, though, it was James who looked stricken. He clutched first at his heart, then at his throat. His knees crumpled. In a moment he lay helpless, the knife glinting not with evil but with impotence in the late afternoon sunlight.

Wolf watched as James' yellow face turned dark purple and he began to cough, fighting for breath. It turned into a racking sound, then the rattle of death. James' eyes closed. His body twitched, and then became still.

Wolf wanted to go back to camp for Powlina and her children. But he dared not, for he would be accused of killing James. In fact, there would soon be a search. He sent a plea to the spirits to protect Powlina. Then he staggered through the woods, binding his wound with his shirt. Keeping thick cover, he began a slow run in an easterly direction.

In the direction of home, not death.

"Come, little man, come out at once!" Naomi urged. *"Sge! Hisga'ya Ts'sdi'ga ha-na'gwa da'tulehu'gu kilu-gwu."*

Isabelle was surrounded by Naomi, Noquisi, and a few Kiowa women who had also survived removal. It was the end of November and cold, but for the fire in the log cabin, although Isabelle was soaked with sweat. She lay on the rug that Naomi had made for Wolf. On this rug, she had welcomed her husband and conceived her child. It was fitting that the child should be born on it.

While waiting for the next birth pain, she thought of the pain of the snake bite. The Cherokees had a saying, 'Today is a good day to die,' and she had chosen an August day to die from her injury. She had dragged this same rug outside and dozed, death-like, hallucinating through the noon heat. The fever made her so crazy she thought Naomi's appearance was a fantasy instead of a miracle. She had no clear recollection of the trip back to Kiowa. Naomi had told her that Yaguska rode with her and held her on Honi, who had not minded that the sick woman lay on his neck.

The women had treated the snakebite with tobacco juice. It was still sore, and still hurt, but the red patch was getting smaller. However, it was nothing compared to the agony that had seized her body this morning before daylight, and did so again now.

"Come, little man. Push now, Mother."

"Aaaaggghhhh." Isabelle made an enormous effort, feeling as if her insides were falling out.

Suddenly, the women began chattering excitedly.

Yaguska stared with large, round eyes at something they held. Isabelle saw the blotched, mottled skin of her newborn baby, the waxy residue on its body, the blood, the cord, its shock of black hair so like Wolf's, and smiled through her pain. "What is it?"

They answered, but she was none the wiser, and Yaguska was still too mesmerized to translate. Finally she grabbed Noquisi's arm as she passed with the baby, wrapped now in a blanket. With the last of her strength Isabelle opened the cloth. "Ahhh."

Her baby was a boy.

Wolf would have been pleased.

And now he would live again in his son.

CHAPTER SIXTY FIVE

KIOWA INDIAN SETTLEMENT NEAR HUNTINGTON NC, FEBRUARY, 1839

It was past the winter's halfway mark when Wolf staggered—hungry, footsore, and weary—through the last leg of his long journey. When he came upon the Valley River just above Fort Butler, he nearly wept. As he neared the clearing at Tomotla, he stopped. He had expected them to be in the meadow waiting for him, looking just like they had as he waved them goodbye. But no one was there. On impulse he gave the call of the whippoorwill. When she heard it, she would know he was close. She'd know he had come home to her.

But there was no answer. He made the call again. Still no answer.

When he reached the lean-to, he slowed his pace for the first time since fording the river.

But still he saw no one, and his heart sank. Where could they be? The door was open, their possessions were still there, but a quick prowl told him no one lived in the hut. No one had built a fire, or used the cooking utensils, in a long time. They had been turned over, strewn around the house, by animals looking for food. And his favorite rug was gone, the one they had never been without.

He slumped in the doorway, almost too weak and weary to grieve. They must be dead. Tomotla had not proved the safe place he had hoped. He had not been here to protect his family—his beloved wife, his son. First he had failed his tribe; now he had failed his family. His despair was complete, and he bowed his head in shaking hands.

After a while, he raised it again. Giving up was not his nature. If there had been an attack, by either animals or humans, there would be more disarray in the house, and his favorite rug would still be there.

He thought further. As soon as his sore feet were rested, he roused himself, and set off for his mother's house.

The last time he had been in Kiowa, although the settlement was under threat, everybody had still been happy, content, laughing. The children were playing and calling out to each other.

These thoughts and the sounds of them were in his mind when he reached the house, so the crying of a baby was, he thought, imagined. He opened the door to the sight he'd been longing for. A fire was burning brightly; his favorite rug was on the ground, and sitting on it was Isabelle, his wife, his love. Beside her was his son, Yaguska, just as he had imagined them.

Isabelle looked up. "My darling! It's a miracle. God has answered my prayers!" She leapt to her feet and helped him into the house. "Oh, you're so thin, but how glad I am to see you!"

He smiled at her, sank onto the rug, and tugged her down beside him. He embraced his son, who had at first run around the room with joy, then fallen into Wolf's arms. The family was complete at last.

But still a baby cooed, softly, close by. After his eyes had become accustomed to the dimness, Wolf saw a wooden cradle in a corner. It had not been there last spring. Someone must have left a baby for his mother to look after. That often happened.

"Whose baby is that? Have you not enough responsibility?"

Isabelle smiled gently. "I hadn't much choice about it. Let me introduce you." She brought the cradle close. Wolf looked at the face of a child who, strangely, looked just enough like Isabelle to perplex him. "Wolf, this is our son. I've called him George. In Cherokee, it's Sequoyah."

He looked not upon a baby's face but upon the sweet face of the afterlife. Was this what the Christians meant by heaven? To look upon a baby, another son . . . Isabelle's son?

He put one arm around Yaguska, another around the cradle, and sank his weary head on his wife's soft bosom.

CHAPTER SIXTY SIX

As Wolf left their cabin to check on the temperature of the ground—he intended to plow as soon as the spring thaw had finished; it was river bottom land and would soften earlier than on the slopes—he cast a glance along the huge timber over the fireplace.

His eyes flicked, as always, to Kwahala's medicine bag containing the remnants of the curse he'd put on James. He'd placed it on the beam as soon as he had returned. Every day he looked at it, and every day he remembered the way James had died. James' crimes had been many and cruel, and Wolf could not find it within himself to feel regret. The blood laws had required that James be punished, and fittingly. Even the missionaries' Bible said to take 'an eye for an eye.'

Still, James had been Isabelle's brother. And every time Wolf looked at his wife, he felt guilt for what he had done. He was unable even to tell her about it, much less say he was sorry.

He sighed, and was giving the pouch another rueful look when Isabelle said, quietly, behind him, "I know that medicine bag means a lot to you."

He started. "Who told you that?"

"I know because you keep looking at it so long and hard."

But he kept his counsel. "Oh, it just reminds me of—the march." He shook his head.

"Do you think everybody got to Oklahoma Territory?"

"Not all will ever arrive, so many were dying," he replied sadly. "Sometimes I feel guilty for being alive."

Her voice became still softer. "I don't know if James is alive, either." Her shoulders drooped. "I guess I'll never know."

Wolf's heart thudded. He should tell her. But he could not. He could kill a man. But he couldn't tell his wife that he'd killed her brother.

CHAPTER SIXTY SEVEN

CHEROKEE NC, NOVEMBER 1999

As wonderful as it was to be pregnant, knowing about the baby increased Carol's worry about the Mattox curse. It had been threatening enough when she thought she was in mortal danger. But it was worse to think that her child—their first-born—might, according to Grandma, be killed by it. She trembled every time she remembered Grandma's warning: 'I just wouldn't want to be in your shoes. Or be your child.'

Daily, Carol thought about this, and daily she became more afraid. Thoughts of how to deal with the problem occupied most of her waking hours. She knew a desperate battle lay ahead, to keep her child alive. She was determined to fight that battle. And win.

But, she wondered, how do you conquer an ancient curse that might not even exist? You couldn't talk it over with anybody and get answers, or fight it with either words or weapons.

It wasn't like fighting another woman. Her enemy wasn't flesh and blood, like Wanda, but the mystical, unseen forces of evil. They were probably stronger than if they had been human. But they were no less evil, and she believed in their existence. If only she could see those forces, talk to them, find out why these things were happening to her. And that, again, made her wish she could find out what had happened to Wolf and Isabelle.

The problem was not just finding out. It went deeper than that. Because of the baby, she had to remove any curse there might be. And she knew this request needed to be made to the ancients, to the people who had put on the curse. She became more and more convinced that nothing else would work.

On a Thursday night, when she felt the baby's first faint, fluttering kick, she took Winston's hand and held it on her stomach. "Do you feel that?" she asked in awe.

"That's amazing." His voice, too, was full of wonder.

Suddenly, she could no longer hold back her fears. She told him, "I spend every day double-checking everything I do, hoping I won't have another accident. I worry about whether the baby is safe, even before it's born. If we don't, somehow, try to find out about that curse, I feel like I'll either die from it, or die from worrying about it."

"We don't even know, for sure, if there is a curse."

This time she was determined. "I need to find out. I want to try and contact the spirits. We both know it can be done, if we believe in it strongly enough. And if it doesn't work, then we haven't lost anything."

His look was sympathetic, but his voice was firm. "It doesn't happen like that. You don't decide what to do. The spirits decide, if they can be communicated with at all. They're fitful and capricious. That's what makes it so dangerous. We could end up even worse off."

Carol replied, "That's hard to believe, when our child, our first-born, could die."

Jolted by this, Winston's thoughts tumbled over each other. He couldn't let his first-born die without at least trying to prevent it.

She plead, "You see what I'm getting at, don't you? If you don't help me, then who will? Who could have a better reason? We have to find out for sure if there is a curse."

He turned it over in his mind. Family was very important to the Cherokee. "I'll think about it. That's all, just think about it."

"Then think about this, too." She smoothed his forehead with a loving hand. "I trust you with my life and the life of our child." She put his hand back on her stomach. "I also trust you to help us stay alive."

How could he deny such trust?

CHAPTER SIXTY EIGHT

THE NANTAHALA GORGE, NC, SEPTEMBER 1999

Most Cherokees shunned the Nantahala Gorge because it was reputed to be inhabited by evil spirits. But Winston and Carol decided it was the place where they should try to contact their ancestral spirits. They went to the bend in its river where he had once saved her life. He thought it was their power spot, their ritual river, and hoped its power could be used tonight.

Winston glanced at Carol sitting on the bank, arms curled around her stomach, sending him anxious looks as he made his preparations. Tonight, they might find out whether the child inside her would live or die.

Responsibility weighed heavily on him, and he felt a chill not entirely autumnal. This was the most difficult and important thing he'd ever tried to do. Was he the equal of his ancestor, Tallaquoyah Wolf? Could he take off the curse that Wolf had put on?

He would soon find out.

They had climbed down the slippery river bank through bracken fern and boulders, Carol worried about hurting the baby; he was weighed down by a backpack full of the things his uncle had said were necessary to make the old magic.

For weeks now, Winston had practiced things best left forgotten—that had been forgotten. Albeit reluctantly, his uncle had recalled them, and then rehearsed his nephew in the age-old rituals.

Pungent smoke swirled from the fire he had built. It was both to attract the spirits and 'go to water,' another tradition he was following tonight. Nearly naked, heated by the fire and cleansed by the river, in one of the oldest ceremonies of all, he threw tobacco into the flames and was glad when the strands burned evenly.

A light wind shivered through the pine trees, but was shunned by sturdier spruces and hemlocks. The sourwoods' perfume was strong.

Winston stood tall, welcoming the elements. *"Sge!"* As he chanted a greeting in his ancestral tongue, the wind changed from a mournful whine to the frivolous laughter of children, and back again.

The fire exaggerated the slow, rhythmic movements he began to make. As they became a dance of shadows, he shouted the incantation again, shaking an ancient medicine rattle in the four directions, then above and below each one, as he had been instructed. The rattle itself, filled with the teeth of his clan's power animal, was potent medicine. It had belonged to an ancestor only two generations removed from the one who might have cast the spell requiring tonight's efforts.

Gradually, Winston's full-throated entreaties changed to low, soothing whispers as he sought the near-trance-like state needed for communicating with the other world. Balancing carefully on a granite river boulder, he closed his eyes and used the formal language his uncle had advised. "Come, spirits, so that I can ask you about a matter of great importance, a matter of life itself."

He continued to assure them. "Your presence will honor me. I need to speak to you on a matter of great urgency." The pines sighed, the river gurgled and, high on a sharp peak, thunder growled. Some might have doubted it was the spirits answering. But not Winston. Despite his misgivings about contacting them, he had been taught that the spirits of his ancestors were all around him and would reveal themselves when and if they wished.

The colors appearing against his closed eyes changed from yellow to orange to black. When at last he glimpsed the purple color which meant the spirits had heard and arrived in his consciousness, his excitement leapt like the fire. The ancient ways were proving as powerful as ever.

Encouraged, he spread his arms. "We need to talk to our spirit guides, on a matter of great importance. We seek our ancestors, to ask if there was trouble between our families a long, long time ago. As one of the Wolf clan, and chief of the Cherokees, I beg you to guide us."

There was no reply. Winston kept silent, eyes closed, connected to both worlds, receptive to every nuance of his senses.

Then, seeming to come out of the river granite itself, a deep, thunderous voice asked, "Who is here with you?"

CHAPTER SIXTY NINE

Relieved at making contact with the spirit world and seeing that Carol had heard the voice, too, Winston assured him, "It's all right; she's one of the Mattoxes."

"I'm your spirit guide; hers is here, too, and we want to help you, protect you from those who would harm you, for certain other spirits are unhappy that she's here."

Winston tried again. "She and I needed to come together. Our families have been entwined for two hundred years in ways that run deeper than the earth itself. We're united by a great and ancient love inherited from our ancestors. But we may also share with them an equally powerful curse of death. That's why we want to talk to our ancestors. I'm a direct descendant of Tallaquoyah Wolf. She's descended from his wife, Isabelle, upon whose brother we suspect a curse was laid by a Wolf. We need to know if the curse exists, and if it's still in effect."

There was silence. Winston thought he saw a small, moving light. Then a different, softer and more sorrowful voice, female, elaborated: "The Mattoxes took a life from the Wolfs, who took a Mattox life in revenge. Those ancient hatreds—the blood laws—were truly terrible."

"Was a curse put on because of that?"

"We don't know," the sorrowful spirit informed him.

Carol moaned. Winston glanced at her but dared not break his fragile communication with the other world. "Who would know? Can we speak to Isabelle and Wolf?"

The soft voice was suddenly replaced by a third voice, this one hard without being strong. Determining whether the voice was male or female was difficult, as the answer shot back. "You should not talk of such things."

"Why not?" Carol cried.

This time the silence was even longer, and just as Winston was wondering what to do, the reply came. "If we bring your ancestors, what do you offer? Can we have this Mattox woman too?" The question was casual, almost flippant.

Winston was horrified. "No! She's carrying our child!" He had been afraid of such unforeseen obstacles, partly the reason he'd resisted an attempt like this. They were just what his uncle had warned against.

How clear the spirits' voices were, Carol thought. Talking to them was just like dreaming, or praying. "Knowing the truth is always the first step toward solving the problem. This truth is in the past. I believe if we can go back to the beginning and find out what happened to Isabelle and Tallaquoyah Wolf, we can better understand what to do now. Please let us talk to them."

The new, hard voice became reproachful. "How dare you ask this? How dare you even speak to us? You're not one of us."

Carol's chin jutted out. "I am, in all the ways that are important. I'm marrying into the tribe. My husband is its chief. My child will be one of you. That's if he's allowed to live. That's why the dying must be stopped," she asserted.

"You can't demand anything. We, the spirits, decide."

"Please help us. Why have so many people died? If we knew that, we might find a way to stop it."

"What if we gave you this information? What could you do about it? It's all done now. It's too late."

"It isn't too late for us."

The voice's flippancy turned into amusement. "If you believe what you're saying, maybe you should find out, for yourselves, what happened." The spirit's enthusiasm built. "Maybe you should live in Wolf's and Isabelle's time. It would be better than just speaking to them."

"I don't think—" Winston began.

But Carol cut in, "We'd like to!" It was the chance she'd been hoping for, the chance to know Isabelle, to find out what had happened. To Winston she said, urgently, "The past can tell us everything! I'm sure it will tell us how we can take off the curse."

Winston knew how much she believed in the importance of the past. But he was worried, as she scrambled to her feet. She stood near the water's edge, as if to better plead with the spirits. "Help us go back to Wolf and Isabelle's time, so we can know exactly what happened."

"We can't do that!" said the sorrowful voice. "It's too harsh a punishment."

"Their punishment should be harsh. And they should know what happened. Besides, they're willing—they've said so, haven't they? That's all that matters." The flippancy was back.

The granite voice said, "They may not go back to that time—"

"—or even to the same time," warned the sorrowful voice. "They may never come back to the present, or not together. They might be lost in the past forever. Either or both might die."

This scared Carol. She was facing death, or possibly, something worse than death. But she owed it to her brother, and now her unborn child, to try her best. She remembered how scared she was that the curse would kill her baby. She had no further hesitation. "I'll take my chances, if it will let my baby live. I'm not afraid of the past." Unlike the unpredictable present, it was something she could deal with.

"The woman won't be a loss to us," the third voice commented, almost idly, "and his heritage will protect him."

Safe or not, Winston felt incredulous at the very idea, and scoffed, "None of this can be done."

"Oh, no? We can do anything we want. Just watch," said the flippant spirit, with a note of glee.

Carol felt a vicious shove push her, hard, into the water. "Ohhh!" And then its cold took her breath away. Immediately, she was swept into the center of the river and pulled down, down, down, into icy water that seemed fathoms deep. Her clothes and shoes weighed her down, just as they had years ago. There was heavy pressure on her head, as if something held her down, and she couldn't breathe. And suddenly, once more, she saw the Indian wearing the red cap with a gold nugget. This time he beckoned to her.

"Help!" she screamed when she managed to come up for air. "Help!" And in that moment, she realized she no longer wore her usual jeans and shirt. Now she had on a very long dress and several layers of heavy clothing underneath it, all of it unfamiliar, and all of it dragging her down. She was powerless to keep from sinking back into the deep water.

Winston ran along the bank and prepared to dive in after her, for the second time in his life.

CHAPTER SEVENTY

KIOWA, NEAR HUNTINGTON NC, APRIL 1839

Baby Sequoyah gurgled contentedly as he watched them work with eyes of darkest brown, sharply focused even at six months, Isabelle thought proudly. She, Wolf, and Yaguska moved along the rows of earth. Yaguska placed corn seed in each mound, she raked the soil over it, and Wolf watered it in. They had covered a good deal of ground today and, talking and laughing to each other, also enjoyed each others' company. Isabelle was so happy she thought her heart would burst.

And for a moment, she thought that was the sound she heard. The shriek was so agonized that it stopped all of them in their tracks. As one, their heads snapped toward the baby. For the sound seemed, unbelievably, to have come from the tiny pallet of deerskin Isabelle had covered with a woolen shawl.

"What was that?" she hurried over to him. "Did you see anything bite him, a snake?" remembering the rattler.

"I saw nothing," Wolf shouted, although he was close behind her. "Yaguska?"

"No, not even a hawk," said the little boy, shifting his sack of corn seed.

"What is it, Sequoyah?" she crooned. Then, crying hard, the baby began to jerk and shake, writhing as if in agony.

"Aaaiiiee!" She let out a high-pitched scream of her own. "He's having a fit and turning yellow!" she told Wolf. "We need to do something! Yaguska, run and get your grandmother!"

Wolf was paralyzed by the sight of his son going through the same contortions James had suffered. He burst out, "This is all my fault!"

Isabelle loosened the baby's clothing and tried to soothe him by rubbing his soft, pudgy skin. Then she stared at her husband. "What do you mean?"

"I've been too cowardly to tell you. But now I confess that I put a curse on your brother, because he killed my brother. It was the blood laws. It was required, but I'm sorry I did such a thing."

"But what does that have to do with Sequoyah?" Frantically, she rubbed her son's legs, trying to make the blood flow. "If you put on a curse, it couldn't have affected our baby, could it?" But now Sequoyah was turning dark, and her efforts were for naught. His screams were quieting, but it was because he was hardly breathing.

"It could, if somehow it went wrong." Wolf bent over with the burden of his guilt. "I was desperate. I made substitutions. Maybe they've somehow made the curse go wrong, although it should have been turned back on me. Instead, it's been turned on my children." A sudden thought struck him. "Or yours." For James had had no children.

Wolf shoved this thought aside. He had to do everything in his power to help Sequoyah. There was no time to make magic to counteract whatever had gone wrong with the curse. He breathed into the baby's tiny mouth, rubbing the little chest between each effort. His heart heavy, over and over he tried to force life into his son.

But finally, Sequoyah seemed not to breathe at all and his skin had turned almost black.

"No!" cried Wolf. Taking out his hunting knife, he lowered it over the baby's throat.

"You're going to kill him!" Isabelle screamed, trying to grab the knife. "He can't even breathe, and you're cutting his throat!"

"Yes." Wolf was terse. "I'm cutting a breathing hole for him. If it works, I can seal it up again with medicines."

Still disbelieving, Isabelle grabbed at the baby. But Wolf pushed her hands away. He aimed the knife and cut his baby's throat. There was a gaping hole and blood enough for a hog slaughter.

But through it, the tiny body took a shuddering breath.

"Look, look! He's breathing!" Isabelle cried, as she waited for Sequoyah to take the next breath.

But there were no more breaths.

Wolf slumped over the small, still body, and wept. "My son, I'm sorry." He gathered the baby in his arms. Mournfully, he chanted, "I'm so sorry, so sorry." Holding his precious, dead cargo, Wolf waded into the river.

"Stop!" Isabelle called to him, and ran to the water's edge. "He may not be dead!" Her baby had taken a breath when all had seemed lost. He might take another. Despite all the blood, despite everything, Sequoyah might still be saved, and she must try.

"Maybe you did a terrible thing," she panted, running along the bank. "James was my brother, but I can understand why you felt reason to kill him." She had also heard that some people on the march had become touched in the head.

But Wolf, still talking to the inert baby, moved deeper into the river. "I've caused your life to be taken from you. I've caused you to die. And now I must die, too."

At this Isabelle waded in, despite being unable to swim, and tried to catch up with her husband. "Wolf! Stop! Don't die! Somehow, we can make everything all right again! You can make good magic and take off the curse. Such a spell must not be allowed to live on." She picked up her long skirts and churned through the water as fast as she could.

But Wolf was by now even further out.

Isabelle became more frantic. "Wolf, stop, please! I forgive you. I love you. I will always love you, no matter what you think you've done. But don't make things worse." As the river rose to her waist, tears streamed down her face and she pleaded, "Don't you leave me, too."

Wolf made no attempt to save himself as the water swirled faster. But he turned back to look at her. "It was hard enough, living with what I did to James. I could never live knowing what I've done to Sequoyah," he told her in the saddest voice she had ever heard. "I could never live with myself. Or with you. If he has died, so must I." And he headed deeper into the river.

Seeing the dark water engulf her husband and baby, and heedless of the danger to herself, Isabelle plunged after him. Then she lost her footing in the deep water, and fell heavily, and began to flounder. "Help!"

The current whirled her around and rendered her helpless. Her clothes and shoes were heavy, just like on the day Wolf had rescued her. She came up, desperate to make one more attempt to save her husband and child. But a powerful force pulled her under again. And then, strangely, her clothes began to feel as light as the Army trousers she had once been so ashamed of.

CHAPTER SEVENTY ONE

THE NANTAHALA GORGE NC, SEPTEMBER 1999

"Help! Help me!" As she surfaced, Carol recognized the deep bend of the river where they had gone to seek the spirits. Then she saw Winston, swimming out of the middle of the river, and cried, "Thank God! You're alive! I was trying to rescue Wolf—or you—I don't know which." Her voice wavered, and she put her hands to her face. "Oh, my God. What happened? It feels like—did we really become them for a while?"

"Seems like we did." Winston helped her up the bank and back onto solid ground, where he took her into his arms.

They had done the impossible, Carol realized with wonder. They had gone back to the beginning, and were safely back in the present. The spirits, too, seemed awestruck. Their whispering sounded like the pine trees.

For a long time Winston and Carol simply held each other. Then Carol whispered, "They had to endure so much, and they lost their child. Isabelle lost her husband, too."

After a while Winston commented, "Those things made them strong, though."

"It made their love strong," she realized. "Love is what keeps us alive. It connects the past to the future, don't you think?"

He drew her closer. "No wonder their love has survived for centuries, even down to us."

"And no wonder the curse has also lasted for centuries." As if just now remembering why they were there, she pushed herself out of his arms and called out to the spirits. "That's why it can never happen again. Wolf and Isabelle's baby died! That must never happen to our child."

"I agree," said the sorrowful spirit, but her voice ended with a gurgle that sounded like the water.

Winston felt something furry brush against his arm. There was a murmuring, as if someone else was talking, but there was no further answer from the spirits. It was time for him to make the most important request of all, and he addressed his spirit guide. "Now we know that the curse just went terribly wrong. It must be ended now. Please take it off."

Finally the granite-hard voice came again, clearly. "We have agreed to resolve the matter in a way that will be best for the Cherokee. Surely you could not object to that?"

"No." Winston's consent was instant. "Everything I do is for the good of our people. You know that, and I've done a lot already."

"True, but do you recognize there is still more to do?"

"Of course."

"You'll be wise to remember it, then. And remember that there must be a balance. We will remove the curse, but we also—"

Winston urged, "What do the spirits want?"

There was a short pause. "Your marriage."

Winston relaxed, so relieved at this answer, even overjoyed, that he could have danced again on the river's bank. "Of course. Carol and I are deeply in love. We're honored by the likeness to our ancestors, and we hold it as a sacred trust from the past. Carol is already carrying our child. Believe me, we'll be married at the first opportunity."

Something settled as a weight on Winston's left shoulder as the third voice returned, no longer flippant, its tone even harder now. "You don't understand. For the privilege of removing the curse, the marriage you must make is to Tsalina—Wanda Running Bear."

This time lightning flashed down the mountainside and the thunder was close and deafening.

Although some of it might have been laughter, Winston thought, as he finally realized whose spirit guide had been speaking so flippantly, all along.

It was Wanda's.

CHAPTER SEVENTY TWO

As shocked as if he had been struck, Winston shouted, "No! I won't do it! You can't ask this!" Looking at Carol's stricken face was like getting another blow.

But the weight on his shoulder increased, and his guiding spirit's voice thundered again. "Remember that as the principal chief, you have a special duty to your people."

Winston closed his eyes. "Yes, but I'm in love with Carol! And surely you wouldn't make a child fatherless!"

Wanda's spirit grated, "Be that as it may, you know that marriage to Wanda was ordained and you had agreed, before the white woman returned and bewitched you again."

He couldn't deny it. But he desperately wanted to refuse to do their bidding.

"The jilting of Wanda was a wrong done by today's Wolfe."

"Well—" Winston was still reluctant to admit it. But he was sharply interrupted.

"If we correct the old wrong by lifting the spell, you must repay us and your ancestors by correcting today's wrong, too. That is what I meant by balance."

Winston's shoulders slumped, and he cast about for a way to escape his fate. His stomach churned, and he flung himself into a macabre dance around the fire once more. He had to make his decision, or else the spirits would become impatient and leave. Most of all, he feared, the curse would not be lifted unless he obeyed their demands.

"We are waiting for your answer."

Finally he stopped, exhausted, his decision made. He didn't want to marry Wanda, but he knew he was guilty of jilting her. But there was something else, something far more important. Most of all, he was determined to lift Tallaquoyah Wolf's spell from the Mattox family, whatever it took because he loved Carol. And because she carried his child—who might die as had all other Mattox first-borns for nearly two centuries. He couldn't risk that. Even if it meant losing Carol, their child must live.

He was also determined to hold the spirits to the crucial part of their harsh bargain. "If I do, will you guarantee you'll remove the curse?"

The pressure returned to his shoulder, but this time it was an almost comforting gesture as the granite voice resumed. "Despite your unhappiness, you will not regret your decision, my son." And finally came the words Winston and Carol had risked their lives to hear. "You have pleased the spirits. The spell is lifted from the Mattox family. Their first-borns will never again die from the Wolf's curse."

Winston closed his eyes, clenched his fist, and wrenched his decision from his gut. "All right. I agree to marry Wanda." He slumped and slowly opened his eyes, just in time to see a host of tiny lights, at different heights, disappear around the bend in the river.

"No!" Now the cry was Carol's. "You can't marry Wanda! Think of all we've been through!"

He could only reply, "I'm thinking of all we don't want to go through. Remember what a tragedy it was for Isabelle and Wolf when their child died? Who could go through that again? How could we put our child through that kind of certain, and horrible, death?"

It was too fresh a memory to deny. She crumpled onto a rock, misery etched deeply into her face.

"This is my punishment for failing to save Wolf and get him to remove the curse," she moaned.

"Of course it isn't. Wanda is trying to punish me."

"Then why are you going to marry her?" she wailed.

Winston knelt and gathered Carol's small, soft body in his arms. He caressed all the places so familiar to him, lingering on her stomach. "So that you can have our son. Or daughter. That's what's most important, and what we have to remember."

"All alone?"

"You won't be alone. Somehow, we'll get through this, together. Our love will be as undying as Wolf's and Isabelle's, and made stronger by adversity. I'll always love you. I'll never stop."

She wept against him, "But you'll be married to somebody else."

He cradled her and his child within her, and as he watched the fire die, he pondered long and heavily about the future.

He had been mightily shaken by their encounter with the past. How long had they been there? Already it seemed like a dream. Did he once again have all his wits about him? Could he live with the consequences of the agreement he'd just made with the spirits? Could he marry another woman—one he didn't love—and give up the one meant for him since their childhood, some might say for centuries?

Carol raised a teary face. "You just don't love me!" she accused.

He cupped her cheeks, brushing away her tears with his thumbs. And then he said, quietly, "I'm doing it because I love you. I'm keeping our child alive. That is the greatest gift of love I could ever give you."

CHAPTER SEVENTY THREE

CHEROKEE NC, OCTOBER 1999

Carol felt strange being a visitor to the little house by the stream that she and Winston had shared for the past few months. She walked slowly around the living room, touching everything. It wasn't just to reconnect after the weeks she'd spent away. She needed to remember them forever.

Hardest to face were the photos they had framed and hung in the hall. As she touched them, her breath caught. There was their trip to Gatlinburg. Biltmore House. The trout he'd caught in the stream.

Watching her, Winston reached out for her. "Carol, don't do this."

She twisted out of his arms, then stopped, afraid of harming her baby. For that is how she thought, now, of the child within her. By agreeing to marry Wanda, he had given up his rights to their child. And she had lost him again, just as she had feared. She had never felt so alone. So unloved. "Do you think I want to leave? I don't have a choice."

"I've been offered a job by a foreign mission our church supports," she told him.

"You looked for another job without telling me?" He slumped against the wall.

She spread her hands. "You make it sound as though I've done something wrong!"

"I know, and I'm sorry."

"Anyway, I didn't exactly look for a job. This just came up." She remembered how surprised she'd been when she'd asked Brian for her old job back, and discovered he was moving on himself, going home, as she had done, he'd told her. On the spot, he'd offered to take her to Australia with him. Without even thinking about it, she had agreed. It was far enough away. Besides, she didn't care where she was, as long as it wasn't here.

"I can't stand for you to leave. You won't go very far away, will you?"

She hesitated. "I'm going to Australia."

"Australia!" He leapt to her side. "But you said it was your church!"

"They contribute to the mission I'll be working at." She added, "I knew one of the Australian anthropologists in Arizona."

"But how can you go so far away?" He raked both hands through his hair. "I can't even think about you being in a place like that."

"That's its greatest appeal to me." She knew she still sounded resentful.

"I'll never see our baby!" He stalked, as though unseeing, around the living room. "I have to be able to see our child!"

Helplessly, she began to cry. "Even if we stayed here, how would you see him? Would you introduce him to your children by Wanda? As whom? It would be terrible to bring a baby into the world that can't be recognized by his own father."

"It's better than having the baby die," he said flatly, "and that was the choice I had."

"I know," she sympathized. "That was the choice I made, too. But surely you know we can't stay here, now. What could I expect to be? Your mistress? And watch you with your wife? That would hurt too much."

He quieted, although his eyes darted around the room as if seeking answers. "I never thought about that part of it," he confessed. "I couldn't think of everything, that night on the river."

She said sadly, "I understand that. But you need to understand that a lesser relationship just isn't for me. And what would my parents think about my having a baby without any father?"

"They're going to think the same thing when you have a baby in Australia." He grasped at logic.

"Maybe when they know about it," she replied tersely. "It's a long way away, and news can travel very slowly." She pressed her point. "Don't you see, that's why I have to go as far away as possible. I've had enough trouble with them as it is, all my life. And I'm sorry, but I can't bear to hear about your life with Wanda." She choked on her next words, but was determined to say them. "I hope you can be happy with her. But this time, if you write me, I'll send your letters back."

As Carol checked the museum's bookshop racks, she saw Wanda Running Bear enter the shop.

With a triumphant smile, Wanda came straight up to her. "I just thought I'd tell you that the wedding invitations are going out this week. I didn't even have to have them reprinted, because the wedding will be on exactly the day I planned."

For a moment Carol thought about replying with her own good news: hers and Winston's baby was due in the new millennium.

But then, Wanda probably already knew that.

"But, honey, you're leaving again, just a few months after you came home, and now you're going even further away!" Marcie Mattox accused her daughter.

"This job offer's too good to refuse," Carol lied.

"But you had a great job at the museum! And you liked it, you said, it was different."

"I know." Carol sighed. "But it wasn't really anthropology, and I realized I made a mistake." Thank goodness her mother didn't yet know about the baby, although her condition was beginning to show. It was going to be hard, but Carol was going to have to fib her way through this, for there was no way the math would add up. Mercifully, she was to leave in two days, so there wasn't a lot of time for either explaining or agonizing about her decision, either to Winston or her family.

"And what about Winston? I thought you two were getting serious. Why, you were living with him, so I hope you weren't just playing house."

Carol gritted her teeth. "Of course not. It simply didn't work out."

Marcie had paid no attention. "And now you up and throw him away. Are you just going off and leaving him? I'm sure I don't know what's got into you, jilting that nice boy like that. And even your daddy is very upset about it. He's taken quite a shine to Winston."

Carol stared at her mother. "I seem to remember you and Daddy were opposed to Winston. Not just once, but twice. You didn't like him being Cherokee."

Marcie was shocked. "Now that's not true."

Carol was incredulous. "You ended our friendship, way back then, by not letting me see him, not giving me his letters. If it wasn't because he was Cherokee, then why?"

Marcie sighed. "It was because of all the stories we'd heard about the trouble there'd been between our families. You know there'd been a lot of talk, from your grandma, about curses and such, and I suppose we'd let ourselves be affected by it. You were young and impressionable. We thought it was for your own good. It was never because he's an Indian, and I don't want you to think that."

While Carol digested this, Marcie continued, rather airily, "And now, well, I won't pretend we were exactly thrilled when you started seeing Winston again, but he's turned into such a fine young man, and your daddy's so excited about his wantin' to go into politics, that we've got to really like him."

Carol could have wept, with joy or sorrow she knew not which. She hugged her mother and stayed in her arms, wanting badly to stay in Asheville with her family, and nurture the love and approval that they finally seemed ready to give, that she'd always sought.

But there was an overpowering reason why she couldn't. Barely able to get out the words, she assured her mother, "Well, you don't have to worry, any more, about a family curse."

"Well, I never did, of course." Marcie held her at arms' length. "Oh, dear, I don't know what you young people are coming to."

And neither did Carol know what might become of them all, especially the tiny person inside her.

But someone who, she thought, might know appeared as she went down the long hallway to her room to finish packing. "I knew nothing good would come of you seeing that Wolfe boy," Harriet observed, fastening her eyes onto Carol so fiercely that they seemed to reach into her very soul. Carol felt Grandma knew everything that had happened, not only a few weeks ago, but also two centuries ago.

She might escape from her problems by going to Australia, but she would never escape from Grandma's all-seeing, all-knowing eyes.

CHAPTER SEVENTY FOUR

NDJIMURRA MISSION, AUSTRALIA, APRIL 2001

"I've brought the mail," Brian Keating told his wife as he arrived home for lunch. His office was about twenty yards away, and lunch at home was not only desirable, it was necessary. The closest town was 250 miles and an overnight trip south.

He threw the pile of mail onto the kitchen table. Carol noticed her mother's distinctive pale blue envelope even before she recognized the bold, up-and-down handwriting. She wondered what could be her mother's reason for using snail-mail. At a distance of fifteen thousand miles, e-mail was far more efficient. Tapes were best of all.

But, Carol knew, occasionally her mother liked to write letters. It was hard to change that ingrained sense of propriety, and Carol smiled at something that once would have made her fume. At least it wasn't the strained silence they had maintained in the Arizona desert, when they hadn't corresponded at all.

"I'll read it later," Carol told her husband. "Lunch is ready, and we're eating in the dining room."

His eyebrows lifted. "Is it contagious?"

"What are you talking about?"

"Has your mother's letter suddenly made you so 'proper' that we're using the dining room?"

She smiled at him fondly. "No. The dining room is the coolest room in the house."

As they sat down she asked, "Are the people from Sydney coming next week?"

"I'm afraid so." He sighed. "I don't think the Ndjimurras are going to be very impressed with two sanctimonious deacons from Sydney's biggest society church. We'll be lucky if the whole clan doesn't go walkabout for a week."

She knew by now that walkabout meant disappearing, without a trace, even in the desert.

"At least the deacons are only staying for a couple of days."

"They wouldn't survive the heat much longer than that."

As Carol savored the roast lamb she'd finally learned to cook, she watched him eat and felt happy that she'd finally been able to let Winston go and love Brian. His love did not take her to the mountain tops, as Winston's had. But with Brian there were no deep rivers to drown in, either.

Brian ate quickly and reached for his broad-brimmed hat. "Timothy not awake?"

"I fed him, and he went back to sleep on the floor of his room. I think it's the heat."

"Well, give him a kiss for me. Thanks for lunch. Got to get back. Gulawarry says he's going to tell me about his mother this afternoon."

"Hope he doesn't just make it up," she grinned. "I think he was the reason I quit."

But she knew Gulawarry wasn't the reason she'd given up the job that had brought her to Ndjimurra Mission. People thought she'd resigned because of marrying Brian and that the baby was Brian's and was the reason she'd joined him. It suited Carol for them to think all of that.

But Carol knew she'd quit because she was finished with the past, whether it be her own or the anthropological one. It wasn't a good idea to delve into the past any more. For the first time ever, it held only sadness for her. She hadn't seen the handsome man in a red cap for a long time. Now she wanted just the present, and the future. And her baby was the future.

When Brian had gone, she stacked the dishes in the kitchen sink and picked up her mother's letter. She fanned herself with it, hearing it crackle, before opening it.

At first skimming the closely written pages, she suddenly began reading every word. "Your daddy's preparing Winston for the next Congressional race. Stanley feels Winston will be the perfect candidate. 'Course it isn't for another year, but they're getting ready. Patrick Yates is the man on the ground, as your father puts it. Naturally . . ."

Carol dropped the thin blue sheets, and went to the window. She wanted to put off reading Mama's letter, to avoid hearing about Winston, about the wonderful life everybody but she was leading.

For, despite the fact that life was tolerable, once again she was in an isolated, desolate outpost of scholarly endeavor. Her life was hard and sparse. Red dust settled on everything—people, furniture, food. She had a constant battle to keep it off, just like all the other battles with the past that she fought every day.

She shaded her eyes against the scorching light. The fierce sun penetrated every corner of the small yellow clapboard house that went with the job of director of the mission. Outdoors, the flies flew right into your eyes, trying to suck out enough moisture to keep themselves alive in the dry, searing country.

As far as her eye could see, to the blue horizon, there was empty red land. Its dead-flatness was only occasionally interrupted by a giant termite mound reaching over six feet high. The trees were all stunted to bush size. Yet the colors, especially where the sky met the earth, were, perversely, magnificent.

This hard life, she thought, was the price she was paying for taking off the Mattox curse. It was proving to be almost as hard as losing Winston. Of course, he'd had to pay a heavy price, too, but at least he got to stay at home. How long would she have to suffer in exile?

Well, who knew better than she that nothing came without its price?

She couldn't put off reading her mother's letter any longer. 'Naturally, because of this,' she skimmed on, 'we're seeing a lot of Winston and Wanda. She's just told us she's pregnant with their first child. We're happy for them. Of course we know you're happy in your new life, and we're glad Winston could find somebody nice, too. Now the only thing we lack is seeing our grandson. I hope you'll bring him home before too long.'

Her mother's words were like spears that went straight into Carol's heart. She would not be taking her son home any time soon, not until people stopped counting on their fingers. She put her head down on her arms at the wooden table and wondered how things could have turned out so badly.

Then she felt a tug on her leg, and she looked down to see her son. "Ma-ma-ma-ma?" Timothy asked, as if wondering what her problem was, and wanting to share it. He had just started walking, and she was still unused to him being higher than foot level. He looked up at her with big, dark brown eyes, as dark as she'd ever seen. Well, not quite. She knew there were even darker ones on the other side of the world. But she wouldn't think about them.

"Darling, I'm sorry I'm crying, and I don't want to make you sad." But his interest had already swerved to a frilled-neck lizard out on the porch, and he dropped back down on all-fours, the quicker to investigate it.

Pride oozing from every pore, she watched him scurry across the floor to the screen door. He was tall for his age, his skin bronzed from the sun. He was going to grow up big and strong, like his father. And his black hair stood straight up in spikes.

And so, despite her misery, Carol felt happy in her heart and spirit. "I'd do anything for you," she told him, as he looked around in surprise. "In fact, for you, I made the ultimate sacrifice. So did your father. How's that for a heritage?" When he went too close to the frilled-neck, she went over and scooped him up, holding him close, smelling his warm, baby smell. "And how glad I am that I did! For I love you more than life itself. Even though I'm suffering, I can stand it better than having you suffer even for a moment."

He wriggled, and began to fret, so she put him back on the floor. Then she turned on the computer in the bedroom they used as a study. "Dear Mama and Daddy," she typed. And then stopped.

She didn't know exactly how to say it, but she was going to ask that they not give her any more news about Winston, his work, or her father's political plans for him. Most of all, she didn't want to hear about his family life. It was just too painful.

CHAPTER SEVENTY FIVE

WASHINGTON DC, JANUARY 2005

Carol looked out the window of the airplane into the pale January sunlight and saw her homeland.

It wasn't the tall, green mountains of western North Carolina. It was the urban sprawl of Washington, D.C. Still, it was home. She always seemed to be coming home from a hot, dry place. She was parched in more ways than one, she thought, remembering having had that same feeling when she had only been in Arizona for a couple of years. Now she'd been away from home for several years. The child sitting beside her was nearly five years old.

He looked up at her with doleful eyes. "Mommy, are we ever going to get there?"

She smiled. Their trip had taken nearly two days. "Yes, darling, we're almost there now."

"And why did we have to leave Daddy?"

Carol thought for a while before replying, "We're going to see a very important man."

Today Winston Wolfe was being sworn in as the new Democratic senator from North Carolina. He'd moved quickly up the political ladder, and now the newspapers and television, even in Australia, were already saying his next goal was the White House.

With a wry smile she thought about how he was replacing the venerable

Stanley Mattox, who had served his people for a long time but, having found a worthy replacement, had retired.

After the formalities in D.C., she would spend a week in Asheville letting her son get to know his grandparents. It would be a time for rejoicing. The only sadness was that Grandma was no longer alive, although Carol was almost relieved that she didn't have to face those eyes that had always seen too much of the truth.

Carol had closely followed Winston's election. Then she had tried to put it out of her mind. But at this, she had failed utterly. It had started her thinking. She simply couldn't resist witnessing the moment Winston become a senator. Most of all, she couldn't resist letting his son see it, to be at least some part of it. Brian, too, had understood.

She imagined Winston taking the oath of office. "Do you, Winston George Wolfe, solemnly swear…" Glancing down at her son, she knew that someday, somehow, she must tell Timothy, as she was sure Isabelle had told Yaguska, about his heritage. That he, too, had a duty to serve his people and his fellow man.

"It's good to see you," Winston told her at the reception for new members of Congress. It was being held in the ballroom of the Cavendish Hotel. He balanced a glass with a canape, she a cup of coffee and a cake for Timothy, who was replenishing his supply at the buffet table.

"And you." They eyed each other. Then, as had happened before, they drank in the sight of each another. There was nothing that hadn't already been said, nothing important, anyway. And there was no need to ask anything. All the questions had been asked, too. And answered.

"Mommy, look what I found—chocolate cake!" The words floated up, but instead of being childish chatter, they seemed as important as words had ever been; as important as the words Winston had spoken in his oath of office.

Instantly Winston's eyes widened, and he looked down at his son. And there his gaze stayed until, filled now with amazement, he looked back up at Carol, who smiled and said, "This is our—my son, Timothy. Timothy Keating." And she saw Winston flinch. "Timothy, this is the important man I told you we were coming here to meet. Say hello."

Winston bent down and helped Timothy keep his chocolate cake from falling onto the floor. "There, that's better, isn't it?"

"Yes, thank you," Timothy replied politely. Then curiosity got the better of him. "Why are you crying?"

Winston looked helplessly at Carol, who in turn feigned having something in her eye. "There's someone else I'd like you to meet," Winston said, to Timothy. "Here she comes now. This is my daughter, Natalie."

"She's little," Timothy remarked to his mother disdainfully, with the superiority of a year and two inches more than the dark-haired little girl who appeared beside him.

"Yes, honey. Hello, Natalie." Forcing down the lump in her throat, Carol asked Winston brightly, "How many children do you and Wanda have?"

"Just Natalie."

Surprised at how near this brought her to tears, she looked around the long room full of people, lit with four huge crystal chandeliers. As if in apology, she asked, "Where is Wanda? I didn't see her at the oath-taking, either."

He took a deep breath. "Wanda and our second baby died in childbirth."

Thunderstruck, Carol whispered, "I'm so sorry. And sorry that I didn't know."

He gave her a pleading look. "I knew you didn't want to hear from me, but I thought your parents might have kept you in touch about things."

She made a rueful gesture. "Eventually, I asked them not to, and not to tell you anything about me. Not because I didn't want to know about you, but because I couldn't stand to hear it. The last thing I heard was that you were expecting Natalie. After that, I couldn't hear any more." And after that, she began to cry.

"And your husband? Is he here?"

"We divorced."

His expression changed, and he murmured, "Why am I not sorry to hear that?"

"You should be; he's a nice guy." After a moment she added, "But it was always a marriage of convenience, to give our son a father and the legitimacy of a name."

Winston looked pained. "I wish I could have given him that."

She lifted her hand as if to brush away his regret. "You gave him much more than that. You gave him life. And anyway, after our, well, our experiences..." Feeling the inadequacy of the word, Carol struggled to finish her sentence. "I just couldn't do justice to loving somebody else. It was unfair to Brian. He deserved better; he deserved somebody who would really love him."

He caught her hands. "I never even tried again. I never remarried because I couldn't love anybody else after our experiences, as you so inadequately put it." He smiled.

"If only..." she began.

He put a finger to her lips. "Let's not cry over the past. Let me remind you about something. We're alive. We're together again, and we're both free. The Mattox curse is gone. Does that suggest anything to you?"

She shifted her weight to the other foot. "It suggests we should try again. But I don't know if I could, it was all so painful. Both times. Besides," she looked at him, "I swore I'd never again live in the past. I'm done with that."

"How can you say that when you look at our two beloved children?"

"I can wish they had both been ours." The sadness of it caught in her throat.

"They can still be ours," he said quietly. "If there hadn't been any pain, or any past, there might have been no children," he pointed out. "You taught me to value the past, and I do now, more than I ever did. Without it, I've discovered, there is no future."

Again her smile was rueful, but this time it was also in agreement.

He looked at her. "May I have this dance?"

She glanced around. "But there isn't any music playing."

"You don't hear it?" He smiled, his eyes holding hers. "You don't hear that Strauss waltz? That's strange." He tilted his head and paused a moment before grinning at her. "Oh, well, we'll just have to make our own music."

In front of everyone, he took her in his arms and began to waltz her around the ballroom, to music that was all the louder for being silent.

And it was bright-shiny new, even though it had been playing for nearly two hundred years.

An experienced novelist, Nancy Sales Cash has been previously published by Pan Macmillan, and optioned by an international film company. Her career includes journalism, advertising, public relations, and television production in North Carolina, New York, London, and Sydney. She has returned to her native western North Carolina to write novels about the magnificent mountains and their captivating history, cultures, and people. A graduate of the University of North Carolina at Chapel Hill with a B.A. in English Literature, she lives in Asheville NC.

www.nancysalescash.com

BEST SELLERS BY NANCY SALES CASH

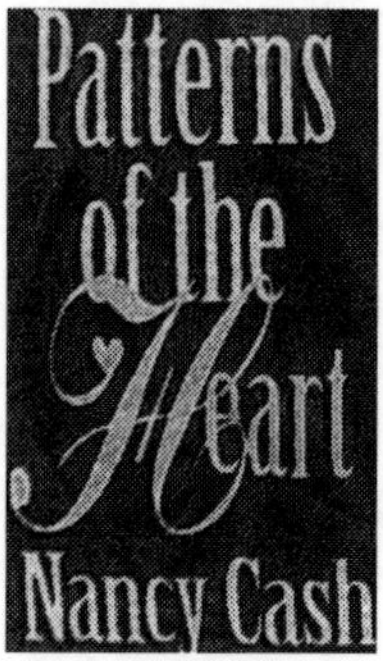

Anya Gordon is the most envied woman in the country. A successful couturier to the elite, she reigns supreme with her adoring husband, Joe, by her side. Finally she can escape the past, a past haunted by the ravages of war and the struggle to build a new life in a strange country. But behind the glamour lies a lost dream, and a secret that could destroy all that Anya has fought so hard to achieve...

A mercy dash back home when her beloved brother has a suspicious accident causes Carol Mattox to re-meet her teenage love, Winston Wolfe. They are bound inextricably, not only by the ancient love of their ancestors, but also by an ancient spell of death. Is Winston her lover or her enemy? Her brother's dying wish forces her to find out, putting her own life and that of her unborn child at risk in a gripping encounter with the unseen forces that control destiny...

TO BUY THESE BOOKS. PLEASE CONTACT YOUR LOCAL BOOKSHOP, AMAZON.COM, OR www.nancysalescash.com